EVERYTHING
he isn't

LAUREN STEWART

Cover Me Darling
Making Manuscripts
Diamond in the Rough Editing
First Editing
Hourglass Editing

For everyone who made it through the past few years with a little bit of humor and a whole lot of hope.

1

SOPHIE

7:00 am Monday through Friday

7:15 am Saturdays and Sundays

No snooze button.

Ever.

Fifteen minutes in the shower, twenty-five for hair and makeup.

Five minutes to feed the cat and make toast while the coffee grounds steeped.

And today, forty-five minutes in a grocery store, patiently waiting for the perfect man to appear.

Hell, I'd been waiting for him to show up since I was sixteen. An entire decade of waiting. I could handle another forty-five minutes.

For the millionth time, I read the sale sign for the five-foot-tall stack of Charmin across from the endcap Liz and I were hiding behind. Twenty-four rolls of toilet paper for only $5.99. Not the kind that scraped your delicate lady bits like eighty-grit sandpaper either. We were talking about the good stuff. Quality stuff. And I was all about quality stuff. Plus, who didn't love a good deal?

I should grab some when we were finished hiding. I mean, waiting.

"I swear," Liz said, "all I want in life is for a man to look at me the way you're looking at that toilet paper."

"Huh?" I blinked and refocused on my best friend as she studied a lock of thick wavy hair to check for split ends.

"I was merely appreciating the way you're ogling the toilet paper."

I squinted. "I don't think toilet paper is something one can ogle."

"You mean we can objectify men but not actual objects?" Liz grabbed a bag of potato chips off the snack display we were leaning against and ripped it open.

"We're not objectifying anything," I scoffed. "All we're doing is giving opportunity a little nudge" —I elbowed her a little harder than I'd intended, but Liz was always doing something to deserve it—"to increase my chances of finding the right one."

"I'm pretty sure you just pay for it, take it home, and use it." She laughed. "I meant that as a statement about toilet paper, but it holds true for men too."

I shushed her.

She managed to keep her mouth shut for about ten seconds before she blurted, "You really don't know how pathetic this is, do you?"

Maybe I should rethink her "best friend" label.

"It's not pathetic. It's brilliant." I peered around the corner again to see if anyone had come up the aisle in the three seconds it took to glare at her. "I need a man who will like Orion. What better way to find someone who likes cats than to see who buys cat food?"

Liz rolled her eyes before shoving a chip into her mouth. "Poor guy doesn't know what he's walking into."

"You'd better be planning to pay for those."

"Of course I am." She rolled the top of the bag over a few times and set it back onto the snack display. "Oh no," she deadpanned. "I must have forgotten to grab my wallet when you dragged me into this life-or-death mission."

"Some of us would rather not die alone, so yeah, this *is* life or death." I snatched the opened chip bag and put it into my empty basket.

"You've got four more years before it becomes life or death." She reached for the bag, unrolled it, and grabbed another chip.

"If you think it's such a bad idea, you could've stayed home."

"And miss all this excitement?" she asked with every bit of fake sincerity she could muster. "Okay, aside from the questionable appeal of men who love cats, what other qualities are we looking for this morning?"

I didn't even have to think about it, my list having burned its way into my consciousness years ago. "Someone smart, sweet, well-put-together, positive, stylish, outgoing, confident, reliable, honest, faithful, who has a job—"

"Glad to hear you dropped the idea that it has to be a *good* job."

"I thought that went without saying." I sighed unhappily. Living in Northern California wasn't cheap, especially not in a small college town like this one. I'd just bought my house a few months ago. The last thing I needed was to have to support someone else. "You don't think expecting him to have a *good* job is asking too much, do you?"

"You? Asking for too much? Impossible. That's what the plan is all about, right?"

"Stop making fun of the plan. It's foolproof."

"Foolproof, foolish." Liz held up her hands as if balancing words on them. "I always forget which one you're going for."

It wasn't as if my requirements for a life partner were anything new. Granted, they were constantly adjusting as I learned the market and gained experience. But ultimately, the latest piece of my plan boiled down to this: The more I knew what I wanted in a significant other, the easier it should be to find him. If I met someone at an art gallery, I would know he was smart, open-minded, and didn't spend every night on the couch playing video games. Since I wanted to be with someone sweet who valued family, chances were slim I'd find him at a wet T-shirt contest. True, the first batch of ventures had been horrendously unsuccessful. Home Depot had been a complete bust, and I tried not to remember what happened at the daycare. But I wasn't a quitter.

"I just want a man who is the whole package and *has* a nice package. Is that so wrong?" I flicked my finger up to make my argument clearer. "All I have to do is figure out where he's likely to be, and then get there before he does. For example, a man who respects women shows it by visiting his mother at the senior center, so . . ."

Her mouth dropped open. "You dragged me there to scope out men? I thought you were just forcing me to be nice!"

"Um . . ." I said, squinting. As if that would help me understand why she put the word *forcing* in there. "It *was* nice. It also happened to be practical." Not successful, but practical.

"Sophie, those seniors' sons were old enough to be our grandpas."

"That's such ageism! What's wrong with dating someone a little older?" I cocked my head to the side. "Plus, I was feeling particularly desperate that day."

"As opposed to today when you're only desperate enough to stalk someone in a grocery store."

Before I could respond, Aaron walked over and pushed his sunglasses up until they perched on his close-cropped black hair. At least he'd been a little excited when I told him about today's mission. Well, maybe more curious than excited, but I'd take the support however I could get it.

"Any luck so far?" he asked.

I shook my head. "Just an elderly woman. She wasn't my type."

"That's such ageism, Sophie," Liz tossed back.

Aaron grabbed another bag of chips I'd have to pay for and then throw away. He ripped open the bag and held it out to us. Liz tilted hers toward him so they could share. How generous of them.

"Since we're hunting your perfect man, are you, by any chance, attracted to heavy drinkers?" Liz asked. "I would be happy to stalk that aisle for you. I could really use a beer right now."

"It's not even noon yet."

"Grab me one too," Aaron said, crunching on a chip.

"You can't drink their beer without buying it first!" I waited for them to laugh and tell me they were kidding. Unfortunately, I'd been friends with them long enough to know it would never happen. That was the problem with having the same friends since high school—we knew everything about each other. The good, the evil, the humiliating.

I could practically read their minds.

Except right now.

Their expressions morphed from jovial to shocked as they gaped at something behind me.

"I can't believe your stupid plan might actually work," Liz said.

I spun around, smacking my elbow on the metal shelf in the process. I covered my mouth to hold in a whimper.

The man walking down the aisle toward us had short, slightly messy, dark hair and the beginnings of a beard. Not ideal, but maybe he didn't shave on the weekends. That would obviously have to change. I preferred stubble-free cheeks, primarily due to my aforementioned fear of eighty-grit sandpaper rubbing on my delicate lady bits.

But underneath the undesirable facial hair was fantastic bone structure—strong, masculine. In fact, he was almost *too* good-looking. There was a slight bend to his nose as if he'd broken it at some point, adding the perfect amount of imperfection and character to his face, as did the thin line of confusion between his blue-but-I-couldn't-be-sure eyes as he surveyed the wall of pet food. His jeans were loose and worn low on his hips, but his T-shirt looked new and pulled across his shoulder and bicep in a decidedly sexy way. Not tight enough to give off the impression that he was showing off his body but just tight enough to prove he had every reason to do so.

"Go talk to him," Liz whispered, shoving me forward.

I pushed back against her. "Not yet." I smoothed my hands over my tightly pulled hair. "Not until I know for sure."

Aaron popped another chip. "How are you going to know 'for sure' from forty feet away?"

"Well . . . I . . . um . . ." I sighed. "Just give me a sec, will you?"

Honestly, my plan hadn't gotten past the possibility phase. Plus, I hadn't checked to see how I looked since we got here. What if most of my lipstick had rubbed off and there was just a thin, feathered line of Ruby Woo tracing the edges of my lips? For all I knew, leaning against this wire shelf of unhealthy snack foods had pulled strands of hair from my bun, and I looked like Medusa's less attractive sister.

"Remind me why we're looking for a cat guy," Aaron said.

"Cats are independent, intelligent, and live life on their own terms. It stands to reason that someone who loves those characteristics in a pet is more likely to love them in a woman too."

"Who cares what he likes? He's fucking hot." Liz flicked her dark hair over her shoulder dramatically. "I'll be whoever he wants me to be."

Aaron caught my eye. We both knew Liz's taste in men—yummy on the outside, empty in the middle. In high school, whenever she started dating someone new, we would place bets on when and why it would end. The game got boring fast—the *when* was always around the three-week mark, and the *why* was always because "he was too needy."

Liz was a cat. Probably a Burmilla, or maybe a Siberian Forest, or any breed that ignored you completely but peed on your bed if—*when*—she didn't think you were paying enough attention to her.

I peered back around the endcap, hoping the cat man hadn't left yet. "Thank goodness."

Liz was right—he was fucking hot. Except . . .

"Don't, don't, don't." I cringed when he side-stepped to the canned food section, my hands tight on the handle of the shopping basket.

"Don't what?" Aaron whispered.

I didn't explain, knowing they'd just laugh at my strong opinions on canned cat food. I fed Orion a well-balanced mixture of good quality wet, dry, and fresh food. But a single, heterosexual man who only fed his cat canned food—or worse, the frozen raw kind—was probably a bit too hip to make a proper life partner. Eventually, we could have that conversation and switch his cat over to a better diet, but I'd rather we did it together.

Cat Man paced back and forth, tossing his hands up and dropping them as he got more frustrated by all the options. Finally, he mumbled something that was probably a curse word, pointed toward the shelf, and spun in a circle with his eyes closed. As soon as he stopped, he opened his eyes and grabbed the largest bag of dry food. He hefted it over his shoulder and headed toward the front of the store.

"Check out the size of that!" Liz said.

"I can't—he turned around too fast."

Liz burst out laughing. "The bag, Sophie. I was talking about the size of the bag of cat food."

"Me too," I said, feeling embarrassment heat my cheeks.

"Good thing we didn't put any money on him," Aaron said. "I would never have pegged him as someone who had enough cats to need fifty pounds of cat food."

"Maybe he likes to stock up, just in case," I said, feeling defensive of a man I'd never met. "Dry food stores well."

"Sorry, darlin'," Aaron said, "but with your luck, he probably has thirty indoor kitties, all named Fluffy or Sammy or Mr. Wiggles."

"No, Mr. Wiggles is probably *his* name!" Liz hadn't stopped laughing at my expense from earlier. "I bet they all sleep with him. So, I'm sorry too, Sophie. I don't think there's any room left in Mr. Wiggles' life for a beautiful, adorably insane woman like you."

I smacked her on the shoulder. "You're wrong." There was always room for love.

"Prove it."

"How?"

"By actually talking to him." She gasped at my fearful expression. "Oh my God. You had this entire thing planned out, but you forgot you would have to speak to whoever passed your stupid test?"

"No," I lied. It had taken a lot of time to come up with the brilliant first part of my plan, so I hadn't had time to worry about what came after that. Every man I'd dated over the last ten years had been someone I went to school with or met through a friend. The setup was done for me. Plus, men always made the first move—welcomed or not. This would be the first time I'd have to do it all myself.

Come on, Sophie. It was just talking. Words—hopefully interesting ones—strung together into sentences spoken aloud. I could do that. In fact, I did it every day on the phone when I spoke to prospective clients of my father's interior design firm. How different could it be to introduce myself to the super-hot cat lover who may be my soul mate?

"If you don't hurry up, you'll miss your big shot."

After forty-five minutes, I couldn't leave with nothing to show for it except for two half-empty bags of chips and Medusa hair.

I could do this. I blew out a quick, decisive breath. "Go wait in the car. I can't do it with you two staring at me." I snatched the chips from their hands and hurried down the aisle toward checkout.

With any luck, I could slip into line right behind Mr. Wiggles and strike up a conversation about . . . something.

Luck was something I'd never had too much of, but things were about to change. And not in a bad way.

2

COOPER

I readjusted the fifty-pound bag of overpriced dog food on my shoulder and waited for the elderly woman in front of me to finish chatting with the cashier about her grandkids. When she looked at me and smiled, I tried to keep the scowl off my face. She seemed like a nice lady and didn't deserve to see the expression I'd been wearing ever since my ex dropped off her mutt at my place this morning. All Helen had given me was a handful of yipping fluff and its miniature purple carrier—no food, no toys, no instructions on how or what to feed the thing. Apparently, Helen's work trip was a last-minute deal, and in that minute, she decided to dump the poor bastard on me.

Helen knew I wasn't a dog person. Or a cat person. Or a people person. Over eight months of on-and-off dating, I would've thought she'd listened to at least *a few* of the words coming out of my mouth. Yet more proof a serious relationship would never have worked out for us, the first being I'd never touched her black-and-brown hairball before today. Forcing Sammy on me was probably Helen's idea of payback for our mutual decision to call it quits once and for all. Why else would she have left her precious little baby with me for the two weeks she'd be in London?

Nothing against dogs, or any other pet for that matter. It was pet *owners* I had issues with. What kind of psycho would willingly choose to be responsible for something that costs a fortune, destroyed the carpet if you didn't let it out in time, and decided when you got up in the morning? Pretty sure that's what kids were for. I didn't want any of them either, but at least kids gave you an excuse to watch cartoons and finger paint.

I shifted the bag on my shoulder again and waited while the old lady filled out her check, got distracted by the cashier's benign question, wrote a little more, and got distracted again. When he asked what she had planned for the rest of the day, I barely stopped myself from yelling, *What the fuck do you think she's going to do? Get shitfaced at a club tonight and go home with the twenty-five-year-old bartender?* If so, you'd think she'd want to write out that check a little faster and get to it.

The goddamn bag was poking me in the cheek now. I hoisted it a bit farther forward, trying to find a good balance. Wasn't working.

"Your cat must be huge," a woman said behind me. "Not that size matters, of course."

When I spun around to see if she'd meant that as a joke, the bag of dog food swung faster than I did, and the momentum whipped all the kibble away from my center of gravity. As the bag side-swiped a candy display, the edge caught on something that tore it wide open.

"Fuck!" As I lost control of everything—and I mean *everything*—all I could do was reach out to stop myself from falling backward and landing on top of the old lady.

Oh, and watch a million tiny ninja-star-shaped projectiles fly at the woman who'd spoken.

"Duck!"

The woman flinched. I lunged forward. Neither of us were fast enough.

Shit. At least she'd had time to cover her face before the majority of it smacked into her.

Everyone within twenty feet was either trying not to laugh or rushing to help the poor woman. I stood there like an idiot, giving myself a second to think of what to say. *Sorry for throwing fifty pounds of dog food at you*, just didn't seem good enough.

"I'm so sorry," I said loud enough to be heard over the other concerned shoppers. "What can I do?"

"Turn back time a few minutes and warn me this was going to happen?" Her hand was still raised, as if she were waiting for another bag to be chucked at her. Dark brown hair kind of fell over her face and kind of...didn't. The force of the hit had destroyed whatever hairstyle she used to have, and pieces stuck up in every direction.

She spat dog food crumbles into her hand.

"I'm so fucking sorry," I said miserably.

The old lady gasped at my language, but if there were ever a more appropriate time to say *fuck*, I hoped I wasn't there for it.

"Totally my fault," the woman said from somewhere under all that hair and behind the hands covering her face.

"Not even a little. Seriously, are you okay?" I asked, along with a few other people who'd gathered around to ask her the same thing.

"I'm not hurt," she said, "but I'm feeling a bit claustrophobic. So, if you could all . . . give me a little space, that'd be great."

Everybody backed off, and after another pathetic apology, I sank down onto my haunches to gather up a billion or so individual pieces of dog food.

"Do you need help?" she asked.

"No, it's fine." Okay, fine it wasn't. But at this point, the day couldn't get any worse, so at least the pressure was off.

The cashier peered over his workstation and said, "Sir, we'll take care of that."

I had to do something to feel less like an asshole. If picking up a bunch of little Xs worked, I'd do it.

"The irony is that five minutes ago I was thinking about how lucky I felt today," the woman said.

"It's my karma. You just happened to be standing too close when it came back at me."

Her head was still lowered but kneeling at her feet helped me get a better look at her. I'd guess she was about my age—twenty-six—and attractive enough to make me wish we'd met somewhere else. Somewhere without ex-girlfriends and all the psychological damage they wrought.

Her lips were full, lacquered with matte red lipstick, and she had a certain formality to her, as if she were going to work or out for drinks instead of the grocery store. She was dressed in black, from her stabby-looking high heels to her button-up shirt that was buttoned *all* the way up. Helen would've never been caught dead in anything that didn't show a lot of cleavage, but the overall effect was the same. This woman was beautiful, expensive, and dangerous. At least for me. Although, in this case, *I'd* been the one to do the damage.

She pushed back some of her hair to watch me.

Fuck.

Her hand still blocked one side of her face, but the eye I could see was deep brown, almost black, the kind that was so dark I wanted to stare into them as long as it took to be able to know what was iris and what was pupil. And then keep staring into them until I knew the woman they belonged to.

Dangerous. Very, very dangerous.

"Actually, there *is* something you can do," I said, refocusing on the kibble. "Help me figure out a way to make this up to you."

"What do you need to make up for?" She smiled. "Did you

accidentally tell a joke so bad someone threw pet food at you too?"

I shook my head without looking up. "I got startled by a beautiful face." Shit. "And I really wish I hadn't said that." The last thing I needed was to pick up the woman I'd just accidentally wounded in the grocery store, especially one who reminded me of my ex.

I'd promised myself I would never get caught up in that shit again, and I always kept my promises. Besides, I was ninety-nine percent sure that the rest of my day would be spent cleaning up this mess, throwing away whatever the little mutt was currently chewing up back at my place, and figuring out the best method of getting piss out of a rug.

I gave up the hunting-and-gathering thing when the store employee came back with a broom and dustpan.

"They can handle it now," I said as we both moved out of the way. "You can throw those chips in my face if it'd make you feel better."

"Do you have any idea how many chemicals are in these things? No one should let them get anywhere near their face." Smiling, she clenched her eyes shut and lowered her hand. She opened them again, one side of her face twitching as she squinted. Proof she did indeed have two eyes, and one was totally bloodshot.

"Am I allowed to apologize again?"

"I'd actually prefer if we both pretend none of this happened." Her brow furrowed and, using my arm for balance, she reached down to fix her shoe.

The light grip of her hand on my forearm made me wonder if I might be ready to get back into the ring again after all. If I reacted like this to a simple touch, imagine my reaction to something more full-bodied with someone who didn't give a shit about my feelings and whose only expectation of me was to get her off.

I bet this woman was too busy being perfect to let herself go long enough to get off. Like my ex.

She took a piece of the kibble out of her shoe and held it out to me between two perfectly manicured fingers. "I think this belongs to you."

"Not quite yet." I grimaced as I took it. "This is embarrassing. I don't usually throw things at people until *after* I pay for them."

"I guess this is a day of firsts for both of us."

When she smiled, guilt overwhelmed every other thought. Not only had I pelted the poor woman with dog food, but I was judging her too? I'd immediately assumed this woman must be like Helen because of the way she looked, but how the hell did I know what she was like?

"Miss, I can take you on aisle two." A cashier took her basket and led her to another counter.

"Actually, I'd rather . . . oh." After a brief, uncomfortable hesitation, she followed, turning to wave back at me. "Bye."

"Sorry again." I watched her until the cashier said, "That'll be $42.17, sir."

"I'll pay for the busted one too." It was my fault the bag broke. Although, it would make me feel better to blame *every-thing* on Helen. Reaching for my wallet, I cursed my ex-girlfriend for changing the way I perceived all attractive women and for forcing me to pay eighty-five bucks for a shitty experience and a sad weekend at home—just me and the mutt.

It was almost as if she'd planned it.

3
____

SOPHIE

Liz and Aaron were standing just outside the sliding doors. Their faces went from hopeful smiles to nervous confusion to outright pity as I walked past them and made a beeline for Liz's car, still blinking like crazy to clear my eyes.

That hadn't worked out as well as I'd hoped. Like, at all. But I wasn't one to quit, not after the way Mr. Wiggles had looked at me with his otherworldly sky-blue eyes and unfairly thick lashes. But mostly it was the way he'd said *beautiful* with his deep, grumbly voice and full lips. It wasn't the word necessarily—women with my body type were called all kinds of variations of beautiful, usually prefaced by "hey, girl" and followed by "let me buy you a burger to go with that booty shake." No, it was the way he'd said *beautiful* and the look on his face afterward. As if he'd surprised himself and regretted being so forward. Humility was on my list. Along with self-confidence, of course. There had to be balance.

"So . . . ?" Aaron asked carefully. "How'd it go?"

"He threw cat food at me."

"We never should've left you alone in there," Liz grumbled.

"He was really nice about it afterward though," I told her.

"I love it when a guy throws cat food at me nicely," she dead-panned. "It's such a turn-on." She picked a piece of it out of my hair.

"At least you're memorable," Aaron said, a few steps behind us. "Can't imagine he'll be forgetting whatever happened anytime soon."

"Yep, I know how to make an impression, don't I?" I rubbed the eye that had caught most of the cat food dust. It was already 75% back to being pain-free, so that was something.

"He'll probably think of you every time he feeds his thirty cats until the whole bag is gone."

"Make fun all you want, but I liked him. Do you know hard it is to find a man who can apologize sincerely?"

"Yes," and "utterly impossible," they said simultaneously.

"Mr. Wiggles apologized about five separate times." It was refreshing to find out something so important immediately after meeting someone versus waiting until they broke your heart to realize they were unable to put two simple words of apology together.

Aaron gave me a sideways hug. "I love how you can always find a way to turn something fairly awful into a positive."

"You'd be good at it too if you had as many shitty things in your life as Sophie does."

"Yep." I smiled. "Even one of my best friends falls into the shitty-things category."

As I opened the passenger door of her car, I saw Mr. Wiggles heft the cat food into the bed of a big black pickup truck at the other end of the parking lot. I wasn't a big fan of pickups—too hard to get into when wearing a skirt. But it wasn't a dealbreaker. Not with a man who liked cats, was borderline too handsome, and apologized when he made a mistake.

I got into the car and pulled down the visor mirror. "No, no, no." My worst fear earlier had been a huge underestimation. "I look like Medusa with bedhead!" My bun was basically gone, and strands of hair were sticking up all over the place. As soon as I saw my bloodshot eye, I slammed the mirror shut. "Is this what I looked like when he saw me?"

After ten seconds of watching my friends look at each other and silently discuss how big of a lie they should tell me, I figured it out on my own.

I'd looked even worse. Deal-breaking worse.

I guess my luck hadn't changed much after all.

As if to finalize that, when I looked toward Mr. Wiggles' truck, he was gone.

Before dropping Aaron off at his condo, Liz took us to the drive-through so I could buy them the lunch I'd promised. I got water. I wasn't a health nut by any means—and I had the hips to prove it—but too much sugar or caffeine made me even more anxious than normal and often resulted in people thinking I was on something illegal. Plus, I could still taste a little of the cat food that had made it into my mouth earlier.

As Liz drove through the maze of small streets lined with California Palm trees in Aaron's condo complex, I finally managed to regain control of my hair.

"Stop the car!" Aaron yelled, pointing at a black pickup parked in a residents-only spot. "I *knew* I'd seen it before! I just didn't remember where."

"How can you be sure it's the same truck?" Liz asked.

"How many people have big, black pickup trucks and a bumper sticker that says, 'Nailed it?'"

I'd been looking at Mr. Wiggles' biceps as he hoisted the bag of cat food into the back, not his truck. The bumper sticker had a picture of a hammer.

"I love that show," I said. Another point in his favor.

They each made their own variation of a pitying "aww" I'd long since learned to ignore.

"It's not for the show, hon," Aaron said.

"Oh. We're sure it says 'it' and not 'her' though, right?" Squinting didn't clear it up at all, so until proven otherwise, I'd give Mr. Wiggles the benefit of the doubt. "He lives in the same complex as you and you never noticed him before?"

"At least now we know Mr. Wiggles isn't gay," Liz said.

True. Aaron was like a heat-seeking missile for any gay man within a two-mile radius.

"Maybe he just moved in," Aaron said. "Pull in over there." He motioned to an open parking space across the way. "If an empty guest spot isn't a sign from the universe, I don't know what is."

"A sign of what?" Liz asked suspiciously. Rightfully so.

As soon as we stopped, Aaron jumped from the car and jogged across the street, passing the pickup and disappearing into the thin walkway between buildings before Liz and I made it to the back of her car.

Hadn't I been through enough today? I stopped to remove another piece of cat food from inside my shoe. Thank goodness I always wore high-necked tops, or I would be finding them in my cleavage forever. "I don't think this is a good idea."

Liz pushed me forward. "Out of the three of us, who's the only one who's ever had any luck with men?"

"Solid point," I conceded.

"Let's see what he's up to," Liz said when we saw Aaron come back out, waving for us to hurry up.

"I'm really not sure about this." I went anyway, breaking into a stealthier tiptoe as we neared the building Aaron had disappeared behind. We turned the corner and saw him crouching behind a bush between a door and a large picture window.

"No way," I said in a hushed shout.

Aaron shushed me. "I'm a Black man hiding in a bush,

Sophie. You think I'm doing this for fun? You wanted to get to know Mr. Wiggles. We're getting to know Mr. Wiggles."

"Not through his window!"

"The only difference between here and the grocery aisle is a piece of glass."

"And the expectation of privacy one has inside their own—"

"Fuck!"

We all froze. None of us said a word. That voice had been very male and slightly muffled. Before I remembered what a disaster this could quickly turn into, I'd already looked through the window.

Mr. Wiggles was standing next to a glass table in the middle of a clean, well-decorated living room–dining room combo. Simple, nice. This guy kept getting better and better. Except he was staring at the bag of cat food he'd just bought, running his fingers through his hair, and cursing wildly.

"I think Mr. Wiggles has anger issues," Liz said. "Is that on your list?"

"Shh!" I reached out to cover her mouth, but she caught my hand before it landed. Probably better she did, considering my aim was horrible, and I would've ended up grabbing her boob.

"Are breasts on your list too?" she whispered, laughing.

I flinched at some of the creative word combinations coming out of Mr. Wiggles' beautiful mouth as he paced back and forth. Then he abruptly stopped and glanced at something behind the couch.

"It's not your fault," he said. "It's entirely *hers*."

Surely, he wasn't blaming *me* for anything, right? I hadn't meant to startle him into throwing the bag at me.

"I didn't mean to scare you, little man." He bent down too low for me to see who he was talking to. "Try not to pee on anything while I'm gone."

When we heard the door open, Aaron whisper-shouted, "Quick!"

Liz ducked behind the bush with him, but I hesitated, looking at the muddy ground at their feet. If I stepped on it, I'd be spending the next six hours with a toothbrush in one hand and my heels in the other. I opted for plan B, which was to flee to the car via the sidewalk.

I got two steps away before hearing Mr. Wiggles say, "Whoa," followed by a pause, and then, "What the—?"

I turned toward him, feeling all my body heat shoot straight to my cheeks, leaving the rest of me frozen in place. Wow. He was even better looking now that I could see him with both eyes. "Oh, hello. Do you live here?"

He squinted at me, closing the door behind him. "Yeah. You?"

"No, I . . . um . . ." All I could hope for now was that he wouldn't turn around and see my friends in his bushes. "This isn't what it looks like."

"What does it look like?" he asked, cocking his head to the side.

"Like I followed you home. I didn't. Because that would be—"

"Weird."

I let out a sigh of relief. I would have gone with *disturbed* or maybe *creepy*. I could deal with weird.

"You sure you're okay after the . . ." He grimaced and pointed at his eye.

"The incident? Yep. One hundred percent."

"Your eye looks better."

"Thanks. So, um . . . you know what would be great?" I looked at my nails for a second. "To never think about that whole thing. Ever again."

"Done. But right now, I can't stop wondering how you

tracked me down so fast and what form of retribution I should expect." It sounded as if it had already happened to him once or twice.

"No retribution. Promise. My friend lives in this complex, but I got turned around somehow."

"I did that a lot when I first moved in—every building looks the same."

"They do." I nodded gratefully. "Anyway . . . I should go find him." Despite my incredible desire to run, I placed one foot in front of another and walked away slowly. "Sorry to startle you."

"Again."

"Excuse me?" I couldn't help but turn back.

"You startled me *again*."

"I guess I did, didn't I?"

We held each other's gaze a bit too long for it not to mean something. Sure, he'd temporarily blinded me a half-hour ago, but my eyes were working great now. And they liked what they saw, minus the stubble on his cheeks.

In that moment—a moment that could've made all the humiliation worthwhile—Liz peeked her head out of the bushes and mouthed something to me. Unfortunately, she also made enough noise to grab Mr. Wiggles' attention.

As he was turning, I shouted, "Wait!"

"There you are, Sophie!" Aaron shoved Liz against the wall before he stepped out from behind the bush. "Did you get lost again?"

"A little." I forced a laugh, silently giving thanks for having Aaron in my life. Then remembering I wouldn't be in this situation if not for him.

Mr. Wiggles looked rightfully confused as Aaron brushed a leaf off his pants and came toward us with an outstretched hand.

"For a second there, I thought you'd replaced me with *another* gorgeous man. I'm Aaron. I live in Building C."

"Cooper." He shook his hand. "I live . . . here."

With a small flick of his head, Aaron hinted we should leave. I agreed. Lord knew what Liz would say if she had a chance to join the conversation.

"I should probably show Sophie the right way to get to my place," Aaron said. "Otherwise, who knows where she'll end up."

He couldn't have come up with something that didn't make me sound quite so inept? I'd already proven that more than adequately today.

"I'm heading back to the store anyway," Cooper said.

"Forgot something?" I blurted.

"I bought the wrong food," he grumbled. "Third bag's the charm, right?"

We all stood there for a moment more, just a few seconds past awkward.

"I should go." He motioned back to his apartment. "He's hungry."

"Nice to meet you, Cooper," Aaron said. "See you around."

"Next time you get lost," Cooper said to me, "feel free to knock on my door."

"I will." I stepped back as he passed me and headed to the parking lot.

He looked back only for a second, but that second was *amazing*.

As soon as he went around the corner of the building, Liz crawled out of the bushes. "Ooooh, I like him."

Me too. "Are you finally admitting my plan isn't as nuts as you thought it was?"

"I'm finally admitting the plan and the person who came up with it are equally nuts. In an endearing way." She took the hand I'd been waving and slowly lowered it to my side.

"It's a step." I sighed, not quite ready to move yet.

My friends flanked me on each side, Aaron slipping his arm around my shoulder and Liz resting a hand on my back.

After a minute, I asked, "That went really horribly too, didn't it?"

"Oh, yeah."

"Think there's a way to come back from it?"

"No way in hell."

After another sigh, I shook it off and headed toward to Liz's car. Move forward. Live and learn. Hope for the future instead of regretting the past. My perfect man was out there somewhere.

"Cooper was too attractive anyway," I said. "And you know how I feel about too-attractive men." They were all assholes.

4

COOPER

I tried not to be too big of an asshole, but I had very few soft, sappy spots. No matter the question, ninety-nine percent of the time my answer was an emphatic *no*. Unfortunately, my little sister had caught me at a weak moment on my way home from work. Jasmine knew how to play me: a frantic last-minute call leaving me barely enough time to speed shave and throw on the suit I only wore to weddings and funerals. Meanwhile, to reinforce her story, Jaz added in some subtle whimpering as she explained how her date had flaked and she couldn't find anyone else to go to "the event" with. Before I realized I could've— *should've*—said no, I was stuck deep in the packed lanes of cars crossing the Bay Bridge with no way to turn back.

I'd never understood why my sister left our beautiful, quiet hometown to move seventy physical miles and about a thousand psychological miles west for art school. San Francisco was bad enough with its chaotic mix of stores, people, lights, and cement. San Francisco with a truck was what hell must be like—nothing but traffic, parking, and crowds. Although, in my version of hell, Helen would be here too.

I picked Jaz up at her apartment and drove downtown, trying to keep my bitching to a reasonable level. By the time we pulled into the parking lot, she'd tossed me enough glares to know we didn't agree on the definition of *reasonable*. So, I paid mightily for the privilege of parking twelve blocks away from the venue without another word. Until . . .

"A musical?" I yelled. "Are you fucking kidding me, Jaz?"

"You'll love it. Wait, that's not right." She slid out of the truck. "You love me and want me to be happy."

"I do love you. I just hope this thing isn't long enough to give that time to change." I grabbed a set of earplugs I kept in the glovebox for emergencies on a job. I didn't think one of those emergencies would involve musical theatre, but I'd never felt better prepared for life than I did right now.

After she handed the usher our tickets, she took my arm and pulled me into the lobby.

"I'll get you back for this someday."

"I'd expect nothing less, big brother."

I tapped the inside pocket of my suit to make sure my earplugs hadn't slipped out sometime between the sixth and seventh check. "I need a drink before it starts." Or five.

At least they had a full bar at these things. I motioned toward the line of excited theatergoers waiting to order crappy wine in plastic glasses. "You want something?"

"Nope. I'm going to find our seats." She let go of my arm and handed me my ticket. "You better not come in late."

"I won't."

"I'm serious," she said, her eyebrow up high. "You're *my* date tonight. If you ditch me for another woman, I'll never forgive you."

"That happened once. You can't judge a man by the decisions his hormones made when he was seventeen." Besides, I hated almost everybody now, especially in groups.

"Hurry up." She kissed me on the cheek and headed toward the orchestra section. While I stood in line, I checked my seat number and the earplugs in my pocket a couple more times.

Someone tapped my shoulder, and I spun around. It was that guy, Aaron, who lived in my apartment complex. What were the chances of running into someone in front of your apartment and then seeing them less than two weeks later seventy miles away?

"Wow," I said. "I guess the world *is* smaller than it looks on a map."

"Are you following us?" Aaron looked as shocked as I felt. "Say yes because it would make my night." He gave me a once— or twice—over. "You clean up well."

"Thanks. You too."

Actually, other than wearing a suit instead of whatever he'd been wearing the other day, he looked the same—short hair, dark brown skin, big eyes and smile, about as tall as I was but lanker.

"She's in the bathroom."

"Who?" I asked.

"Sophie."

"Oh, great." Aside from a low, steady ache of guilt for pelting her with all that pet food, I didn't really care. That said, seeing an attractive woman was never a hardship. Unless she was my ex, of course.

"Since she bought the tickets," Aaron said, "I'm in charge of drinks and whatever we do after the show. We got a hotel room for the night, so we'll probably go dancing. You're welcome to come to the club with us, and depending on how that goes, maybe back to the hotel too." His smile was so big, I flinched. "You and your . . . date?"

"That's quite an offer." I considered clarifying that my sister had dragged me here against my will, but why bother? Besides, while not too many straight men were as well put-together as Aaron or would look so genuinely happy to be here, he might not be gay. For all I knew, he and Sophie were together, and if I went dancing with them, I'd be stepping on toes that weren't my own. Or agreeing to a threesome. Neither of which I was interested in doing.

"Thanks, but I think we'll head home after this."

He frowned. "Offer stands if you change your mind." We both moved with the line. "Speak of the devil . . ."

As soon as I saw her, I understood why he'd used that expression. Sophie stood about fifteen feet away, her mouth open slightly in surprise. Her black dress drew a map of where I'd like to run my hands, and the fullness of her dark red lips made me wonder how that lipstick would look smeared on a few key areas of my body. If I wasn't taking a permanent break from beautiful, high-maintenance women, I would gladly sell my soul to that one.

None of that would be happening though. Especially not with a woman like her.

"Look who I found, Sophie!" Aaron called, putting his hand on my shoulder.

With the same look of shock, she walked toward us, her purse rocking into her hip every other step. "How unexpected!" She stopped next to Aaron. "I can't believe you're a theater lover too."

"Actually, I'm—"

"Sir?" the bartender asked impatiently. "What can I get for you?"

"Um . . ." I reached into my back pocket for my wallet before remembering where I was and that I was wearing a damn suit instead of my usual jeans and T-shirt. "Jack and soda plus whatever they're having."

"You don't have to do that," Sophie said.

"It's no problem," I said, staring at the hand she put on my arm. "I still owe you one."

"Sir? The show's about to start."

"We'll have a Cabernet and a Pinot," Aaron said.

I glanced at the bar menu, did some quick math in my head, added in a healthy tip, and set the cash onto the bar. What I *didn't* do was spend too much time wondering how long they'd been together before Aaron knew what she drank. He hadn't even hesitated.

Good luck to him. Hopefully, he wouldn't end up as miserable with Sophie as I'd been with Helen.

"Aaron," Sophie hissed out of the side of her mouth, blurring her smile for a second.

"What? He wants to pay." Aaron shrugged innocently. "And I think we should give him whatever he wants."

Her eyes popped open wide, and her cheeks flushed. "Aaron!"

My abs tightened as I tried not to laugh. When that didn't work, I turned back to the bar and watched the bartender pour our drinks. I wasn't clueless—I knew when I was being hit on. But with people being more open with their lifestyle, orientation, and fluidity these days, you could never be sure what was going on until it was spelled out. Just because Aaron wasn't shy about his interest didn't mean the two of them weren't together. When I was a kid, I didn't take other people's stuff, and I didn't like to share mine. Things hadn't changed since, especially when it came to sex.

"Aaron's right. And what I want now is to buy you some wine."

"Then I guess we're both getting what we want," she said, holding my gaze.

Shit. I felt myself weaken. No! I would not backslide. *Think about baseball or work or anything else that could snap me out of it.*

"Jasmine," I blurted. "She'll declare emotional war on me if I'm late. I should go." I grabbed my drink and headed toward the orchestra section, throwing a quick, "Enjoy the show," over my shoulder. That's what people said at these kinds of things, right?

I'd downed the booze before I even stepped into the theater, tossing the cup into a garbage can as I took the program the usher shoved at me. I should've gotten more than one drink.

Jaz tapped on her nonexistent watch as I shuffled sideways down the aisle, apologizing to everyone as I passed. Thankfully, they all stood and folded their seats up to create more room. It was still uncomfortably tight for a guy my size, but if they'd stayed seated, their eyes would've been level with a cock that was still picturing Sophie in that dress.

"What took you so long?" Jaz asked as I sat. "Let me guess: You had to buy someone a drink, and by *someone,* I mean a woman."

"Technically—"

"You're Cooper Wahl, aren't you?" the woman on my other side asked.

I clenched my eyes shut a second, knowing the look I'd see on Jasmine's face when I opened them again. Yep, that was the one.

"Answer the woman," Jaz grumbled, her arms folded tightly across her chest.

I turned to the woman, wishing I didn't know why she recognized me. "Yes, ma'am."

"Oh my God!" She smacked her friend on the arm. "Sally, this is the Do-Her guy!"

"It's Get 'er Done." My sister leaned across me to glare at her. "Not 'Do-Her.'"

"Close enough," the woman said.

"Not at all close enough," Jaz mumbled.

I appreciated her defense of the ill-conceived business name I'd chosen eight years ago, but I was used to it. *Do-Her* wasn't even the worst I'd heard. Fortunately, or unfortunately, that stupid name was nothing if not memorable. The name, along with a high quality of work, had made my business grow beyond my wildest dreams. The only reason it stayed small was because I turned away twice as much work as I took on.

"We came to see a show that one of us better enjoy," I whispered to my little sis, "and it's not going to be me."

She mumbled obscenities under her breath while the women on my other side ignored all social cues I was giving off and blabbed on about recognizing me from the television interview I'd done for a local station a while back. A favor for one of my clients. One I regretted almost instantly for exactly this reason.

"You can fix anything, right?" the woman closest to me asked as I tried to ignore Jasmine's increasingly painful grip on my arm.

I cut her off as soon as she started explaining her parent's marital issues. "Unfortunately, that's not the kind of problem I fix."

"But they say you can fix anything."

"*Things* I can handle. Not people." Besides, I was the last person anyone should come to for relationship problems. Thankfully, the lights went down.

"But—"

"Shh!" Jasmine shoved me back into my seat.

"We can talk during intermission," the woman said quietly.

"Uh . . . sure. I'll be at the bar."

"I used to think it was so cool women were always lusting

after my brothers," Jaz grumbled. "Turns out, it's really fucking annoying."

"Relax," I whispered. "She wanted my help, not my sweet, sweet lovin'."

It was almost too dark to see her eyes roll. "For a guy who makes his living figuring out what other people can't, you're totally clueless."

"Is it over?" I asked as soon as the house lights went on at intermission.

"Good thing you don't want to ruin this for me." Jasmine stood and filed out behind the people on her other side, squeezing herself around the few who weren't leaving. "The first act is over, but don't worry, the second is longer."

"Oh, good," I muttered. "I can get more liquor now, right?"

She sighed dramatically. "I take it back—feel free to leave me for the first woman you see."

"I'll keep that in mind," I lied. I wouldn't abandon her anywhere for anyone.

We followed the crowd toward the lobby, and she grabbed my arm when I faked a lunge toward the emergency exit. We were in line for the bar when I saw Sophie and Aaron across the lobby.

"Wow, you actually look almost happy to be here," she said. "What's suddenly got you so excited?"

"Nothing." I turned and focused my eyes on the prize—the long row of liquor bottles resting on top of the bar.

"Really? Because it seemed like you were gawking at that woman in the long black dress and spraying your pheromones everywhere." She pretended to gag.

"*Heeeey*, respect the pheromones! They've led to great pleasure for a lot of women."

"Eww!" She slugged me in the arm as I laughed. "The worst part of that was making me wonder what you meant by 'a lot.' Damn you. Now *I* need a drink."

"Serves you right." I kissed her cheek. "So, how many drinks is it going to take to make me forgive you for dragging me here tonight?"

"Hello again," someone said behind me. We'd said about twenty words to each other, and I already recognized Sophie's voice. Something about it shot straight to my gut and everything lower. It was feminine, expressive, filled with laughter even when she wasn't.

Goddamn, I'm weak. I slowly turned around, faked a smile, and did a quick round of introductions.

"Have you seen this show before?" Aaron asked my sister.

"No, but I've listened to the soundtrack about a million times, so it feels like I have."

They all agreed while I stared at the arm Aaron wrapped around Sophie's waist.

"What about you, Cooper?"

"Um . . ." With all eyes on me, I asked for Jasmine's help by nudging her with my elbow.

"Yeah, Cooper." She pulled away and stood next to them while everyone waited for my response. "What do you think of the show so far?"

I didn't want to be the asshole who brought down everyone's mood by saying what I really thought. I didn't enjoy lying, but I could bend the truth to avoid insulting everyone in the room. "Uh . . . the set pieces are designed and built well. Now, who wants"—needs—"a drink?" I sure as hell did.

Sophie and Aaron passed, but Jasmine wanted a rum and Coke, so as they wandered away from the line, I ordered our drinks, making mine a double. When I turned around, Sophie and Aaron were gone. Good.

"You don't deserve this, you know," I said, giving Jaz the smaller of the two cups.

"You're such a good big brother, you're going to give it to me anyway." She took a sip before breaking the big news. "By the way, we're going to a nightclub with them after the show."

"No, we're not."

"It's Friday night, Cooper. Live a little. Plus, I already said yes, and I know you wouldn't let me go somewhere with people I just met without having a ride home."

Guess what my second least favorite thing to do was—go to any establishment referred to as a *nightclub*. Bars? Sure. After-hours places? Yep. Taco trucks? Hell yes. Nightclubs? Never.

"Sophie will be there," she taunted.

Was I really that transparent? "I thought you didn't want me paying attention to anyone else tonight."

"I changed my mind. You're useless to me. Other than taking me to the nightclub and driving me back to my place after, of course."

"Of course," I repeated before sighing. "We're not staying long." After all, I had to drive home and wouldn't be able to numb myself with liquor.

"Who is she anyway?"

I took a long sip before answering. "A woman I met while buying dog food for Sammy, who is probably pissing on and chewing everything in my place right now because I fell for my little sister's manipulation."

"You still have Helen's dog?" She looked surprised even though she knew my ex. "When is she coming back?"

"It was supposed to be for two weeks, but her trip might be extended." I shrugged. "What am I supposed to do, pawn the little guy off on some other idiot?"

"That's so Helen. She's the reason I thought you were done with women like that. Apparently, I was wrong."

"Women like what?" I knew what she meant.

"Superficial, well-dressed narcissists who make you hate yourself," Jasmine said, as if she knew Sophie was any of those things.

True, Sophie was the kind of beautiful few men were strong or smart enough to resist. Sexy, intelligent, sophisticated, moderately uptight. The hard-to-understand type I was unhealthily addicted to.

Used to be addicted to.

Sophie and Helen had a few things in common, but at least Sophie had a sense of humor. And more curves than Helen could dream of having. She smiled a lot more, too, although I wasn't sure how I felt about that yet. I found most people annoying. That went double for happy people.

Jasmine continued, "In fact, I seem to remember you saying that the next woman you dated had to cuss like a sailor, have her own toolbelt, and not own more than two colors of lipstick."

I didn't remember saying that, but it sounded about right.

"Is it wrong to want a woman who's independent and unafraid to just be herself? Before you answer, you should remember we shared a bathroom for over a decade so I know how much makeup you own, and I've heard plenty of words come out of your mouth that would make Mom cry. Are you really that unusual?"

"Of course, I am." She smacked my arm. "I'm a special fucking flower, just like Mom and Dad told me I was whenever a boy broke my heart in high school."

"I don't think those were the exact words they used," I said. But I remembered how pissed off my brothers and I were whenever some stupid shithead treated her badly.

"You have to admit the toolbelt thing is dumb though." She looped her arm around mine to drag me back toward the theater. "Besides, those things might be what you want, but I don't think you've ever known what you *need*."

That was true. At least when it came to women. My last mistake was in London right now probably laughing it up and having a much better night than I was.

I hated happy people.

5
———

SOPHIE

The Castro district nightclub was dark, loud, and reeked of cologne. I'd only been here once, but it was Aaron's second home. I never understood why he didn't just commit and move to the city. Probably the same reason he wouldn't commit to a relationship, something he and I shared but for vastly different reasons.

We found a table near the back. While Aaron and Jasmine spoke excitedly about San Francisco, I focused on finding out what was wrong with Cooper. The man liked cats, the theatre, going to clubs, and was the hottest guy in a gay bar. A gay bar. That in itself was a minor miracle.

So far, he'd banked more in the *pro* column than anyone I'd ever met, but that could change in a single chorus of "It's Raining Men." Everyone had faults, and I was determined to suss out his before the night ended.

Unfortunately, the club was mind-bendingly loud even at the back-corner table we'd claimed, so everything we said had to be shouted. We yelled at each other for about half an hour, filling in the basics. If I understood him correctly, I found his first flaw—his job. Interior design and what sounded like wide-ranging handyman services were opposite sides of the industry, but it meant there was a chance—albeit a small one—that we might end up on the same project some day or he might have met my father in a professional setting. There were two deal-breakers right there. Plus, while there was no shame in doing any honest job, when one half of the couple was a handyman and the other was on the cusp of running a high-end design company that had appeared in every home magazine on the West Coast, there was bound to be conflict. Cooper didn't seem insecure, but I'd never met a man who handled being on the low end of the financial seesaw well. So I added his profession to the *con* column and hoped that would be the only one.

Aaron stood. "Who's ready for round three?"

"My turn," Cooper said, pulling out his wallet.

I looked down at my empty glass.

"It's on Cooper, Sophie," Jasmine yelled. "I'm sure my brother would love to get you drunk."

"What the fuck, Jaz?" he snapped before leaning toward me. "My sister thinks she has a good sense of humor, so obviously, she's wrong about a lot. That last comment being one of them."

"I was joking!"

He nodded. "While also proving it's time to take you home."

"Relax, brother." She leaned back in her seat, arms crossed over her chest. "Enjoy your big once-a-year night out. I'll just sit here quietly and pout."

He hesitated another minute before heading toward the bar with Aaron to order another round.

"I swear it was a joke," she said as soon as we were alone. "I forgot you guys don't know each other well enough for sarcasm yet."

"Is it ever too early for sarcasm?" I asked. "Besides, I knew you were kidding."

"Good!" She sat up straighter and scooted her chair closer to mine. "Because I'm starting to like you, and Cooper seems into you."

"I'm not sure how into me he is. We just met."

"Yeah, but he's picky about who he flirts with."

Picky was good. There was nothing worse than an overly flirtatious man, especially one as attractive as Cooper. Because the flirtation would work ninety-eight percent of the time. Another reason why "too attractive" was on the list of things I didn't want in a man, and Cooper was definitely pushing the line.

On second thought, there was something worse than an overly flirtatious man—an overly used man. I had an overly used boyfriend a few years ago. And while I had no physical proof, I was almost certain he compared all those uses and even gave each woman a colorful descriptor to designate how good she was at sex. None of my ex-lovers, including him, had ever complained about my skills, but my list and an expectation of monogamy had limited my experience in that particular area.

Cooper and Aaron were tall enough to make them out over the crowd. Cooper turned his head and shook his head at someone I couldn't see.

"I bet somebody just tried to pick him up," Jasmine said, amused. "Granted, I'm his sister, but I don't get what makes him so appealing, especially to gay men." She tilted her martini glass all the way back for the last few drops. "Maybe it's because he's so broody, and they see that as a challenge."

"Is he?" Broody wasn't good. I'd dated broody for four miserable months. Broody never called me back, never wanted to go out, and always made me work to squeeze out even the most basic response from him.

Obviously, Cooper's sister knew him better than I did, but Cooper hadn't seemed broody to me, so I'd reserve judgment but keep an eye out for any brooding.

A minute after the guys brought back our drinks, Jasmine stood. "Come on, big brother. Dance with me."

He grimaced, pointing to the ceiling. "I don't think this is the kind of music siblings are ethically allowed to dance to." He made a good point. The beat was fast, but there were serious sexual overtones to the lyrics, and everyone already dancing looked to be either biblically familiar with each other or they were about to be.

Luckily, nothing ever stopped Aaron. "I'll dance with you, Jaz. Let's go."

She happily took his hand and let him lead her onto the dance floor.

Without turning toward me, Cooper scooted his chair closer until our thighs touched. Probably to have a better view of the dance floor or to talk without having to yell. But good luck trying to tell that to my body.

I'd been around many attractive men before, but this felt different, like my first high school crush. If I looked down, I wondered if I'd see all my arm hair leaning in his direction and mini bolts of lightning passing back and forth like some sort of science experiment.

Silently, we watched Aaron and Cooper's sister grind and laugh for a minute. Out of the corner of my eye, I checked for brooding.

"How long should we pretend you're not stalking me?" he asked. The heat of his breath on my ear sent a shiver through me that stopped at my crotch.

I laughed uncomfortably. "Remind me which one of us threw cat food at the other?"

"That was pretty charming, wasn't it? It was also proof I wasn't stalking you. I've never been good at subtlety or games. If I'd seen you before that moment in the store, I would've thrown cat food at you *then*."

"If we're not following each other, what should we call it?"

He squinted. "We could call it fate."

The corner of his mouth lifted, and my heart clenched. *Fate:* a noun that pressed every single one of my girlish fantasy buttons. I knew better than to make too much of the comment though. In general, men didn't believe in fate. They believed in chemistry, coincidence, and making things happen—*things* meaning sex. It was useless to try to convince them otherwise. I'd tried. Multiple times. All I got were panicked looks and unreturned phone calls.

"If the whole idea of fate wasn't total bullshit," he finished.

Maybe I understood men better than I thought. "Then let's call it a series of weird coincidences."

"I'm good with weird."

Well, *that* would come in handy.

"Sorry I cut out so fast the other day in front of my place," he said. "I had to go back to the store."

"For more cat food?" I teased.

"Dog food." He clenched his eyes shut, slowly shaking his head. "Turns out dogs eat dog food, and I'm the idiot who bought the wrong kind. Twice."

"You have a dog." I'd meant it to be a totally normal, benign question, but I'm fairly sure each of the four words expressed my disappointment perfectly. Cooper had a dog. He wasn't a cat person after all. So much so that he couldn't even recognize a picture of one on a bag of cat food. Twice.

He was a dog person. Dogs were nowhere near my *pro* list. Dog people enjoyed spending all their time outside doing outside things like hiking and going to the beach. Dog people took pleasure in throwing balls or frisbees around and asking, "Who's a good boy or girl?" in a sing-song voice. I didn't like any of those things. In fact, I actively hated all those things.

Of course, I wasn't perfect either. Not even a little. It was the journey that mattered, constantly striving to be better tomorrow than I was today. So, I suppose I could learn how to throw a frisbee and speak in a weird voice to an animal that won't understand what I was saying. But I'd never enjoy it.

It was fine. Cooper had many other good things going for him, other attributes that were on my list. The theatre, for one, and he ran his own business. At least, I thought that was what he'd said. The volume of the club made it difficult to hear anything not screamed.

"How'd you like the show?" I yelled.

He gave half a smile and sipped his drink, letting my innocuous question linger as if I'd said something inappropriate.

"You didn't enjoy it?" I asked, defensively. "Touring companies always make changes from the original Broadway productions, but I thought they did a fantastic job with this one."

"I'm sure they did. I'll have to take your word for it."

"You didn't watch the show tonight?"

He tilted his head from side to side. "Watched? Yes. Listened to? That's why I brought earplugs."

"You don't like musicals?" The loud music might have covered the despondency in my voice, but he must have seen it in my face. "Why did you go then?"

"My little sister asked me to."

I dropped my gaze and focused on the ring of condensation on the thin cardboard coaster at the base of my drink so I wouldn't give anything else away with my expression. He cared about his family, was intelligent, and was more attractive than I could've ever hoped for. But he was also a dog person, he didn't like theatre or the city, and he didn't dance. That *I* didn't dance either was unimportant. My perfect man would dance reasonably well. Plus, there was still the open question of Cooper's broodiness.

While none of those things made him a bad person, they were all on the *con* side of my list. Every time I'd veered away from the list, let my emotions or my hormones overrule it, I ended up depressed and alone. And I wasn't sure how much more of that I could take.

Just then, Aaron came rushing back to the table, pulling Jasmine along with him.

"You're never going to believe what Jasmine told me about Coop!" He turned to the man in question. "Can I call you Coop?"

"No." At least he wasn't indecisive.

Aaron looked at me and said, "Cooper is the man behind Get 'er Done."

"What's 'Get Her Done'?"

"It's *'er*'—without the *h*," Jasmine said, as if that made a difference.

"How comfortable is that rock you've been living under, Soph?" Aaron sighed. "Cooper is the guy who can fix anything. Been on the local news and morning shows a couple times, right?" Jasmine nodded while Cooper looked miserable. "You look a lot different without the beard."

"So I hear." Cooper rubbed his cheek. "I'm thinking of growing it back."

"Don't do that!" I blurted.

"Okay," he said slowly.

After studying his face for a second and imagining it hairier, I remembered the countless lengthy discussions Aaron and Liz had over the pros and cons of bearded men. I'd never paid much attention because I was strictly in the *con* camp when it came to facial hair. But they'd always used the Get 'er Done guy as the reference for the *pro* column.

It took a minute to put together the bits and pieces. Supposedly, Get 'er Done could do miracles with almost any problem—

construction, technology, managerial, decision-making, and a number of other things.

"Tell them about the name," Jasmine said.

Cooper sighed. "It was in homage to my ten-year-old self's favorite childhood movie. What can I say? I was eighteen when I started the business. Had I known how stupid the name would be eight years later, I would've opted for something a little harder for people to laugh at."

Aaron rubbed his lips together as if trying to think of the right way to say something. "Are you sure the laughter isn't their hoping that your services include getting *her* done?"

"That's come up a few times," Cooper said into his glass as he took a drink. "But to be clear, that's neither something I offer nor take as payment."

"A friend told me you're a magician—you put your hands on something, and two minutes later, it's fixed."

He squinted at Aaron. "I'd be leery about everything else your buddy has told you because that's not even a little bit true. What I do isn't magic, and it usually takes me more than two minutes to do it. Most of the time, it's a *lot* longer."

"That's good to know," Aaron said, his eyebrow lifted. "Isn't it, Sophie?"

"Eww!" Jasmine grimaced while Cooper shook his head, and I tried to hide mine.

"What about phones that keep crashing?" Aaron asked. "Sophie, give him your phone. It sucks, but she's attached to it for some reason."

"Because I don't trust salesmen who say they can transfer everything to a new phone without screwing something up," I snapped.

"I can probably fix whatever's going on with the phone," Cooper said, "but you're on your own with the trust issues."

"See?" Aaron laughed. "It took you, like, thirty seconds to figure her out."

I set my phone on the table in front of Cooper and took a deep breath. "Don't mess anything up."

He held my eyes for a moment. "I try hard not to mess things up. But don't worry, I'm more successful at that in my professional life than my private one." He asked me a few questions about the phone, scrolling through my settings. A minute later, he handed it back to me.

"No problem," I said, putting it back in my purse. "It wasn't a test. It's—"

"Fixed. Aaron was right—you should back everything up, wipe it completely, and get a new one."

"That's impossible." I tapped and swiped through my most vital apps to make sure everything was still there. It all was, and it didn't freeze or turn itself off like usual either. "How did you do that so quickly?"

"I told you—he's a magician!" Aaron said.

"Because I said you were right?" he joked. "Again, not magic. I'm just good at figuring out how stuff works, and I don't want to talk about myself anymore. It's someone else's turn." He looked directly at me.

I shrugged. "I'm really bad at figuring out how things work. Myself included."

When Cooper smiled, my breath stopped. He had fantastically full lips, perfect teeth, and a goddamn dimple in his left cheek. A dimple! How had I not noticed that before? Or how beautifully bright his blue eyes were when they looked into my boring brown ones.

Damn him. Damn me. Served me right for making so many assumptions before getting to know him and realizing how incredibly wrong he was for me. I'd been too distracted by my body's reaction—something that very rarely acted in my best long-term interests. It hummed just looking at him. Hell, if my body were in charge, I'd already be straddling his lap with my dress hitched up around my waist. Fortunately and unfortunately, my body wasn't in charge. The list was.

The dog, not liking the same things, his job. All cons. But it was those eyes and that dimple that were the dealbreakers, pushing him way over the "too attractive" limit. Plus, now that I thought about it, I *had* seen him look a little broody at the theater and once or twice here at the club.

I pushed the remainder of my drink to the other side of the table and scooted my chair a few inches away from his. I needed to stop drinking and get away from him as soon as I possibly could.

Because facts are facts.

And Cooper's *con* column was now insurmountably bigger than the *pro* side.

I slumped down in my seat a little as soon as my brain convinced the rest of me that he wasn't "the one." Best case, we'd have just enough time together for me to start caring about him before it twisted into another bad relationship. He'd tell me I was crazy and asking for too much. I'd tell him that he'd never even tried to make it work. Finally, we would both run out of fight and walk away, only remembering what we hated about each other and none of what had drawn us together.

I already liked him enough not to waste his time on a relationship that would never go anywhere and keep both of us from being available to one that would. It was best to cut things off now before they had a chance to ruin everything. Like split ends or gangrene.

This way was smarter, kinder to both of us.

Unfortunately, when he smiled at me like that, it became so much harder to plan the best way to let him down easy tonight and not to just *be* easy for the night.

6

COOPER

The night air was cool, a welcome respite from the hot, stagnant air inside the club. Aaron and Jasmine continued dancing to the muffled beat coming through the door as we made our way through the crowd on the sidewalk outside. They went ahead, gossiping as if they'd known each other forever. Sophie and I followed at a safe distance.

In the last few hours, I'd done more talking than I had over the last few months combined, and more loud talking than ever. I wasn't used to sharing that much about myself. Or sharing anything at all. It wasn't comfortable, but oddly, it wasn't as excruciating as it usually was either.

I'd also spent much of that time adjusting my cock. Every time Sophie laughed, touched me, or we got caught staring at one another, my cock gave me an unwelcomed reminder that it was ready to go at a moment's notice.

Her cheeks were flushed, either from the heat inside the club or the three drinks she'd had. I respected a woman who knew her limits. Of course, from time to time, I also respected a woman who didn't have any limits. I'd kill to see Sophie relaxed, that black dress hung over a chair—no way was she the type who threw anything on the floor—and her hair spread out on a pillow.

She certainly had the beautiful thing down—the kind that only got harder to define the longer I was around it, each moment doubling my determination to figure it out. To figure *her* out. Like a puzzle with an infinite number of pieces—her looks, mannerisms, words, charisma, and whatever the hell was going on behind her smile.

Part of the reason I was good at fixing shit was my ability to assess an object, situation, or person. Including myself. While I had innumerable faults anyone who knew me would attest to, I was fortunate enough to have inherited physical characteristics most women found attractive. My looks had gotten me into a lot of situations I wanted to be in and some I should've stayed away from.

Which one was this?

As we walked toward my truck, Sophie glanced at me every few steps, her brow furrowing more and more each time. "Why are you looking at me like that?"

"Me?" I wondered how she'd react if I told her the truth. That I was trying to decide how to feel about her. A battle raged between my head and my body, and remembering the horror show of my last relationship wasn't doing shit to convince my legs to run away from this one.

She stopped and put her hands on her hips. "What?"

"You're very attractive." A completely honest understatement.

She squished up her nose, embarrassed. "So are you."

"Thanks." Without thought, I stepped closer. I could have her up against the window of the closed café behind her in less than a second. Just a quick taste of her. Then maybe my brain would clear, and I'd do what was right for my mental health.

"Cooper . . ." Her eyes darted from my eyes to my lips and

back again. "Can I ask you a couple questions? Just to clarify a few things."

"Sure." I managed to hold myself together when she put her hand on my chest.

"Are your parents still together?"

"Yes," I answered warily, not sure where this was headed but knowing it wasn't in any direction I wanted to go. "They retired early and moved to Palm Springs a few years ago."

"Good for them." She barely paused before asking another. "Jasmine mentioned you had three brothers. Do you all get along?"

"More or less."

"What's the less?"

"Only one of them is local—Beckett. Jasmine lives here in the city, but the other two live out of state, so I don't see them too often. When we do get together, we have to squeeze all the family drama into a single weekend. It can be a little intense."

"Makes sense. Do you like cats as well as dogs?"

I blinked at the speed she switched topics, as if she just wanted pat answers without caring what they were. This wasn't curiosity or even small talk. This was a deposition.

"Yes," I said, "but only because I don't like either of them."

Her brows came together. "You don't like your dog?"

"He's not mine. He's my ex's. I don't like her either if it makes you feel better."

"It doesn't."

"That's too bad," I said flatly.

Funny how quickly hope could turn into disappointment. For a second there, I thought she was different. I should've known better than to doubt myself. Again.

"Describe your perfect day," she said, either not noticing or not caring that I had pulled away, literally and figuratively.

I didn't want to share my thoughts or feelings. Something

that had never failed to disappoint the woman I was with. It wouldn't this time either. Usually, it was a slow and steady letdown that dragged out over a few months. Apparently, Sophie wanted to condense it all into one evening. Fine. If she really wanted to know what I thought, she'd get it in all its unpleasant glory.

"My perfect day." I sighed, wondering how far I'd get before she regretted asking. "Wake up. Not too early. Have sex. The warm, lazy kind when neither person is totally awake, so we start out moving slowly, doing whatever feels best. Then it turns into more and we let ourselves go, not caring about what else we have to do that day, or morning breath, or if the neighbors can hear the screaming and the headboard slamming into the wall. Then coffee. Good coffee, not the shitty kind. Then a long shower. With sex. Up against the tile or from behind. I'm not picky. Hang out for a while not really doing much of anything. Maybe go for a walk in the afternoon, watch some TV, and . . ."

She swallowed. "More sex?" She hadn't looked at me once since I started talking.

"Sure, if that's what you want," I said, complete with a cocky-ass smirk.

Her gaze slowly moved from the concrete near her feet, up my body, and finally to my eyes. "That's a lot of sex."

"You said my perfect day, not a realistic one." I shrugged. "Now I have a question for you. What's the job I'm interviewing for, and does it come with dental?"

"I didn't mean to offend you. I just had to be sure." She straightened. "You're a great guy, but I'm looking for someone . . . else."

That would've taken a little time to heal if I hadn't already shut everything down. "Wow. Anybody else or someone in particular?"

"Not *anybody*. Someone smart, interesting, who has their life in order. It's nothing personal."

"Right." I started walking again. "How could anyone take that personally?"

She rushed to keep up. "Not that you aren't interesting. And smart. You are."

As if I needed her reassurance. "I know."

"Good," she said, smiling. "I didn't want you to think I hadn't realized that."

"Appreciate you letting me know though." My voice was tighter than I wanted it to be, proof I cared more than I wanted to. "I was really worried there for a sec. I'm just glad you didn't judge me before you got a chance to know me." Although, to be fair, we'd both made assumptions about each other. The difference was that mine had been right.

"I'm not judging you, Cooper. But it doesn't take a long time to figure out that we're vastly different people who have quite different values."

"Like honesty and integrity, those kinds of things? Sure. I get it. Who'd want someone like that?"

At least she caught my sarcasm. "You're mad at me."

"Not mad." I stopped and shook my head. "In fact, I was thinking the same thing."

"You were?" She looked insulted.

"Yep. We'd be a disaster in the making."

"Oh." She glanced ahead toward Aaron and Jasmine, then back to me. "I'm . . . glad we agree." She stared at me, hopefully not waiting for me to break down crying.

"Yeah," I said. "I'm not looking for long-term." Expectations I wouldn't live up to, needs I wouldn't fulfill, feelings I wouldn't have.

"But you *are* looking for something short-term."

I couldn't tell if it was a statement or a question.

"I might be open to that . . . with the right person." Whoever she was inside didn't change how gorgeous or curvy she was on the outside. Women like her messed with my head too much to date, but I wouldn't turn down having all the benefits and none of the danger. "Why do you ask?"

"No reason," she said quickly.

I nodded. "I'm glad we cleared everything up then."

"Me too."

I'd never had trouble finding women who were interested. Women who didn't need me to share a piece of myself before the first date. After Helen, I thought I'd learned to stay clear of high-maintenance, hard-to-read women, to not get mixed up with another one just because she was tough to figure out, and I fucking *loved* that.

"Sophie!" Aaron shouted. "I'm going to the hotel."

"I'm going with him." Jasmine slipped her arm through his. "Cooper, you can pick me up there whenever you guys are done."

"Actually, we're *already* done." Hell, we were done before we even started.

7

SOPHIE

On Saturday, I had a date with a large glass of Pinot Noir. At the end of the night, I grabbed the bottle of wine, and we went out to my backyard to stargaze. Aaron, Liz, and I had all fallen in love with Davis during college and decided to stay in the small-by-California-standards town. My house was just far enough from where I'd grown up in Sacramento that my father didn't expect me to drop by his place every day while also being a quick commute to the office where my father *did* expect me to drop by every day.

I hadn't lived here for long—only four months—but the first area I'd tackled had been the backyard. Lots of seating, a table for food and drinks, and a wood-burning fire pit in the middle of the covered patio. On the grass, I'd set out a side table for my date and a lounge chair for me.

It was the best date I'd had in a really long time . . . until Liz called.

Aaron must have told her about our trip, including every minute we'd spent with Cooper and Jasmine. But he didn't know how Cooper and I had left things. I couldn't tell him. He liked

Cooper too much for me to break it to him without a little more preparation.

Luckily, Liz didn't like anyone very much, so I could tell her the truth. When I reached that part of the story, she stopped doing her regular "uh huh" and "then what happened" reactions.

"I missed something," she said, cutting me off. "This guy can put up with Aaron, he's even hotter in a suit, you liked his sister, and there was a ton of chemistry between you two. But you decided to end things before they started?"

Now that I knew the direction this conversation would take, I wished I hadn't said anything at all. "I didn't say there was a ton of chemistry. You're missing the larger picture."

"That he didn't pass your stupid test?" Her voice boomed through the phone. "Fit into all your little boxes? *That* picture?"

"Stop yelling at me. I didn't do anything wrong."

"You didn't do anything *right* either." Her sigh was long. The ensuing silence was even longer.

"He didn't want me either!" I hated how much that had hurt my pride. "He's looking for something casual, but not—"

"Hang on," she said. "This might actually be good for you. He's not everything you've ever wanted. Fine. But he's hot and offering you free milk. It seems like a waste not to get some, doesn't it?"

"Am I supposed to know what that means?"

"Why waste a gorgeous, seemingly-decent guy just because he isn't soulmate material? Remember my parents' favorite misogynistic saying: 'Why buy the cow if you can get the milk for free'?"

"It's hard to forget the most awkward conversation of one's adolescence."

Shortly after we met in high school, Liz's parents discovered the only parent I had left was a workaholic I barely saw, and I was being raised by our housekeeper. So they tried to be the family I didn't have. Unfortunately, that also included a sit-down to explain to two seventeen-year-olds why holding onto our virginity was so important. As if that hadn't been awkward enough, Liz pretended not to understand, forcing her very conservative parents to explain the idiom in great detail. Little had they known that their daughter gave her proverbial free milk to a member of the basketball team the year before. I'd end up giving mine away a few months later, beginning a string of failures that continued to this very day.

"Just because you're not going to fall in love with the cow, buy it, and keep it in your barn forever," Liz said, "doesn't mean you shouldn't drink some free milk every once in a while."

I had nothing against casual sex even though I'd never had any. I wanted the emotional *and* the physical, having both instead of only one. If you're spending all your time sleeping with a man you could never love, when would you find the man you could? Granted, if I were getting the milk for free from anyone, Cooper's name would definitely be near the top of the list, in the number-one slot. Not that it mattered. I didn't want free milk. Did I?

"You still there?" she asked.

"I think I'm lactose intolerant," I said miserably.

"You're not. Besides, the whole point of it being free is that it's not a forever commitment. You can stop drinking whenever you want. You should do it."

"Maybe."

"That means no," she grumbled.

"No means no. Maybe means maybe."

"Oh, please, Sophie. Your yesses mean, 'I need a second to completely overthink it, and then I'll say no'." She cursed. "I have to get to work before all my binge-drinking customers die of thirst. Can't let all those student loans I took out go to waste, right?" She fake sobbed. At least, I thought it was fake. Bartending was supposed to be a transitional job for her until she found something permanent and great. It had been a long, hard transition.

She blew out a deep breath. "But first, I'm going to say what I almost told you a minute ago and then decided would be too blunt." She said that as if she normally wasn't.

Liz, Aaron, and I were always direct, knowing we wanted the best for one another and we were each strong enough to hear the truth. Of course, when I was on the receiving end of all that directness, it helped to have a drink or two in me first.

"Wait a sec." I topped off my wine and took a big sip. "Okay, I'm ready."

"You need to get rid of that damn list. I don't know what you're so afraid of, but whatever it is, it's holding you back."

That wasn't nearly as bad as I'd expected. My father had taught me a lot of things, some good, some not so good. But one thing I took to heart was that the fastest way to know which areas you needed improvement was constructive criticism. I trusted Liz. But no one was right all the time, and this was one of those times.

"I'm not afraid of Cooper," I said. "We just aren't compatible."

"How do you know? You barely gave him a chance." She paused then said, "Hey! Maybe you should ask the guy who can fix anything to fix *you*." She exaggerated a regretful sigh. "If only we'd thought of that before you totally blew him off."

"Wouldn't have worked anyway. Apparently, he avoids enormously painful jobs that would take an entire lifetime if not longer to get right."

"Smart guy." The laughter in her voice fizzled into a serious tone. "Have you ever wondered if the man you should be with is nothing like you think?"

I scoffed. That was impossible. I'd updated and refined my list after every awful date and every horrible breakup, adding all the things I didn't want and all the things I did.

"It's not as if you've had great male role models," she said, telling me nothing I didn't already know. She hated my father. From the second she met him and every second since. Occasionally, I agreed. But then I remembered what he'd been through—what we'd been through—along with everything he'd taught me about business. Everything I had was because of him. And someday, he'd hand over the reins to the interior design business he'd built from nothing. All I had to do was convince him I could do it—be more than just his office and advertising manager.

"I will take some time to think on that," I said to end the discussion.

"You know I love you, right?" She cursed again. "Answer that later. I gotta go."

After we hung up, I thought about what she'd said, the tinge of defeat in her tone as if she'd already given up on me. As if I were hopeless. I wasn't.

I'd worked hard to be the person I was. It was totally normal to be a little afraid of letting someone into my life, my body, and possibly my heart. I'd be an idiot to let just anyone in.

Besides, Cooper had probably already forgotten all about me.

8

COOPER

"Come on, little man. No one's looking and no one cares." There was nothing pretty about a grown man begging. "Please!"

Despite Sammy's size, apparently, he was in fact a dog, so he shouldn't have a paralyzing fear of taking a dump on someone's lawn. We'd already passed three other dogs on our trip around the football-field-sized courtyard in between the condo buildings, and they'd all looked happy when they did it.

I shoved the poop bag—seriously, this is something that actually exists, a bag that smelled like baby powder specifically made for shit—into the back pocket of my jeans and took a deep, calming breath. Maybe my readiness and excitement for this horrific weekend to be over was making him nervous.

Between obsessing about my near relapse of terrible dating decisions when I was with Sophie and wondering why the hell I let Sammy sleep in my bed, I'd gotten three hours of decent shuteye. Exhaustion left me even grumpier than normal.

"Cooper!" someone yelled.

I didn't know my neighbors, mostly because they were people, and being civil would only encourage them to talk to me again.

When I'd moved out of my parents' house as a happy, hopeful eighteen-year-old—minus the happy and hopeful parts—all I'd wanted was a place of my own. To be rid of the continual claustrophobia involved in sharing a house with three brothers, a sister, two parents, and the neighbor girl who moved in when her mom abandoned her. My mistake had been to buy this turn-key condo in a small complex near my shop instead of some land with a decent-sized cave on it. Something tall enough to stand in without smacking my head and deep enough that no one would ever find me.

When I stopped to look at who was screaming my name, I ruined Sammy's forward momentum, which he really needed. "Sorry, bud."

"This whole time I thought it was Sophie you were following!" Aaron walked across the grass toward me, waving his hand over his head as if he were still dancing, today in a matching red and white track suit. "It's me though, isn't it?"

"Damn, I hoped you wouldn't figure it out." Out of the corner of my eye, I saw the little shit taking a little shit. "That's the spirit, Sam!"

Aaron looked over at Sammy. When he let out a half-sigh/half-squeal and moved toward the little guy, I grabbed his arm and held him back.

"Wait until he's done. Please. We've been out here half an hour already."

"I'm in shock." He glanced at me then back at Sam. "Never in a million years would I have guessed you'd have such an adorable puppy. What is he? A Yorkipoo?"

"Dear God, I hope not." For his sake. The little guy already had enough problems convincing anybody he was a dog. "Is that really a thing?" Maybe Aaron was fucking with me.

"Yorkshire Terrier and Poodle cross—Yorkipoo."

Poor bastard. "I don't know. He belongs to my ex. For some

unknown reason, she decided to stick the little monster with me until she gets back from a work thing in London."

"Don't worry." He patted my shoulder. "I'm sure there are worse options than you."

"Possibly, although I don't think Sophie would agree." I bent down to pick up Sam's business with the bag, dropping the leash because it wasn't as if I'd have a hard time catching up with him.

"Uh oh. What did she do?"

I had to laugh at the seriousness on his face, the worry in his tone. "Nothing I won't recover from." I might even get some of my pride back eventually. "Does she dump a lot of guys before they even ask her out?"

He cursed under his breath. "She didn't."

"She did. Apparently, she wants 'someone else'."

"That woman and I will have words the next time I see her. She didn't even tell me."

"It probably slipped her mind." I took some solace from his disappointment while hating my need for the support.

"It's her dad's fault," Aaron said after a minute.

"He spoiled her?"

"He *ruined* her." Aaron shook his head. "Honestly, that man belongs in one of those." He motioned to the shit bag as I dropped it into a garbage can.

"Ruined how?" I'd known a fair number of troubled women —gone to school with a few, been hit on and groped by more than a few, and just ended a relationship with one of the worst. I hadn't gotten that vibe from Sophie. Then again, I'd been wrong about a lot lately.

Unfortunately, I still hadn't learned my lesson. I let another pretty face who thought she was better than me to get under my skin.

"I shouldn't have said that," Aaron said. "Sophie's like the sister I wish I had. My real sister is a serious bitch. If you ever meet her, run. Sophie is amazing but also confused about a few things."

I wasn't sure if that made me feel better or worse. She hadn't looked confused. That body, the smile, her overall presence. They all exuded confidence. Probably what made her so damn attractive.

"I need to do some stuff," I said quickly. I didn't, but stewing in my own weakness for a woman I barely knew wasn't productive or fun.

Sammy was at the end of his leash, and I didn't want to yank him toward me, so I called his name. When he ignored me like usual, I called him again. When that didn't work, I walked over to him and picked him up, holding him at eye level. "I let it go when it was two weeks, little man. Now that your mom has once again proven she cares only about herself and we're stuck with each other for a while, things are going to change around here."

His little sad puppy eyes didn't work on me. My cup was already filled to the brim with shitty feelings and regret.

"You shouldn't take what Sophie said personally," Aaron said.

"You guys need to stop using that fucking expression." I shook off the pulse of irrational anger running through me. "I'll be fine. Lots of people don't like me, I don't like a lot of people, and none of us have died over it yet."

Possibly sensing my frustration, Sammy got antsy. As I bent over to set him down, Aaron took him from my hands and kept walking. I followed behind Aaron, confused and frustrated. Tomorrow, after a decent night's sleep, I would go to work and never think of Sophie again. Or any other woman who looked like she cared more about her lipstick than anyone around her. I *liked* who I was. Why would I want someone who didn't?

Aaron didn't say a word until we got back to my place. "*I* like you, Cooper. And the other night, it was very evident Sophie likes you too. Maybe she needs a little time to realize it." He seemed like a good guy other than being a little too happy.

"It's okay, my new friend. She's not who I'm looking for either." Gotta remember that.

He stopped smiling to study me, but it was brief. "Want to meet up for another walk soon?"

"Sure. I'm out here a lot."

"I'd be happy to walk him for you," Aaron said. "I'd have to check, but I could probably even take him into work. Does he have a carrier?"

"It's purple."

"Perfect."

"Is it?" I sighed. "Thanks. I may take you up on the babysitting offer." I wasn't too busy with work stuff right now, but you never knew when something interesting might come up. Life was always full of surprises.

9

SOPHIE

I arrived at the house in the upscale Riverview neighborhood at eight o'clock sharp on Wednesday morning expecting Dennis and his crew to already be working. The clients, Sandra and Troy, had called last night to say they wanted to replace the wall of sliding glass doors in their living room with French doors to open up the house to the backyard and pool area. Their spending an extra week at their cabin in Lake Tahoe gave me additional time to beg the guys to add another project to the to-do list.

Changes were an undesirable yet normal part of the remodeling process, something I'd anticipated when setting the initial timeline, but this was my first solo project, so I needed everything to go as smoothly as possible.

The more profit we made meant fewer opportunities for my father to wonder if he'd made a mistake trusting me to temporarily take over Dillon Design for him. After putting in three years of after-schools, every summer and break during college, and the last four years of full-time work into the Dillon family business, I was still proving myself every day. Although even calling it a "family business" was a stretch. The Dillon family consisted of me and my father.

Eleven years of nothing but office work until two weeks ago, when he had his heart valve replacement surgery. Once he finally accepted he'd be out of commission for a while, I'd gotten an intense, horrible, hurry-up-and-why-can't-you-get-this-faster tutorial of everything he'd never let me do, in addition to all my normal admin and scheduling work.

Even after he fully recovered from the surgery, he'd have to take it easy and avoid stress. As if he were capable of avoiding stress. He lived on stress. Stress, bourbon, and red meat. Which, as he so often forgot, was why he needed the surgery to begin with.

It didn't feel great that my big shot was happening because my father literally had no one else, but life was what you made of it. I had six more weeks to show him he wasn't the only one who could run Dillon Design.

None of the workmen had arrived yet, so I let myself in and headed for the main room of the house.

"Shit." They'd barely touched the kitchen and were way behind schedule. Hopefully, they'd spent the last four days finishing the master bedroom ensuite and would start the kitchen today. I headed down the hall and groaned. The bathroom was still torn up. They'd set the new sinks, vanity, and tub in place but hadn't connected anything. All the tile was still in boxes with the custom-made lighting fixtures sitting precariously on top. I carefully picked up each fixture and bent over to set them onto the ground, cursing like a contractor, except under my breath.

Over the past few days, I had called a gazillion times to ask how it was going, and Dennis' answer was always, "Fine." I should've known they wouldn't do as good a job for me as they did for my father.

I bristled and hissed like my cat does when he's seriously pissed off. If I were a little more hands-on, monitored their work more closely instead of trusting them to do it, we could still turn it around and get everything done by the deadline.

"Now that's the kind of ass I'd like to take a big bite out of."

I flinched at Dennis' voice, straightened, and turned around to face him.

"Excuse me?" I snapped.

"I love it when you visit, Soph." His creepy, middle-aged grin destroyed what would've otherwise been a decent face. "Makes the day so much better to have something pretty to look at."

"How's my father's ass, Dennis?" I asked, ignoring my nausea.

He grimaced. "What?"

"I assume you speak to everyone you work for in the same manner, so what did my father say when you said that to him? Or does he not have the kind of ass you enjoy biting?"

"Relax." He backed up a step. "It was a joke."

I held up my finger. "Hang on. I need a second to silently congratulate myself for not paying you for your comedic skills."

"Okay, okay." He held up his hands in fake submission and walked away, mumbling something I didn't think was a compliment.

"In fact, I'm not sure *what* I'm paying you for because you don't seem to be doing any construction either." I followed him into the kitchen. "Why did you tell me things were going well?"

He didn't have the balls to face me, but his voice was big. "Because I work for your dad, not you. *He* pays me to get the job done. Which it will get."

"When? There's not enough time to finish it!" Until last night, the owners had planned to be back on Monday and expected things to be at least livable by then. I didn't even bother to tell him about the French doors.

"Goddamn it, Sophie!" His volume thundered through the house. "I told you it'll get done."

"Then I asked you *when*." I walked around the opposite side of the island, keeping up with his strides while leaving space between us. "Now it's your turn to answer. That's how conversations work."

"Who the fuck do you think you are coming in here and telling me how to do my job? What I can and can't say?"

"Your employer."

"No fucking way. Your *daddy* pays me. Not you. You just write the checks. So why don't you go back to doing what you're told and keeping those pretty lips shut while the rest of us do the real work?"

"You're right, Dennis. I'm not your employer. Anymore."

"What? You can't fire me!"

"And yet I just did." I shrugged with all the feigned calm I could muster. "Like you said, I write the checks, and I'll only be writing one more with your name on it. Don't worry, I'll mail it to you."

He stared at me open-mouthed.

I shooed him away. "You can leave now."

"How 'bout we call Peter and see what he says about it."

"Sure. Do you want to explain how you sexually harassed his only daughter or should I?" I reached into my bag and grabbed my phone. "Why don't you fill him in on that part, and I'll tell him about the yelling, cursing, and general disrespect. Then I'll give the phone back to you so you can go over all the time you've wasted and work you haven't done."

"Fuck you, Sophie." He laughed darkly. "Good luck finding someone else who can do this job right and who's willing to work for your dad."

"Not to mention someone who's not a pervy asshole." I pointed toward the door. "You can go now." I tried hard to keep the realization off my face, but he was right. Finding someone who fit that criteria would be next to—if not completely—impossible, and our other crew was starting an even bigger job downtown. But what choice did I have?

"Goddamn bitch," he muttered as he stomped off, taking the opportunity to call me a few more names before slamming the door behind him.

I rubbed my shoulders, the muscles releasing as my anger drained away, replaced by a different kind of pain. The kind I'd feel tomorrow night at dinner with my father when I told him I'd fired Dennis, and the entire crew that was supposed to finish this job was gone, along with my ability to prove I knew what I was doing.

I looked around the room. The cabinets that were in place didn't have doors, and a few hadn't been installed. The walls weren't painted, only primed. There was no sink or lighting, and the old countertop and sink hadn't even been taken out yet. Definitely time to panic.

No. Everything can be fixed.

Problem: I needed a new contractor. Someone I could trust who came with great references, who wasn't an asshole, who my father didn't hate, and who didn't hate him. Unfortunately, my father had pissed off half the industry in the last fifteen years. That was one of the things I'd planned to change. Hopefully, the last ten minutes weren't a sign of things to come.

How hard could it be to find a brilliant, capable, trustworthy contractor who could start tomorrow?

Solution: Find someone who doesn't exist.

I took out my planner, my shoulders tightening as I flipped through each page of the contact section until there were no more pages. No more contacts. No more possibilities. No more hope.

Don't you dare give up. You can do this.

I did an online search for local contractors with a four-star rating or above. Scrolling through the most relevant businesses, passing any my father had already done business with or whom I'd heard negative things about. What I needed was a magician.

Then I saw it.

"Shit."

Get 'er Done had a four-point-nine-star average rating. It was also the most reviewed on the site. I checked three other websites to make sure the first wasn't an outlier. It wasn't.

"Okay." I took a few deep breaths and paced around the empty room.

On the bright side, at least I knew the person I needed did exist.

On the darker side, I'd just told that person I didn't want him.

All I had to do now was convince him that, professionally speaking, I did.

Perfect. Problem . . . solved.

10

SOPHIE

I tucked my blouse in a little tighter as I made my way across the parking lot toward the address listed on the Get 'er Done website. Cooper hadn't answered his phone either time I'd called, and I was tired of waiting. I bet he was the type of person who never listened to his voicemail messages. His email inbox probably had a thousand unread messages in it too.

Two more reasons I'd been right to call it over before we'd begun.

Running a successful business took organization. Organization was practically my middle name, one I much preferred to Elizabeth. If I helped Cooper get his business in order, he'd be more likely to help me with the Riverview remodel.

Unfortunately, I needed him *now*. In a purely professional way. Looking too deeply into his eyes, or getting free milk, or imagining him naked would *not* be happening during our meeting. I knew better than to mix my business and my personal life. Too many things can go wrong, and at the end of the day, I believed in my business skills more than any man I'd ever known.

Hopefully, Cooper could separate the two. Hormonally and

emotionally, men as a group were better at compartmentaliza-tion than women, and Cooper was very much a man. In fact, it had been difficult to stop fantasizing about how much of a man he was since I'd met him. And that was why I was storming toward the front door of his workplace versus accidentally-on-purpose running into him at his apartment again.

I had deliberately forbidden myself from looking him up online after the night at the club. Online searches were a sure way to lose five or six hours—or days—fixating on something or someone completely irrelevant to my life. But Cooper was no longer irrelevant. I needed him.

After reading through about seventy online reviews, it seemed Cooper did a lot more than he'd let on the other night. His work went far beyond television interviews and fixing phones. The before-and-after pictures on his website proved he could do the job I needed him for. All I needed to do was convince him to do it.

The parking lot was filled with line after line of warehouses and auto repair shops, all the same color, shape, and size, a letter tacked onto the end of the street address the only distinguishing feature between each building.

I double-checked the address listed on the Get 'er Done website and compared it to the one painted on the front of the building: 36-C. What were the chances? My mind went to the exact place I didn't want it to—Cooper's arms sliding around my waist from behind, his hands cupping my size C breasts as he kissed my neck.

"Stop," I grumbled. I needed to focus.

The sound of a power tool started and quickly stopped as someone yelled, "Fuck." About halfway down the building, I saw a rolled-up garage-style door. I looked for the Get 'er Done sign or logo. Nothing. So, I peeked through the open roll-up door.

Large machinery lined every wall with smaller tools taking

up every horizontal space. Various lengths of two-by-fours and sheets of plywood were leaning against the concrete pillars that kept the ceiling from toppling down onto the mess. It was chaos in its purest form, and while it wasn't my field of expertise, it seemed may have been a little hoarding thrown in for good measure. How could anyone work in this environment? At least it didn't smell as bad as it looked. In fact, it smelled good. The scent of sawdust covered the more nauseating smells typical in workshops, like machine oil, paint fumes, and whatever the hell might have died under all that crap.

A woodworker's paradise. My worst nightmare.

I let out a breath and reminded myself of the three goals I'd set on the way here: Cooper would say yes to everything I wanted, I wouldn't have to be here any longer than necessary, and he wouldn't take advantage of the spot I was in and demand double his normal rate.

A dark-haired man stood with his back toward me, surrounded by worktables, broken high-end furniture, and partially disassembled appliances.

"Excuse me!" I called.

The man shifted to the side, repositioning the long piece of wood and running it through a table saw. If it wasn't Cooper, it was someone with an equally impressive ass.

"Cooper?" I yelled louder as soon as the whine of the machine lowered.

The man, who wasn't Cooper, glanced at me over his shoulder and turned off the saw. He set his earmuffs and safety goggles down on one of the many tables as he came over to me.

"Can I help you?" He ran his hand through short, deep-brown hair.

"I'm looking for—"

"What the hell are you doing here?"

I spun around and saw Cooper walking through the open door.

Somehow, in the last five days, I'd forgotten just how attractive he was. I thought about the first day we'd met at the grocery store and then outside his place. Same mussed-up hair, same jeans and T-shirt ensemble. Even the stubble on his cheeks looked about the same. How I could've possibly forgotten about those eyes was something I'd never understand.

Then my mind swung forward to my talk with Liz. Nope. I wasn't here to buy the cow or even consider drinking the milk. I was here for business. If I were to blend the two, I'd just end up doubly disappointed.

"Hello, Cooper. I—"

He didn't stop walking or even look at me as he passed. "Whatever you want will have to wait a minute." He reached his hand around to his back pocket and pulled out what looked like a thick bank envelope, holding it out to the other man. "Take it."

"Why?" The man looked more closely at it. "Shit. How much is in here?"

I tried not to listen, to give them their privacy and keep my eyes diverted. Luckily, they were both ignoring me anyway.

"Did you know there's something called a 'registry' where you can see all the shit someone needs for a baby?" Cooper's back was to me, but the feigned naivety was obvious from his tone. "All in list form and ready to buy. Just like that. Crazy, right? Beth told me about it. Apparently, your wife doesn't trust me enough to pick stuff out on my own. More proof of how smart she is, Roy. You should definitely keep her."

"I plan on it, but . . . you gotta be kidding, man. How much is in here?" He opened the envelope and flipped through a thick stack of bills. "It looks like what you pay me in a year."

"Not nearly what I pay you in a year, but enough to get the shit on the registry."

"*All* of it?"

"Isn't that how it works?" He lightly smacked Roy on the shoulder. "I'm kidding. But it's a gift, so you have to take it. You and Beth should go shopping. I can finish up here."

"You sure?"

He nodded. "But remember, it's for baby stuff. Don't let Beth blow it all on strippers and tequila ... again."

Laughing, Roy rolled his eyes. "Dare you to make that joke in front of her."

"Hell, no! I'm not man enough or stupid enough to do that, especially while she's pregnant. Speaking of ..." Cooper pointed his thumb over his shoulder in my direction. "Did that one tell you what she wants?"

"*This one* didn't have the chance," I snapped back, regrettably proving I'd been listening to their entire conversation.

"She just got here," Roy said, glancing back and forth between us. "I'm going to leave now. Take my beautiful wife shopping. Thanks, man. I really appreciate it."

As soon as Roy had gone, Cooper spun around. At least he was smiling ... sorta. "With my good deed for the day done, now I'm ready for you." His eyes narrowed. "Did you change your mind already?"

"About ... ?" As his smile grew wicked, I shook my head. "I need to ask you something."

"I agree." He nodded knowingly, although he couldn't possibly know what he was agreeing to.

"You do?"

"Sure. Just because we don't like each other doesn't mean we should waste the spark between us." He tilted his head back and forth as if he were weighing his options. "Sure, as long as we keep it casual"—he adjusted the waistband of his jeans sugges-tively—"I'm in."

I put my hands on my hips. "You're in? Meaning, in *me*?"

How generous of him. "Unfortunately, I'm going to have to pretend I didn't hear—or see—any part of that amazing offer. And I'm leaving if you even touch your zipper." Not that I didn't feel the spark, but I had bigger priorities.

He sighed. "Why are you here, Sophie?"

I inwardly cringed at the way he said my name, as if it left a bad taste in his mouth. He could dislike me as much as he wanted if he agreed to work with me. I straightened up as much as I could and put on my most professional and uncaring visage. "I need your assistance with something."

"I know. That's why I offered."

"Not everything is about sex, you—" I shut my mouth. He hadn't been like this the other night or any of the other times we'd met, so I guessed I was talking to Hurt Cooper. And hurt people hurt people, right?

I started again, this time with more patience. "I need Get 'er Done. Professionally."

"Oh well," he said it disappointedly, but I could tell he didn't really mean it. Or believe it. Whatever spark there was between us was gone now. "I have work to do. Should I keep guessing which of your problems you want my help with, or are you going to tell me?"

The last thing I needed was for Hurt Cooper to start listing all the issues he thought I had. "I'm looking for a new contractor. My last one . . . it didn't work out. I need someone really good for the next two weeks, and I'm willing to pay well for it."

"How well?" One of his eyebrows went up when I said the number I was comfortable with. Then silence.

I grudgingly gave him another, higher number. More silence.

He made me wait a few more rounds, but eventually we got to a number that made both of his eyebrows raise. I got a nod too.

"I need to be able to trust you can do it."

With his brow furrowed, he studied me for a minute before answering. "I've never cheated anybody, and if anything, I'm a little too honest. So, professionally speaking, yeah, you can trust me."

"But not about anything else?" I asked, shocked that he'd admit to that and unhappy I'd brought up his personal life.

"Depends." He motioned for me to follow. "I think I've proven I don't see the point in lying, and I don't hold grudges unless it's absolutely necessary." When he opened the door to a large office at the back of the shop, he didn't look as annoyed. Hopefully, that was a sign I hadn't passed the "absolutely necessary" threshold yet.

"By the way, you were smart not to want to get involved with me," he said as I surveyed the chaos of his office. "I steal the covers, don't put the caps back onto pens, and have been known to drink straight from the milk carton. But only when it's almost empty. A lesson taught to me by growing up with three disgusting brothers and a sister who's a lot less ladylike than she seems."

"Okay," I said, drawing out the word. "Are there any other irrelevant-to-me issues you want to clear up before we start?"

"Since you seemed to enjoy interrogating me so much, I figured I'd lay it all out now." He held up a finger. "I thought of a couple more." He grinned as he pushed an enormous pile of paperwork off to one side of his desk and rolled a chair over for me. "My credit score is incredible—almost as impressive as my oral skills but not nearly as exciting. My favorite thing to have for dinner is breakfast, and it usually takes me all weekend to get up Monday morning." He slumped into the chair behind the desk and motioned for me to sit. "The rest can wait until you tell me what work you need done."

I brushed off the seat and sat. "You're an unusual man."

"Like I said, you made the right choice." He pulled a yellow writing pad from a drawer and grabbed a pen. Without a cap on it. "Tell me about the job."

"Jobs. Plural. If everything works out like I hope it will." Regular work from a high-end, established design firm held a lot of weight, hopefully enough to entice him to work for me.

"I don't usually take on steady work," he said. "I like the challenge of tackling something new and bore easily, so if it's installing the same shitty, pre-fab cabinets and crappy tile, I'm not the guy you're looking for." He chuckled. "Again."

"I didn't mean to hurt your feelings the other night." I knew it bothered him more than he'd ever admit. It made sense—a man who looked like Cooper probably didn't hear *no* very often, and, apparently, he'd taken my reasoning much more harshly than I'd intended.

"You didn't," he said, leaning forward to catch my eye. "When I walked into the shop and saw you, it took a second to recall how we'd left things—with both of us feeling exactly the same way. Plus, like my business cards say, I fix problems. It doesn't mention I try not to create *others*, but that's only because it wouldn't fit on the card." Then under his breath, he added, "Probably should look into getting bigger ones made."

"That's good to know." I giggled and then stopped myself, remembering I was supposed to be keeping this professional if for no other reason than *he* seemed to be able to. I sat up straighter and cleared my throat. "My clients want high-end, custom work. Their greatest fear is visiting a friend's house and seeing the same design they just paid an exorbitant amount of money for. Right now, I'm working on a master ensuite and kitchen project. Along with new fixtures, cabinets, and the normal stuff, I'm also looking to do something truly singular for the kitchen lighting and built-ins." I pulled up his website on my phone and scrolled through the pictures of projects he'd done that were similar in feel to my design style and explained what I liked about them.

"Of course, that pantry is horrible." I pointed to a built-in at the edge of a picture of a kitchen that was otherwise gorgeous.

"Ouch. No, really, don't hold back."

"Too honest?"

"No, the honesty is appreciated. I just forgot how blunt you are." He leaned back in his chair. "Plus, I agree. It had sappy sentimental value to them or something. I don't touch sap or sentiment."

"That seems healthy." I leaned down to my bag. "Do you have time to look at some ideas?"

"I have something to finish and deliver it by six. So, if you don't mind doing it while I eat my lunch . . ." Glancing at his watch, he stood and headed through a door at the back of his office, flipping the wall switch to light up a break room. "You can have the next twenty minutes."

"I'll take it." I quickly grabbed my bag and followed him.

As he heated up something from the fridge, I laid out my design boards at one end of a gorgeous knotty pine wood table.

"Did you make this?"

"The Chinese food or the table?" he asked, setting one on the other. "No and yes. You get to guess which one is which." He grabbed two plates and utensils. "You're welcome to have some. Unless eating with me would make you uncomfortable."

Just being around him made me uncomfortable. But not in any way I wanted him to know about. "As long as I guessed right that you made the table not the food, I'd love some." Stress killed my appetite, so I hadn't eaten since my fight with Dennis. Cooper hadn't agreed to do the job yet, but if the grumbling of my stomach was any indication, I was extremely confident he would.

"Thank you," I mumbled, covering my mouth. "This is delicious."

"I know." He showed off his dimple. "It's a local place. I've eaten there about once a week since I was a kid."

"Creature of habit."

"Gotta have at least *one* good one, right?"

After a few more bites of chow mein, I showed him photos of the space, my renderings, and a few pattern boards. I'd worked hard on these, so I appreciated that he took our plates to the sink and washed his hands before touching them.

"These are good," he said as he flipped through a few.

"You sound surprised."

"I am. Pleasantly. I hate being asked to make ugly things." He went back to one of the kitchen angles. "Like this." He pointed to the lighting I'd planned to install over the kitchen island. "Too trendy. They'll hate it a year from now. Plus, it's too clunky compared to the rest of what you have."

"It wasn't my original idea, but"—I yanked the sketch out of his hand to look more closely—"you really think they'll hate it?"

"I really do."

I looked again, silently cursing that he'd picked out the one piece I'd been unsure of. "I'll take it under advisement."

"A modification of a custom piece I did about a year ago might work really well in the space. I'll have to find a picture of it." He took the board back and asked a few questions about the homeowners.

"They want the kitchen and living room areas to blend into the backyard," I said. "They do lots of entertaining, like holiday parties and pool parties for the kids."

He looked up, scowling. "People find those entertaining?"

I laughed until I realized he wasn't kidding. "Wow, you really *are* broody."

11

COOPER

I got to the Riverview house about twenty minutes before Sophie and I had agreed to meet. I wanted to check out the neighborhood and the exterior of the house, maybe even go around back since she'd assured me the owners weren't home.

Most people didn't have a single clue about what they really wanted. That went for home renovation and every other area of their lives. By the time they came to me, they'd either tried and failed or not tried at all because they knew they'd fail. Either way, they'd already spent way too much time overthinking and were too deep in it to make good decisions. My job was to break that news to them. Fortunately, that was when my reputation came in handy—I was the guy who supposedly could fix anything. So, they let me.

Except none of that mattered today because I'd never met the owners of this place and never would. They'd hired Sophie. I was just here to follow directions. Problem number one: I didn't follow directions very well. Problem number two: Sophie's directions were crap.

The list of projects that she emailed me at midnight told me what she expected from me, most spelled out in excruciating detail and a few she probably wasn't aware of. I ignored most of it. I'd seen her designs yesterday. I didn't need an itemized to-do list. Her email also provided information about Sophie herself—she was even more of a workaholic than I was and, despite her intelligence and innate eye for good design, she had no idea what she was doing.

As soon as I read that email, I should've told her I couldn't help her. Or this morning after she'd texted to remind me of the meeting we'd arranged twelve hours ago "in case you forgot." I'd love to meet the man who could forget anything about Sophie in twelve hours—I could ask him how he did it. Too bad he didn't exist.

I already had more work than I could handle and hadn't hurt for money in years. Unfortunately, when I found out how much the job paid, all I could think about was the look on Roy's face and the awkward hug he'd give me when I told him. I paid him well—way more than he'd make working for anyone else—but he had a baby on the way, and all the shit that came with them was expensive. I'd covered the initial gear they'd need for the kid, but the pricey part was upkeep. Like dogs. Roy didn't know it, but I wanted to set him up well enough so he could take as much time off as he wanted when the baby was born without worrying about his bills.

Unfortunately, making that happen involved working with Sophie. Being around her was dangerous, as if every minute doubled the chance I'd backslide. As fucked up as it was, her not being interested only made things worse. I had an unhealthy need to figure out why she blew me off—and not in the good way.

After Helen and I finally called it quits for good, I decided to give myself some time to break out of that headspace and learn why I had a fetish for women who wanted more from me than I was willing to give. Helen was the worst, not the first. But hopefully, she was also the last. I may have just committed two weeks of my life to prove to myself I could handle it. Or maybe it was the exact opposite—to prove to Sophie that she'd been wrong about me.

When I heard Sophie call my name, I came out from the side yard. She looked as perfect as always—hair tightly pulled into a knot at the nape of her neck, makeup perfectly applied, sweater and skirt that showed off her curves while still being conservative. All black. It crossed my mind to ask her if she ever wore any other color, but then I realized it didn't really matter and I didn't really care. Ours was a work-only relationship. The last thing I wanted to do was get to know her. I already knew enough.

She smiled when she saw me. Of course, she did. I fucking hated happy people. They made you agree to all kinds of shit you wouldn't otherwise.

"Thank you so much for doing this," she said. "Did you get my email with the attachment?"

I nodded. "All five pages of it."

She glanced back at me as she unlocked the front door. "You didn't bring it with you? Never mind. I think I brought an extra copy."

"Oh good," I said as I followed her inside. This should be fun.

"Where should we start?" She set down her gigantic designer bag and pulled out a copy of the list she'd sent and set it on the counter between us.

I didn't even look at it. Instead, I watched her expression go through at least three stages of grief. When she got to "acceptance," she put her hands on her hips and let out a big breath. "Can I show you around? Tell you what to do?"

"Yes to the first. No to the second," I said. "Like I told you, I don't work that way. I can't have someone peering over my shoulder all the time."

The corners of her mouth turned down. "I thought you meant the actual construction parts. Like what kinds of screws to use and where to put them."

Did I say this would be fun? I meant torturous.

"I saw your sketches," I said. "I'll know more once I see where the last guy left off. At that point, you're going to have to trust I can do what you need. If you can't manage that, I'll give you some names of other people who will do an adequate job of making you happy by giving you exactly what you want. If that's even possible."

"For someone to make me happy or to give me exactly what I want?"

"Either."

"Fine, we'll do it your way. No list." She pulled out a brand-new pack of yellow sticky notes, ripped the wrapper off, and started writing on the top one with a Sharpie. In complete silence, I watched her walk around the kitchen, alternating between mad scribbling and sticking notes on almost every surface.

"What are you doing?"

"These are just reminders." She stopped writing long enough to look at me. "So you don't forget anything."

I ripped one off the center island and read it. "You're kidding, right?"

"I should've made them for Dennis, but he worked with us for a long time and had his own way of doing things. Or more accurately, *not* doing things." She immediately started scribbling again.

I followed a couple of steps behind and ripped each sticky note off as soon as she moved to the next spot. I had a nice stack by the time she realized what I was doing and let out a humph of disappointment.

I leaned against the doorway between the kitchen and the

pantry area. "They want these cabinets to come out and be replaced by a coffee bar, right? And have it match the pantry doors. I read your notes. All of them."

"This is extremely important to me." She studied me for a second, clutching her pen and the remaining notes. "I need everything to be perfect."

"That's too bad because it's not going to be—nothing's perfect. But I promise it'll be so close only you and I will ever know it's not."

She didn't look convinced, so I tried again.

"I'm arrogant enough for you to trust that, if nothing else, I won't want to put all that self-confidence at risk by doing shitty work."

"Alright," she mumbled, as if she expected everything to collapse around her the second she let go of a small amount of control.

It was one job, albeit a big one that in addition to me and Roy I'd have to ask my younger brother Beckett to help me with. Then Sophie and I could go our separate ways. Roy would be set, I could go back to my quiet, easy life, and she could go find someone who enjoyed being told what to do.

"Now you get to show me around, answer any questions I might have, and then step back and let me do my job."

For the next fifteen minutes, I inspected the work that had been done in the kitchen and the master bathroom. Sophie only spoke when I asked a question and kept her sticky notes to herself. When I was done, we sat on two stools at the kitchen counter and talked money. Good money.

"This is the amount we agreed on yesterday." She pointed to a number about halfway down the spreadsheet. "I assume that's still acceptable?"

"It'll do," I said, skimming the rest of her budget when she reached down to grab a pen from her bag.

When I'd started Get 'er Done, I hadn't known enough to price my work properly, but as I gained more experience and my reputation grew, so did my prices. I wasn't cheap. But if these profit margins were normal for Dillon Design, they were at the absolute top of their game.

"You're not supposed to look at that page!" She snatched it away from me. "I'll forgive you if you take the job."

"Nice to know you're not above a little blackmail," I said. "Are those your regular rates?"

Something in my expression or tone gave away how impressed I was because a proud smile bloomed on her face.

"No, but it turns out I'm a surprisingly good negotiator. This is my first solo contract, which is why it has to be perfect—" She stopped herself before I could. "*Close* to perfect. I wanted to secure a big buffer for any unaccounted expenses that might pop up."

"That's a hell of a nice buffer." Even taking into consideration the cost of the useless labor of her previous contractor.

"I'll take that as a compliment." She flipped to another page and told me about the huge bonus I'd get if I could switch out the sliding glass doors for French doors.

Shit. There was no way I could turn this job down.

"Will you do it?" she asked, hope filling her big, beautiful eyes.

"Before I agree to anything, it's important we understand each other—I'm doing this for the money, not to be nice or so you'll like me."

"Understood."

"You can have me for the next two weeks," I said, immediately regretting using that expression because neither one of us would be *having* the other in the next two weeks or any time after that. "Not a second more. We'll start on Monday, but scratch the doors off that list of yours right now. It's already going to be tight, if not impossible, to get it all done before the owners get back. Unless you want me to do a shitty job. It might look good, but it'll cause problems down the line."

"I'll talk to the owners. Of course, for what they're paying if you can find the time . . ." She bit her lip.

I'd never knowingly gone into something I knew would be a mistake. The work itself we could handle without any problem. It was everything else I wasn't sure about. Primarily her. But I was going to do it anyway. Hell, I always said I enjoyed a challenge, and this would be the biggest I'd encountered in memory.

"If I can find the time, for what you're paying me, you can have whatever you want."

12

______

SOPHIE

Like every other Thursday night, I got to my father's house at 5:45 and let myself in. This part of Sacramento was hardly dangerous, but I wished he would lock his door, nonetheless. Even after almost dying, he still believed he was invincible.

"I'm here!" I called.

"Did you bring the green beans?" Lucy, my father's house-keeper-slash-everything, yelled from the kitchen.

"Yep." I held up the bag as if she could see them. "Be there in a second." I made a quick detour to my father's study, knocking on the door and waiting for permission to enter.

"Come in," he said.

He was sitting in the new electric lifting recliner I'd bought after his surgery to help him stand. He hated it almost as much as he needed it. In the two weeks since his surgery, he'd lost at least ten pounds. The slacks and button-up shirt he insisted on wearing even during his recovery hung heavy and made him look even thinner.

"Hi, Dad. How are you feeling?"

"As one would expect after being forced to take those horrible opiates the doctors prescribed."

"So, really good, then?"

He sighed, already frustrated with me.

One thing he'd never managed to correct was my over-whelming sense of optimism. Not that I didn't have pessimistic days, weeks even, where it felt like the whole world was conspiring to take me down. But at the end of each day, I reminded myself that it hadn't yet, and I had no intention of letting it happen tomorrow either.

I screamed when I saw what he was holding. "You can't drink while you're taking painkillers!" I rushed toward him to snatch the glass of what had to be his favorite bourbon from his hand.

He pulled the drink to his chest, covering it with his other hand. "It's one finger. That's hardly what will end up killing me."

He was right. His stubbornness would kill him first. It was way stronger than the booze.

This was a battle I'd never win. "One finger. That's it." Not that he'd listen. After all we'd been through together, all he blamed me for, it still stung that he was choosing to not follow instructions that would keep him alive.

"I'm going to help Lucy," I said. "Let me know if you need anything before dinner." I grabbed the decanter on my way out. "Unless it's more bourbon."

The kitchen was large by today's standards, let alone back when my parents had completely redesigned the house. Being ahead of the curve was what gave Dillon Design an edge over all the other companies that had popped up at the start of the HGTV house-flipping era.

The fifty-six-year-old woman who'd taught me every word of Spanish I pronounced correctly was standing in front of the stove wrapping a thick salmon filet in aluminum foil. Eight-plus hours a day for the last six years, Lucy cleaned, made sure my father took his medication, fed him breakfast and lunch, and cooked his dinner before she left for the day.

She was the sole reason that he was still alive, and why I had most of my sanity left.

"How's your week going, *Ángel*?" she asked as she set out a colander and cutting board for me.

"About the same as all the others." I walked around the island and gave her a quick hug. "Yours?"

Without a single word, she told me everything. She didn't even have to take her eyes off the stove.

"Even worse than normal?" I cringed at the thought. "I don't know how you do it." I understood why I put up with him—he gave me life, a home, taught me everything I knew about business, and—if prayers were ever answered—would give me Dillon Design someday.

Plus, I knew how much it still hurt when I thought about my mom not being here. She'd been part of his life for longer than she'd been part of mine. He thought he'd grow old with her and spend every day of that together. How badly did he still hurt?

But why Lucy stayed was still a deep, possibly dark mystery.

"Or *why* you do it." I dumped the beans into the colander and gave them a rinse in the sink.

"Peter is a good man who doesn't know what to do with himself right now. Once he starts working again, he'll be better."

"That's a long time to deal with his worse-than-normal state of being."

"He's not so bad." She squeezed my arm and winked. "I've known men like your father. They may roar like lions, but inside they're kittens. Don't worry about me—I can handle him."

I didn't doubt that at all. I just wondered why she bothered.

"Besides," she said with a tiny grin, "he's good to me." Either she needed to reassess her standards, or he was a completely different man when it was just the two of them.

"Are you sure you don't want to stay for dinner tonight?" I asked her for maybe the five hundredth time.

She shook her head for the five hundredth time. "It's good for you two to have some time to yourselves. It's especially good for him."

Maybe, but *good* wasn't the same as pleasant, or even tolerable.

Once the food was ready, Lucy brought our plates into the dining room while I finished setting the table. She yelled for my father to come in, grabbed her purse, and said, "Buenos noches!" on her way out the door.

Like usual, we spent the first ten minutes or so focusing on our food, his health, and the unpredictability of California weather.

"How's the job in Riverview going?" he asked, as if I didn't call him with status reports on all our contracts almost every day. Granted, I'd skipped yesterday for obvious reasons, which meant I had to tell him about now.

"Great. Except, um . . . Dennis quit," I lied.

He raised one eyebrow. "That doesn't sound like him at all."

"Strange, right?" I stared at my food—one bite at a time—and tried not to blurt out something that would drive me deeper into the lie. I made it three bites. "He said it was for personal reasons."

I couldn't tell him the truth. If he knew what Dennis said to me, he'd either have risked his health by going after the asshole, or he'd say I should be able to handle a little name calling. I wasn't sure which would upset me more.

I'd called Dennis this afternoon to get our stories straight— nobody else needed to know, especially my father. I told him that once my father was back to work, he was welcome to say his "personal reasons" were over and he'd like to come back. That gave me another month and a half to figure out how to stop that from happening. Behavior like his was never a one-off. No way did I believe I was the only woman he treated like that.

"I'll make some calls first thing tomorrow."

"Actually I . . . um . . ." I stabbed a green bean. "I already hired someone."

He didn't lift his head from his plate, didn't say a word. As if he knew I wasn't telling him everything.

"I think you'll like him," I continued. "He owns a very successful business."

"What's it called?"

Covering my mouth, I swallowed. "The company is called . . . Get 'er Done. A local news station interviewed him a while back. You may have seen it."

He scowled. "Get 'er Done? I don't know what that even means."

"Well, he'd already applied for the business license with that name when someone pointed out it could be confusing."

"So, you hired an idiot?"

My fork clanked when it hit my plate. "It was a simple error in judgment that didn't hurt anyone. He was eighteen and started his own company. I think it's admirable. He's good at what he does, which I think is the most important thing. Don't you?"

Why did I feel so defensive of Cooper or his business?

He set down his utensils, wiped his mouth, and laid his napkin in his lap. "The most important thing is to keep our clientele happy, so Dillon Design is the first they think of when someone asks them for a recommendation." Each word was precise, a quick strike meant to remind me how stupid I was for forgetting the lesson they held. "The most important thing is to make sure our designs continue being shown in industry magazines. The most important thing is to keep moving this company forward. Always forward, always better." He picked his utensils back up. "You know that."

"I do." It wasn't worth disagreeing. Especially after I'd spent years working my ass off for it. "Ironically, Cooper—that's his name—said the mistake actually turned out to be great for business. People think it's funny, and it gets him noticed."

"Please enlighten me as to how other peoples' jokes benefit my business." He never stopped cutting his green beans. Didn't look at me once. Just sliced each one into perfectly even pieces, lifting each and setting it down an inch away in turn.

"It's not as if anyone knows Dennis' name," I said, trying to avoid letting my frustration slip into my voice. "None of our clients will ever know Cooper is working for us. They'll only know about the high-quality work they see. That's what counts, right?" It was a rhetorical question that part of me hoped he'd answer. Ever since I could remember that fact had been drilled into my consciousness—it was all about quality. The highest quality. Dillon Design didn't need to be a household name—it had to be a respected one.

"I suppose so," he said as he carefully finished dissecting his dinner.

I needed reassurance, to hear him tell me I was doing a good job and hadn't completely screwed everything up by getting rid of that asshole Dennis. That my confidence in Cooper was based on logic, not anything more basic, more human, more hormonal.

Unfortunately, that wasn't something my father had ever offered me. Or was even capable of. Before my mom got sick, he'd been a good but not great dad. Her diagnosis broke him. His workaholic tendencies became an addiction, an escape. Something he could control. After she died, his business was all he had. Well, he'd still had me, but I was just a kid back then. Someone to blame.

In a way, he left me before she did.

We spent the rest of our meal in silence, neither one of us eating much. There was no way to tell what was going on in his head, but mine was like a tennis match between "why bother?" and "maybe there's a way to make him understand."

Eventually, the game was over, and I realized that the less he knew, the better I'd feel.

After I cleaned up the kitchen, I went into his den to say goodbye.

"I'm taking off," I said, silently sighing when I saw another whiskey in his hand. "Thanks for dinner."

"Come here. I want to tell you something." He waited until I was standing right next to his chair. "Watch this new man like a hawk until you're two hundred percent confident he can do the job we're paying him to do. Keep on him, make sure he understands whose project it is and who's in charge."

My father had taught me more than my degree or any design classes I'd ever taken. The foundation he gave me had created who I was as a businesswoman and, while I might not be confident in every part of my life, I'd never doubted that.

All I needed was more hands-on experience with design and a chance to show him what I was capable of.

"You have nothing to worry about, Dad."

"Sophie." He grabbed my hand as I turned to leave. "Don't ever trust a man before he's earned it. I know you, and I know how you are."

I pulled my hand out of his to grab the glass of bourbon he told me he wouldn't have, a stab of anger and frustration filling my chest.

What did that mean? How I was? He knew nothing about me other than that I was good with spreadsheets and placing orders. He'd never let me do anything else myself.

Was that why I felt an insane need to prove myself, or why I shouldn't bother?

"I won't disappoint you, Dad." As long as Cooper didn't disappoint *me*.

13

COOPER

Apart from thousands of walks with Sammy and one with Sammy and Aaron, my weekend was spent setting up the equipment we'd need for the job. I wanted everything ready to go Monday morning. During and in between those tasks, along with every time Sophie called or texted about something she thought I needed to know but didn't, I wondered why the fuck I'd agreed to do this.

On day one, Roy, Beckett, and I were out on the back patio doing a quick overview of the plan for this week while we ate lunch. When Sophie opened the sliding glass door, they both stood, looking to me for answers. I had none. Only questions. Questions like, why, for all that was holy, was I going to start work every day for the next two weeks hoping she'd stop by to check on our progress instead of call? Especially since all it would do was give us another opportunity to disagree about something.

"Roy, right?" she asked, walking toward him with her hand out. "Nice to meet you properly. Without anyone calling me any names."

"I didn't call you any names. Name-calling is for insecure bullies."

"Exactly." She glanced at me with an eyebrow raised and then turned away. "You must be Beckett."

"Impressive." Beckett took her hand gently.

She laughed and said, "Actually, it's pretty obvious. There's more than a little family resemblance between the two of you, especially the eyes."

True, except his comment had been directed at *me*. I may have said too much when I asked for his help. Should've foreseen this situation and kept my mouth shut. Beckett wasn't known for his subtlety. Sadly, being in grad school for psychology led him to believe he could psychoanalyze his brother without repercussions.

I cleared my throat and stepped forward. "This is—"

"Sophie," she offered. "I'm the—"

"the Designer," I finished.

"Actually, I was going to say boss," she said. Subcontractors weren't employees, but knowing she was kidding didn't stop me from pushing the issue.

"*I'm* their boss."

"Yes," she said, another smile creeping onto her face, "and I'm *your* boss."

One thing I knew for certain was that nobody could possibly be that happy all the time. Maybe it was a reaction to the guys being here and not wanting to look like an asshole, or maybe I was an asshole, but I suddenly wanted nothing more than to wipe that permagrin off her face and see all the ugly underneath.

"I'll call you my partner, associate, coworker, and a couple other options, but I don't have a boss." Never had, never would.

"Great." Beckett cut me off before I said anything else. "Now that we all don't know who's in charge, can we move on?"

"I didn't mean to disrupt your workflow," Sophie said, her eyes lingering on me for a moment longer, just enough to prove I'd gotten under her skin a little. Now that I knew how, you could bet I'd be doing it every chance I got. "I stopped by to see how you were doing and if you need anything."

"I'm good," my brother said, smiling. "You good, Roy?"

"I'm good. It's Cooper you need to worry about."

I'm glad someone thought this was funny. *Two* someones.

"That's it. Lunch is over." I shooed the guys back inside. "Get back to work, you assholes."

She followed me into the house. "Did you get a chance to pick up the paint I ordered for the bathroom?"

"You mean the one you reminded me about five times? Yeah, I did."

"Great. I want to look at it in the space. Where is it?"

"At the store," I said without stopping. "They know me pretty well over there, and you're a good customer, so they're going to let you switch it out for another color."

"Why would I switch the color?"

I stopped. "How should I put this?" I turned to face her. "A man lives here, right? In this house?"

She nodded.

"Then I'm not painting the bathroom pink."

"It's not pink! It's blush!" she said at about the same volume she'd used in the nightclub. Without any music to compete with, she lowered her voice. "Blush will flatter their faces when they look into the mirror every morning."

"Flatter their faces?" I turned around and headed toward the room in question. "You know what a man *really* wants every morning? Not to have a pink fucking bathroom." And a blowjob, but I wasn't going to do that either.

"It's not pink, Cooper," she said, still following.

"It's not going up on these walls, Sophie." I grabbed the

square foot swatch I'd asked the guy at the store for, knowing this exact conversation was bound to happen.

I held the swatch up to the wall next to the vanity. "Do you really think this is going to flatter their faces? Or is it more likely to start a fight about why they let their designer put this ugly fucking color on their walls?"

She twisted her mouth sideways. "I suppose it does look a bit pink in the space."

I craned my ear toward her. "What'd you say?"

"I said it's pink." In the time it took her to say, she'd flipped off her grumpy face and put her smile back on. "A soft white or ivory might work better."

"Great idea."

"I'll be back as soon as I can," she said, already moving.

For the next few days, the guys put in about twelve hours of hard labor per day. I put in more. I'd never tackled this many projects at the same time before. We were good at what we did and worked well together, but it was a lot to ask of them. As it turned out, it was also a lot to ask of Sammy. He wasn't used to being alone all day long. When I worked at my shop, I could go home for lunch and hang out with him a bit, but I didn't have the time to take an hour off this project every day.

After the first few anxiety attacks Sammy had whenever I approached the front door, I couldn't handle the guilt anymore and started bringing him with me to the jobsite. As long as he had a toy and a chewy treat, he happily stayed on the patio and out of our way. I even bought a plastic baby playpen to keep him safe whenever we were moving something in or out that might hurt him. Good thing I also brought lots of shit bags because he sure didn't have any hang-ups about using the yard.

Roy was as much a Sammy fan as I was, but Beckett stopped

whatever he was doing to go check on him every once in a while. It was worst during our lunch breaks. Maybe I needed to cut them down to fifteen minutes, so my brother only had time to feed himself.

"Don't you dare, Beckett," I said in the classic big brother voice that I hadn't used since we were kids.

Mouth open, Sammy stood on his tiny hind legs, impatiently waiting for Beckett to drop a piece of meat from his burger.

"He wants it."

"Of course, he wants it. He's a wild animal. Aren't you, buddy?" I roughed up the fur on top of his head. "But you won't be at my place tonight when he decides to purge it from one end or the other." Sammy had never actually had an accident in the house, but it wasn't a good idea to train the little beast to beg for human food. "Come here, you little bastard." I scooped him up with one arm, carried him over to a lounge chair far away from where the guys were eating, and set him on my lap.

"What are you looking at?" I asked him, brushing his fur out of his eyes. Did these things need haircuts? Maybe I should ask Helen the next time she texted to tell me she'd postponed her return home again. I was getting the impression she wanted to make the London visit a permanent thing and was abusing the good fucking will of her dog-sitter while she figured it out.

"Why can't you admit you like having him around, Cooper?"

"Because I don't." Of course, at that moment, Sammy stood on my thighs, put his paws on my chest, and started licking my chin. "See? He's horrible. I hate him." I put my finger in front of his face. "Stop. That tickles and is disgusting. I've seen you try to lick your own ass with that thing."

When both guys broke into laughter, I set the dog down on the ground and ignored his jumps and pleas to be let back up. When I stood, he ran back to Beckett for more begging. My little brother "accidentally" dropped a chunk of bun onto the ground in front of him, letting out an exaggerated and totally fake, "Oops."

"Damn it, bro. Now you'll never get rid of him."

"Get rid of whom?" Sophie asked, stepping through the open sliding glass door and onto the patio.

Fuck, she looked good today. Not that she looked any different than she usually did—always in black, always with her hair pulled back from her face and up from her neck. Oh, the things I could do to that neck.

Seeing someone new to annoy, Sammy ran right up to her and used every bit of power he had in his tiny little legs to jump. With all that effort, he made it up to her knee, and while I gave him props for getting closer to her thighs than I ever would, I didn't envy his tumble after.

Since she hadn't been expecting a little ball of fluff to attack, Sophie gasped and stepped backward, probably before she even realized the fluff was a dog. Then she leaned down to check on him, apologizing profusely and telling him how cute he was. As if he needed to get a bigger head about it. His little body couldn't bear the weight.

"He's fine," I said. "He's practically weightless, so he doesn't so much fall as glide down like a feather." I scooped him up, dusting him off once he was tucked into my side. "See? He's not hurt."

"He's yours?" she asked, her head tilted and her eyes thin in doubt.

"Hell no. I hate dogs." Then why did I sound so damned offended by her tone? Because she looked at me as if the mere idea of me taking care of something or someone besides myself was impossible.

"I'm dog-sitting, remember?" I snapped, not sure who I was angry at. "I must have mentioned it right before you told me you were looking for any guy who wasn't me."

"That is *not* what I said." Her eyes filled with a fire I hadn't seen before. Good. It was about fucking time we had this conversation. I'd been trying to piss her off enough to fight me for almost a week.

"Maybe you've given that speech to so many guys you don't even hear yourself anymore. Trust me, as someone who'd never heard the 'big talk' before, that's what you said."

"It's not as if you didn't jump at the chance to get rid of me," she shot back. "Unless I wanted sex, of course, which is probably your version of the 'big talk'."

"Would you have rather I—"

"We're going to head in and finish off that tile around the shower," Beckett yelled. He took Sammy from me, out of harm's way. "And I'm taking him with us. Unless the homeowners would have a problem with him being inside."

That was probably something I should've asked during one of our many phone arguments, in between her doubts that things would be finished on time and my picking fights with whatever I could. Sadly, this might have been the healthiest relationship I'd ever had with a woman outside my family.

"As long as he won't have an accident," Sophie said without looking at him. Her eyes were too busy shooting daggers at me.

"That's the difference between dogs and people," I said with a smirk. "Dogs can be trained."

Neither of us moved until Beckett slid the door shut behind him. As soon as we heard that click, it was as if it triggered something in her, brought her calm professional mask back on.

"Cooper?" She centered herself. "Sometimes I wonder if you are just arguing for the sake of arguing. It's my contract, and that means I'm in charge."

"You wanted me for my expertise but haven't let me to do a single thing without your permission. It's like you're sitting around deciding how much I can fuck up between the time you send a text and I respond to it. That's a shitty way to prove how in charge you are. Haven't you ever trusted anyone before?"

She turned her head to the side and took a few deep breaths as if willing herself not to lose control or say what she was really thinking. That was the side I wanted to see—the honest side, the real one.

"It's a good thing you didn't take this job so I'd like you," she said.

I couldn't hold back the smile, sure as hell couldn't stop the laughter. Apparently, neither could she. With it, I imagined all the tension and bullshit releasing too.

"I want us to have a good working relationship," she said, wiping her eye. "To be equals, and equals don't continuously fight with each other."

"Equals can fight as much as they want. As long as they also listen to each other. Trust each other."

"How?"

That one word helped me figure it out, figure *her* out. Like the last piece of a puzzle. She needed reassurance, to know I considered her an equal. She could've just asked, but she probably didn't even know she needed it. Not to mention I hadn't been supporter-in-chief lately.

"You're a thoughtful designer and a fantastic negotiator. Way better than I could ever be. You're also good with spreadsheets. Like *really* good. But there are things I'm good at too."

She nodded. "That I could never do."

"At least not right now. So, if we're going to make this work, we need to let each other do what we're good at."

"This job is important to my future, and I think I get a little too worked up about it."

"Maybe a little," I said. "I think we've both been approaching this all wrong. You and I are like this." I held my hands up a few

inches apart, fingers curved into half circles. "Opposites. Unfin-
ished. We should be using each other—"

Her eyes popped open wide.

"Let me finish," I scolded, despite loving how quickly her
mind had jumped there. "We should be using each other's *skills*
to build something beautiful." I slowly brought my hands
together as the two half circles became a whole.

"And focus on the good stuff in there." She stuck her finger
through the center.

I smirked—couldn't help it. "That is often where the good
stuff happens, yes."

She rolled her eyes. "Deal." We shook on it. "Also, you're a
pervert."

14
______

SOPHIE

During my infrequent visits to previous job sites, I'd been impressed by how Dennis and his men worked. Regardless of what I thought of the man, I never doubted his skill. Now I did. Not only did Cooper and his crew get along better, but they moved around and with each other as if it were choreographed.

Cooper and Beckett were family, siblings. Something I didn't have but had never bothered me before. Since construction wasn't Beckett's profession, he wasn't as proficient as the other two men, but there was no serious eye rolling or shouting. Lots of inside jokes and teasing, but no real arguments. The same way Cooper had been with Jasmine at the theater. I wished I could meet them all, see what a whole, healthy family was like.

I'd had a whole family once, a long time ago. My memories began when my mother got sick. As my father receded more into his work, I was left to take care of her most of the time, cuddling up next to her and playing with the controls of the adjustable twin-sized bed she got when she could no longer comfortably go to their bedroom upstairs, talking about whatever an eleven-year-old thought was important. Maybe that was why I had so few memories of anything before that—because those were the moments I needed to remember, and I was afraid I'd lose them if any others popped up.

Fortunately, nothing could bring me down today. The sky was blue, the job was moving forward, and I'd had the best phone call with a client ever. Over the last few days, I'd worried my father was right, that I'd made a mistake in hiring someone with a stupid business name and that no one would take us seriously. I had to call Sandra and Troy to tell them that the French doors probably weren't going to happen, so I decided to test my father's theory. With a lot of word play, I managed to drop Get 'er Done into the conversation without letting on that they were currently working on the house.

Sandra's squeal may have caused long-term damage to my hearing. She'd gone on and on about the great things she'd heard from friends. Apparently, when Cooper had agreed to work with me, I'd been even luckier than I thought. I'd given a day's notice for a two-week job to a man who was almost impossible to book. Once I told them I'd decided to bring Get 'er Done in to finish their home, they both immediately said they'd check with their offices to see if they could work remotely for an additional week to give Cooper more time.

Celebrating my business savvy alone sucked, so I started bringing the guys lunch every day. What started out as what I considered a clever way to monitor their progress—without annoying Cooper—had very quickly become a way to spend more time with him . . . I mean, them.

"You aren't required to feed us," Cooper said as I passed out the food. It had taken a few tries to figure out what they liked. Today, I brought over their favorites, along with a salad for myself so I could sit with them longer.

"It's no big deal. I put it on the business account."

"Are you sure your dad will be okay with that?"

I lifted my head up to look at him. "How did you know it was my father's business?"

"Did you really think I wouldn't look you up the second you left my shop? 'Dillon Design: Let our family turn *your* family's house into a home.'" He quoted a few other things from our website. "Great house in that family shot. Do your parents still have it?"

"Yep," I said, opting to leave out the fact that only *one* of my parents still lived there. Or lived at all.

"That's good. Beckett still lives in the house we grew up in. With a few changes, right, B?"

His brother nodded, swallowing before he spoke. "After our folks moved out, I took their bedroom. Cooper helped me change enough of it to stop me from thinking about my parents whenever I was in there . . . doing stuff, you know?" He grimaced dramatically as we all chuckled, knowing exactly the kind of *stuff* a gorgeous man in his early twenties did a lot of.

"Hey, Soph," Cooper said as we were finishing up. "I have a question for you."

"I have an answer for you: No, you may not call me 'Soph.'" I probably hated the nickname as much as Cooper hated his. "Unless I can call you 'Coop.'"

Beckett popped his head up, eyes wide and lips in an O-shape. "If she gets to call you Coop, can I?"

He looked at his little brother. "No, but neither does she."

"What if I promise no bad jokes?"

"I don't think that's a promise you can keep, bro."

I laughed, enjoying the totally normal, healthy teasing between the brothers.

When I stood and started cleaning up, Cooper put his hand on my arm. "I really did want to talk to you about something."

It wasn't as though he'd grabbed me anywhere pleasurable, but I found myself staring at where our skin touched, thinking how his hand would feel elsewhere on my body. Luckily, we were working together now, or I might've been tempted to find out. Oh, who was I kidding? He was tempting as hell. But I could control myself in action if not thought. Dirty, dirty thoughts.

Cooper waited until the guys had gone inside before starting. "About your dad . . ."

"No," I blurted, shaking my head. "He has nothing to do with this project. It's mine, and I'll make it successful completely on my own."

"With my help." His smirk was barely visible, but it was there.

I let out a breath and cocked my head. "Is it considered helping when you're being paid to do it?"

"If the person who's paying is really desperate, and you're their only option?" He grabbed a paper napkin and used it to sweep crumbs off the table. "Then yeah, I would call that help."

"What makes you think you were my only option?"

"Because I went from not being the man you wanted to the one you *needed* in less than a week." He crumbled the napkin into a ball and tossed it into the garbage. "Aren't you going to ask me why I used the word 'desperate' too?"

"I think I'll skip that one, thanks."

"Let me know if you change your mind." His amused expression turned serious. "Back to your dad."

My smile fell. "What do you want to know?"

"Is he a bit of a . . ." His voice trailed.

I expected the question would be business-related, not personal, but as I watched him struggle to find the right word, I feared the worst.

"Dick?"

"Excuse me?" I snapped.

"Two of my old clients called me this morning. Two." He held up the appropriate number of fingers as if saying it twice hadn't been clear enough. "A man called my clients to interrogate them about me. Not like someone checking me out before hiring me, but like he had a personal ax to grind. He wouldn't identify himself, but they both felt the guy was weird enough to warn me."

"You assumed it was my father even though you know nothing about him."

He shrugged innocently. "I figured interrogating people was hereditary."

"I thought you didn't hold grudges," I grumbled.

"I don't like to make assumptions," he said after a sigh, "but when I do, they're usually right." He paused just long enough for me to wonder what kind of assumption he'd made about me. "You give away a lot without meaning to."

"Like what?"

"Like this job is do or die for you. That it's your first big solo gig and has to go perfectly. Other than your dad, who do you have anything to prove something to?"

I might have been angrier if he hadn't been right. About everything. It probably had been my father, and good excuses or not, he *could* be a dick. It was never his intention, but his caring so much about each and every project and always being the most experienced person in the room led to a lot of frustration when things didn't go right or when people screwed up. Having someone he didn't know at all doing the work must have been killing him.

Except Cooper wasn't the only one doing the work. I was here, too, someone he *did* know. So if he'd called to harass Cooper's clients, it meant he didn't trust me either. Nothing I said to my father would change his mind. Cooper didn't need to know that though. He already had enough reason to dislike him.

"I'll talk to him." I didn't know how or when, or if my father would hear a word I said, but I'd try.

"I appreciate that, Soph," he said, smiling. Crap. I'd totally forgotten about that dimple.

"Not a problem, Coop." I rolled my eyes. "Now, don't you have work to do?"

15

COOPER

Every morning at seven o'clock, Sophie texted to let me know what fucking day it was and how many we had left—something I let go because she'd stopped all the *other* reminders—the guys and I worked our asses off and earned every penny she was paying us.

Amelia, the girl my parents had unofficially adopted and who was still living with Beckett in our old house, even called me to give me shit about overworking him. Beckett was in grad school studying psychology and taught classes at the university, and apparently my ambitious work schedule was forcing him to teach his classes without showering first. I informed her he could shower whenever he wanted to, as long as he was in and out in no more than three minutes and didn't have to leave this job early to do it. As soon as I hung up with her, Beckett gave me shit for giving her shit. One of these days that boy was going to realize he was in love with Amelia and put all of us out of our misery.

After I told the guys about the bonus we'd get to replace the sliding glass doors, they put in even more time. Roy prayed his wife wouldn't go into labor, and Beckett took his run at six instead of eight so he could get here when I did.

We finished installing the last French door two hours before the family came back from their extended vacation. No sooner had we taken a deep breath than Sophie shoved rags and mops into our hands and told us to get rid of the construction dust and dirty footprints we'd tracked in.

"I can't wait to get that paycheck," Roy muttered.

Beckett wrung out the rag, dropped it, and pushed it around the floor with his foot. "And a shower."

"What is it with you and showers?" I asked. "Do you really need me to give you permission. Dude, you should take a shower because you fucking stink."

Like any good brother would, he wadded up the wet, dirty towel and threw it at me. Almost got me too.

"Nice arm, little bro." I tossed it back, aiming for his face. "You took up the wrong sport in high school. An arm like that was wasted in track."

"Except, if I weren't a runner"—he dropped the rag and tugged his T-shirt over his head, holding his arms out and posing—"I would look more like you and less like this."

True, I was more bulk muscle to his lean, but... "I can take you any day of the week, you little shit." I ran at him. He gave me a good fight as we grappled on the floor like in the old days.

Sophie shrieked from the doorway, "What are you doing?"

We rolled apart, Beckett jumping to his feet as if he'd never been down. I was laughing too hard to get up, so I grabbed the rag he'd dropped and pretended to mop.

"They'll be here in a few hours!" she said.

"Relax, *boss*." I stood and dusted myself off. "After working two weeks straight, we were bound to get a little stir-crazy. We're just letting off some steam. You should try it sometime."

"Maybe I will." She threw up her hands. "Maybe I should get

down on the ground right now and roll around with someone in the middle of a travertine floor that doesn't belong to me."

I popped a brow. Fuck it. I'd made it two weeks without falling into any old, unhealthy patterns. That deserved celebration.

"Now that the job is over, and we're not working together anymore," I said, still amused, "let me be the first to volunteer to be the person you roll around with."

We both shut up as the utterly inappropriate and desirable idea settled into our consciousness.

Her mouth tightened, and she tilted her head. "Actually, I prefer runners."

Roy and Beckett groaned while I closed my eyes and mouthed a dramatic, "Ouch."

"Now can we concentrate on finishing the job?" she asked. "I would hate for the homeowners to miss all your hard work because they were distracted by the enormous mess you left behind."

We all agreed that would be a travesty and divided cleanup duties. On the way out to my truck to drop off a bunch of painting supplies, Sophie stopped me.

"You do great work," she said, shielding her eyes from the sunset.

"What? I missed that. Could you speak up, so the neighbors can hear you?"

"I was right to trust you."

Not quite loud enough for the neighbors, but I'd take it, especially because it came with another one of her stunning smiles. I was starting to like them more than I was annoyed by them. Just like I didn't hate the truce we'd slipped into.

I thought I'd spend two weeks proving she was wrong about me. Turns out, I'd been wrong about *her*.

When she held out a check, I looked at all the shit I was

carrying and shook my head.

"Wait until I put these—"

She folded the check in half and put it into my pocket. Not that any pocket would've been safe, but her choice of the front one meant her fingers came awfully close to my cock.

I thanked her to cover my groan. When she didn't back away, I asked, "We good?"

"I just wanted to say that you're everything you promised. More. All while putting up with me—something you might consider adding to your business cards. So thank you." She lifted onto her tiptoes holding the beltloop of my jeans for balance.

Goddamn it. I'd made it two weeks.

When she leaned toward me, her eyes already closing, I froze. She could've told me to give back all the money and ordered me to do it all again tomorrow, and I would've agreed. My cock had already.

The disappointment didn't hit until I felt her lips land. The kiss I'd been hating myself for thinking about, for wanting more than breath, didn't happen. I'd been off by two inches. A kiss on the cheek was fine from your seventy-year-old auntie or someone European. But the softness of Sophie's lips was torture, providing just enough proof of how great they'd feel on mine. Maybe it was enough to imagine them on other parts of my body and provide a more vivid image to jerk off to later.

I knew she meant well, that it was her way of connecting with me, laying to rest all the tension and miscommunications between us. So I tried to keep the deep, *deep* sadness out of my expression when she pulled away.

"It was my pleasure." I'd never said something less true. Although, *pleasure* was definitely one of the words going through my mind. Lowering a paint can in front of my erection, I walked around her and headed to my truck.

"Cooper?" She waited until I'd stopped. "I know you probably have loads of other work to do, but when you're not busy, I'd like to run something by you. Another job."

At that moment, I could've walked away and avoided further punishment. Gone back to my life. Maybe it was the way the light hit her face, making her beauty almost ethereal. Or maybe it was my cock speaking for me. Whatever the reason, I said, "How about tomorrow?"

She nodded. "That's perfect. I'll text you the address."

We got all our shit cleared out right before the owners came home. Sophie asked me to stay and meet her clients, but I was dirty, confused, and tired. Instead of taking a shower and crashing like I should've, I invited the guys out for a beer where everybody would be filthy, tired, and confused. Roy opted to go see his wife instead. Go figure.

"Just me and you, little brother," I said. "We can drop Sammy off at my place on the way." Nobody that tiny could hold their liquor—he'd just end up embarrassing himself.

The bar was packed, dark, and smelled like stale beer and folks whose jobs didn't include espresso makers, corner offices, or white collars. It was exactly where I needed to be. I bought the first round. And the second. My little brother had busted his ass for me, and being a teacher's assistant and tutoring on the side didn't pay big bucks.

"You can pay me back when you're charging three hundred bucks an hour," I said when I handed him round three.

"With therapy, right?" He held his bottle up in thanks.

"If I ever go to therapy, it definitely won't be with someone who knows enough about my childhood to fuck with me psychologically."

"Speaking of childhood, I haven't seen you smile this much since we were kids. She's good for you."

"I can't say for sure what pronoun Sammy prefers, but I think he's a boy, Beckett."

"I meant Sophie, dumbass. What I can't quite figure out is why you don't seem to like each other all the time." He shrugged. "Is arguing foreplay for you guys?"

"What's foreplay?" I took a swig of my beer and hoped that was enough to change the subject.

"You're talking a lot more too."

"Fuck, I know. It's disgusting. You think she's rubbing off on me?" I held out both arms and looked for any of her residual happiness that might've made its way onto me. "Get it off! Get it off!" I sat back in my chair and took another swig of my beer. "Close one."

It was easy to say you enjoyed the work after it was over, once you'd forgotten all the annoying little details inherent in it. Arguments and ego blows aside, Sophie had done me a favor. My brother and I hadn't hung out much since the rest of our family left the area. I worked all the time. Beckett was busy with school and was apparently dating someone who wasn't the girl he'd been in love with since he was twelve.

"For real?" I asked, not holding in my shock. "You have a girlfriend?"

"She's not my girlfriend. We're just seeing each other." He drained his beer. "And, you know . . . she's in between apartments, so she's going to stay at my place until she finds a new one."

"What does your roommate think about that?"

"Amelia doesn't care. She's fine with whatever."

"Right." I nodded slowly. "Why wouldn't she be?"

I wondered if I should tell him or if it would be funnier if he found out the hard way. Before I could decide, my phone rang. I groaned when I saw the caller ID.

"Hey, Cooper!"

I shouldn't have answered. If I had any lingering doubts about Sophie, Helen's voice evaporated them all, along with every bit of happiness in me.

"Are you finally taking your dog back, or should I sell him on the black market?"

"That's the reason I'm calling, actually."

"Here I was hoping it was just to chat." I hoped the sarcasm could travel five thousand miles.

When she spat, "I'm trying to be nice," I knew it had.

"A little too late for that." I handed Beckett some money and motioned toward the bar, so he'd stop rolling his eyes at me. He snagged the cash from my hand and took our empties with him to the bar.

"When are you picking up your dog, Helen?"

"I have a bunch of vacation time saved up and was hoping to travel around Europe for a little while." Of course, she was. "I have a friend who'll take Sammy until I get back. If I give you her number, will you call her?"

"You're just going to dump him on somebody else?"

"She has another dog, so—"

"Yeah well, what if Sammy doesn't like their dog?" He wouldn't take a shit around the other dog, and that couldn't be healthy.

"What do you want me to do?" She sighed. "It's not as if you want to keep him."

I didn't. But I didn't like the idea of the little guy being tossed around like a kid from a broken home either. "How much longer will you be gone?"

"I'm not sure. A week?" That meant two. Minimum.

"He can stay with me." Why stick him with someone else

when he'd already chewed everything within his reach at my place? "But it better not be another month."

"Thanks, Cooper. You're the best." She was such a liar.

16

COOPER

When I opened the door, Aaron was standing on my stoop smiling at me. It was way too bright and way too early in the morning for that kind of shit-eating grin. With Sophie and Aaron, it was all day, every day. Made me wonder which of them was patient zero. Beckett was right—I'd been spending too much time with Sophie lately, so that shit better not be contagious.

I rubbed the sleep from my eyes. "Why the fuck are you so happy all the time?"

"I'm not," he said seriously. "I just can't pull off that broody thing like you can. Plus, I take dental hygiene very seriously and like to show off all my hard work. Can't do that if I'm frowning."

"You have a point. And very healthy-looking gums."

"Thank you." He bowed his head. "Now, it hurts me to say this to you, but go put on some clothes."

"Why?" I looked down at the boxer briefs I'd slept in.

"Because we're taking Samuel for a walk."

"Sammy's fine with the patio now. His legs are so stubby, he gets winded running from one side to the other. It's the equivalent of a normal dog running the length of a football field a couple times."

He sighed dramatically. "Samuel *is* a normal dog, and all dogs need to get out of the house occasionally. So do their humans."

"I'm *not* his human."

"Yeah, well, I don't think you needed the 'his' in that statement either." He pushed past me. "Samuel! Where are you, sunshine? It's Uncle Aaron!" The little fluff came running as soon as he heard the voice of someone who actually liked him. "Cooper, go pretend to be human and get dressed. We're leaving in two minutes."

When I came back from my room, Aaron was standing at the door dangling my sunglasses from his fingertips and holding Sammy with his other arm.

"If you want my shades, you better take the dog too."

"Oh, please. Do I look like someone who'd wear five-dollar sunglasses?"

"No, but those were ten dollars."

He held them out. "I don't want to alarm you, but there's sunlight out there."

"Why did I agree to this?" I took my sunglasses and put them on as I locked the door behind me. "Do you always get what you want?"

"I'm gorgeous, have a great job, am the whole goddamn package, and yet you are by far the most interesting man I've met in months, so obviously, I don't get *everything* I want."

"Maybe that's because you spend all your free time with a woman."

"Two, actually. And while you're factually correct, the woman you're referring to is a magnet for stunningly attractive men."

My gut clenched at the thought of Sophie dating someone

"stunningly attractive." I didn't know where the feeling came from—it wasn't as if I wished I were the kind of guy she wanted. I liked who I was and had no plans to change into somebody else anytime soon, especially for a woman.

"Unfortunately, her judgment is off-the-charts bad," he continued. "Do you have any idea how many closeted gay men she's gone out with? I figure, why not recycle them?"

"Good for you. Recycling is important."

I let Aaron follow my lead as we slowly made our way out of the complex and toward the public park down the block. Because, like I said—I wasn't planning to change anytime soon. As we walked, I could tell Aaron was struggling to keep his pace adequately slow. Everything about him screamed overachiever, someone always in a hurry to get to the next step, the next opportunity. I was more of a take-it-as-it-comes-if-it-comes type of guy.

The city had set aside a large portion of the park for dogs, two huge chain-link fenced-in areas side by side—one for normal-sized dogs and the other for the little ones. They were all still bigger than Sammy because he was abnormally small, but he seemed to enjoy their company. I'd taken him here a few times, including last night after I'd gotten home, which was why he'd been too exhausted to wake me up at six this morning by licking my face with his disgusting little tongue.

As soon as he saw the other dogs, he started running, spinning around in midair when he realized he was still attached to something. I unclipped his leash and shooed him off to play.

"He's absolutely adorable," Aaron said, watching him plow into a small group about thirty feet away.

"He's a decent-looking fella. A little needy though."

"Aren't we all? Needy, anxiety-ridden, and self-loathing."

"No, thankfully." I looked at him, noted the tightness of his mouth, the way he kept his eyes locked on the pack of tiny dogs. "At least, that's not the goal."

He sighed. "You and I are very different people."

I didn't even consider pushing for more information—that wasn't in me, but I was curious. Another puzzle to figure out. If he wanted to share, he would, but until then, I'd deal with what I knew about him. It couldn't be easy to be a gay Black man, no matter where you lived.

"You're a lot nicer than I am," I said, nodding.

"I dress better too."

"Definitely. Don't forget better looking."

"Too obvious to bother mentioning." After a chuckle, he continued, "Sophie told me you two are meeting later." His voice went up at the end, but it wasn't actually a question.

"She wants me to take a look at another job." That I shouldn't agree to do. "I hope she understands there's a good chance I'll say no. I had to push off all my other work to help her with the last one."

He followed me over to a bench near the gate where we could sit down and still keep an eye on Sammy. "It'll be nice for you two to spend some more time together though."

I let the comment linger a while but didn't bother keeping the doubt off my face.

"Not that I'm hinting or anything. Honestly, you two together would be awful for me." He grimaced. "Can you imagine how adorable your babies would be?"

At least he started laughing before I took him seriously. Although now that he'd put the idea in my head, Sophie and I would make great-looking babies. Smart too.

"Nah, with my luck, we'd end up with a kid who looked like Sammy but without all the hair." I grinned at the thought of a couple of hairless Sammys running around and Sophie chasing after them in her suit and heels.

"Think she wants babies?" Fuck if I knew why I asked that, why it had sounded like a serious question I needed an answer to. To get rid of the suddenly curious look Aaron was giving me, I added, "She's so neat and organized. I can't imagine her on the ground, getting dirty or covered in fingerpaint."

"Oh, I think you can. In fact, I'd guess you've spent a fair amount of time imagining her like that."

"Fuck off," I said, laughing. I didn't deny it though. Knowing nothing would ever happen between us didn't stop me fantasizing about it.

"I'm just giving you shit," he said. "She's an attractive woman, and you are a heterosexual man. It was an easy joke to make." He stretched out his legs in front of him. "Unfortunately, until she gets rid of that list, it'll keep getting in the way of any real relationship she could have."

"What list?"

He looked at me as if I were stupid. "The plan, or whatever she calls it. Her requirement list."

"Requirements for a relationship?"

"For a man."

I let out a half-hearted chuckle. "That explains so much."

I shouldn't have been surprised—I'd seen her planner. She had lists for everything. To-do lists, doing lists, and done lists, along with delegation lists, follow-up lists, shopping lists. Why would it be any different in her personal life?

Aaron's eyes were wide. "I— I assumed she'd explained it to you when she first . . ." He struggled for the right word.

I shook my head. "No list or plan was mentioned."

Sammy followed another dog to the gate as it was leaving, so I got up and grabbed him before he could escape and go home with another family. Disloyal bastard. I set him back down, watched him run straight for another dog as if his first friend had never existed, and sat back down next to Aaron.

"If I don't make the list, who does?"

"You should ask her about it. Maybe you'll be the one to convince her to burn it. I used to think it was adorably ridiculous, something she'd grow out of. Liz and I enabled her for too long. The man who would make her list doesn't exist, but a man who would make her happy does."

"You mean she's not happy now? I've seen her not smiling, like, twice, and neither time lasted longer than a minute and a half."

"There's a big difference between smiling and happy, Cooper. Anyone can smile. See?" Instantly, he slapped on another shit-eating grin.

"*I* can't."

His smile wilted. "Then maybe you don't have as much to hide behind it."

We watched Sammy play for a little longer, both silent with our own thoughts.

I knew Sophie's need for control was hiding some damage, but I still didn't know what kind or where it came from. Sure, I hoped the smile she always wore was genuine, and I liked the way it felt to help her out. But people didn't change—only their perceptions did.

When we were ready to go home, I grabbed Sammy and handed him to Aaron.

"Can I keep him overnight tonight?" he asked as we began the walk home. "We can watch movies, make s'mores, and do our hair."

"Wow. I'd almost hate to miss all that fun. I'll pack a bag for him—some food, his favorite toy, the pillow he usually sleeps on. I got him a brush the other day, so I'll toss that in too, for when you do each other's hair."

Aaron stopped to stare at me a second, smirking and rolling his eyes.

"What?" I snapped.

"You love him."

I held my gut as if I were going to puke. "I admit that he's grown on me a little, but love isn't even on my radar."

"My mistake." His grin didn't falter. "I'm sure you'll know when you're in love."

17

SOPHIE

Orion's meow broke me out of my thoughts and forced me to stop staring at my phone. I forbade myself from texting Cooper a reminder of our meeting today. Apparently, he neither needed nor appreciated them. But temptation was a real thing.

"It wouldn't hurt you to show a little patience, you know." I put down the cat food and watched Orion attack it as if I'd never fed him before. I'd never understand why someone who wore nothing but classic, slimming black clothing would adopt a white long-haired cat. Probably because he'd looked so lonely, standing apart from his littermates. He'd needed a companion as much as I did.

There was a chance Cooper had changed his mind after we spoke and wouldn't show up, so when I showered this morning, I'd made a mental list of my other options. It was a short list because I didn't have any other options.

The glass ceiling project was supposed to be inspiring and meaningful, not tainted by ill feelings and regret every time I looked at it. I'd waited this long to find someone skilled enough to do it, and I could wait a little longer if I had to.

I'd been dreaming of a way to look at the stars from my

bedroom, to have a way to remember my mom, since I was twelve. It had to be perfect, not hurried, or half-assed, or anything less than perfection. *Close* to perfection.

Cooper was the first person I trusted to do it right.

But not right away. First, I'd ask him to finish my walk-in closet—a smaller job that would take a few days and give us a chance to see how we got along when the other guys weren't around.

I tried my best not to stare at the door or jerk at every sound that could've been a key in the lock. I hadn't even given him a key yet.

Yet. That could be a problem. Typically, contractors had keys to enter a jobsite when the homeowner wasn't there, and I suddenly felt idiotic that it hadn't occurred to me. If I gave him a key to my place, I'd eventually have to ask for it back, as if he were an ex-boyfriend after a bad breakup. Maybe it was a mistake to have him here, in my home. What if he got the wrong idea and thought this was my way of inviting him to do a more intimate type of work?

Not to mention he'd have 24/7 access and might come over to work while I was in the shower. Or walking around the house naked. Not that I walked around the house naked, but what if I decided this was the week I wanted to start?

Orion got up and walked between my legs—his way of demanding to be held. I wondered if Cooper needed to know this was my house at all. I leaned down and picked up my cat.

"Would you tattle on me if I pretended this was Liz's place?" I asked, scratching him under his chin. "Since she'll be away for a while, she would need someone to take care of the world's cutest cat, right?" That way I could still live here, and Cooper never had to know it was mine. It would only be for a few days, would make me feel better, and wouldn't affect Cooper's life or work at all.

Orion knew someone was here before I did, twisting out of my arms and running into my bedroom before I even heard the knock. On the way to answer the door, I reminded myself it might not be Cooper. It could be a neighbor. Or a deliveryman. Or a Girl Scout.

"Morning." Roy stood on my front step, a toolbox in each hand.

"Good morning."

Cooper had sent a replacement. I could accept that. All I really wanted was someone who could do the job as well as he could. Roy was competent. Besides, today was a walk-through and discussion, not a commitment.

I led him inside and offered him a cup of coffee.

"My wife isn't drinking anything with caffeine right now, so I'm not either." He stared at the coffee pot the way I stared through a Neiman Marcus window. "Except on special occasions."

"Today *is* a special occasion," I said, taking out another mug. "I'm trying to bribe you into doing another job."

"Bribery works." He set his stuff down to take the mug and gulp down about half the steaming liquid.

"Doesn't it burn?"

"Yeah, but in a good way. Plus, I should finish it before Cooper gets here. Not sure if you noticed, but he's an ass about wasting time."

"I love that about him," I said under my breath, then it hit me. "You mean Cooper's coming? Here? Today?"

Roy tilted his head in confusion. "Unless he changed his mind in the last twenty minutes."

"That's great! I mean, obviously, I assumed he'd be here on time." It was nice to be right about someone occasionally. "I thought maybe he was ill and sent you to cover today."

"He sounded fine when I spoke to him. I just needed to drop

off some stuff that went into the wrong truck yesterday, and this place is closer to mine than the shop is." He set down his cup. "You don't happen to have any soft cheese or sushi to bribe me with too, do you?"

We chatted about his wife and their baby on the way. He drank two more cups of coffee and ate a large chunk of brie I had in the fridge. Five minutes later, I heard another knock on the door.

It wasn't a neighbor, or a deliveryman, or a Girl Scout either this time.

"Please don't make me regret this." Cooper's arms were folded over his chest, pressing his biceps forward so they looked even bigger than normal.

"I'll do my best."

After he said hello and thanks and we both said goodbye to Roy, I opened the door wide and invited Cooper into my house. Not that I planned on letting him know it was mine.

"I like this neighborhood. Its got character, history."

"I think so too." I led him into the living room.

His eyes traveled around the space like a speed reader moving through words, noticing everything at once and cataloging the important stuff for future reference.

After a minute or two, he looked at me, his brow tight. "It's . . ." He spun around again as if to make sure he hadn't missed anything. "Sterile-looking."

My heart dipped in my chest. "Sterile-looking." The first word he thought of when he saw my house, my *home*, was "sterile."

"I meant clean. Very clean." At least he read my facial expression correctly and was trying to clarify. But the damage was already done. "Does anybody live here?"

"Yes," I said flatly. "A very clean person." I suddenly felt much better about my decision not to tell him it was my house.

"It's got lots of potential." He peered around me to look out the sliding glass door that led to the backyard. "Great trees too."

At least we agreed on something.

"It's still a work in progress," I said, unhappy I felt the need to defend a lack of clutter. "The homeowner is a close friend. Liz has great taste but not the finances and time to do everything at once. So over the past four months, we've been tackling one project at a time. I'm proud of how they came out."

"Great. Can't wait to see them."

Cooper flinched when Orion brushed his leg and rubbed his face against his jeans.

"That's a cat," he said brilliantly.

"I'm aware. Leave him alone, Orion. Cooper doesn't like cats," I said as I picked him up. "Or maybe he doesn't like cats the same way he doesn't like dogs?"

"Sammy's barely a dog."

My eyes widened. "That's the first time I've heard you admit you like him."

"The little guy has a certain amount of charm. Especially when he sticks his nose under my chin to wake me up in the morning. Definitely could do without the licking though." He scratched the cat on the top of the head. "Orion's a good name. The god of war or something, right?"

"According to the ancient Greeks, Orion was a hunter Zeus put into the sky. He's remained there ever since as a constellation."

"So is your friend into mythology or astronomy?"

"Um . . . both, actually. When she was young, she wanted to be an astronomer. Except she kept calling it astrology, which was really embarrassing." I hoped I wasn't blushing at the memory when my teacher finally explained the difference. "Anyway, I'm house- and cat-sitting while she's away, so you're welcome to bring Sammy over while you work."

"*If* I work." He paused. "Think Orion would be okay with that?"

"Cats are good at taking care of themselves," I said with a little pride. "They're independent and know what they want."

"They also do nothing but sleep twenty hours a day, treat the only people who care about them like shit, and are easily distracted by shiny objects."

"No one's perfect," I mumbled. As soon as I set Orion down, he ran down the hall and disappeared. "Anyway, Orion will be able to handle Sammy."

"I'll think about it. It might be good for the little man to have a four-legged friend. I don't know if you've noticed, but I'm not always the best company."

"Really?" I shrugged. "No, I hadn't noticed that at all."

He grunted a laugh. "Let's get to work, boss."

I ignored the mocking title and motioned for him to follow me. "Let me show you my favorite part of the house." Hopefully, he wouldn't call my bedroom sterile too.

18

COOPER

I followed Sophie through the clinically clean living room and down a hallway toward the master bedroom. Everything was flawlessly designed, reconfigured, and well maintained. The one thing missing was personality. Like, any of it. No matter where I looked, I couldn't get a sense of the person who lived here apart from their compulsive tidiness.

A home should reflect the people who lived in it, have pieces of them around to create a place worth making memories in. This one didn't have any of that—no photos, no ugly throw blanket that they couldn't throw away because it was a gift from a family member, no pillows with funny sayings on them, no signs of life. Hopefully, whatever Sophie wanted me to do would be something along those lines.

"Wow." As soon as I stepped into the master bedroom, I understood why this was Sophie's favorite. When these old houses were built, bedrooms were never this big. Somebody must have knocked down a wall between two bedrooms, and instead of the small loft space above the room, that extra space had been used to almost double the height of the ceiling.

It was already my favorite too. Dark hardwood floors. The

real shit, not the kind that came from a big box store. Muted paint color on the walls. Understated curtains pooling just the right amount onto the floor.

The centerpiece was the gigantic king-sized bed frame. Had to be custom-made by someone who knew what they were doing and then spent another couple of decades refining their skills. I'd never seen anything like it.

"What do you think?" she said from beside me. "Nice?"

"*Nice* isn't the word that comes to mind." I checked out the detailing, carefully running my hand along the mirror-smooth edge of the headboard. "She isn't just a piece of furniture. She's art."

"*She's* nice art though, right?"

When I looked at Sophie, she had a hand over her mouth, trying not to laugh.

"Very nice art." A piece this large could get heavy fast, but the artist had carved each line into something incredibly delicate, almost lacelike.

"Um . . . if you're done fantasizing about the bed, can I show you what I need your help with?"

"I'm gonna need another minute with her." A man could live and die in that bed. Happily.

Before I said fuck it, jumped on her, and spent the rest of the day star-fished in the middle of her, I diverted my eyes and refocused on Sophie. "She's really beautiful."

"I agree. It took a while to find someone with enough skill and humility to exactly follow my drawing. Miraculously, I found an artist who works with reclaimed wood, and her studio just happens to be in San Francisco."

My brows popped up. "You designed this? That takes a lot of talent—from the designer and the builder."

I knew she could handle the business side of things without breaking a sweat and thought she had a good design eye. I'd been wrong. This piece proved she had a *great* eye for design.

"Thanks. I'll let Laney know. And if you ever meet my father, feel free to mention that to him."

"If I ever meet your father, I'm not mentioning anything that proves I've been anywhere near a bed with you."

"Good point," she said with a laugh. "Are all beds female or just this one?"

"Anything that gorgeous has to be female. You of all people should know that."

When a flush of pink hit her cheeks, she spun around and opened a door that led into a dimly lit closet. Whoever had expanded the bedroom hadn't done much for the closet—a couple of walls, the door, drywall, and that was it.

"I sketched out where everything should go," she said. "Shelving, hanging space, shoe racks."

"I think Liz is a nudist," I said as I followed her in. The place was so empty it made my closet seem full.

Sophie hmphed. "She put all her things into the covered clothing rack next to the dresser so they wouldn't be in the way. You must have missed it while you were drooling all over the bed."

While it was a walk-in closet, two people couldn't actually do much walking inside of it. When our arms and sides weren't bumping, we were in an extremely intimate face-to-face.

When she showed me how far she wanted the lower shelves to come out, she bent over at the waist and backed up right into me. Instinctually, my hands went for her hips. I caught them an inch away from touchdown and yanked them back.

If I could trust my head around her, I would've thought the time from when her ass touched my cock to when she jerked away was a lot longer than necessary. I could've sworn I heard her sigh somewhere in the middle too.

"And that's it," she said, moving as far from me as the space allowed.

Too bad. I'd hoped things were just getting started.

But they weren't, so I refocused on what I was good at. "What about lighting?"

She pointed to a couple of boxes in the corner and showed me where she thought it should be installed. Like usual, I disagreed and showed her what I thought would work better, and she told me I was wrong.

I'd always claimed to like women who knew what they wanted, and how they wanted it, but after meeting Sophie I might have to rethink that.

I shook my head. "This whole side for shoes? It's way too much."

She looked at me as if I were the crazy one. "You probably have one pair of work boots, a pair of loafers, and some sneakers. Am I right?'

"No, I have two pairs of work boots."

"It's amazing how often you prove my point for me."

I could just make out her eye roll in the darkness.

"To be clear, this isn't a Dillon Design job."

"Is freelancing allowed at Chez Dillon?" I asked. Maybe she was trying to set up something separate from her dad's company. Smart. I didn't know much about her dad other than that he wanted my old clients to badmouth me, and he made his daughter a bigger ball of anxiety than she was naturally, but either reason was enough to not need any others.

"It's too small a project for us, and I'm giving Liz a really good deal because she's a friend. It's more of a favor than a money-making endeavor." Then she quickly added, "You'll be paid your normal fee, don't worry."

"I wasn't."

"So, you'll do it?" Her shoulders lifted, her little nose squished up, and her hands came together in a begging position.

Before I agreed to the last job, I'd asked myself why I would put myself through that. I knew it would be a special kind of torture, and it was. Seeing the look on her face now—the excitement, the hope, and, yeah, the begging—made the torture worse. Plus, since she was house-sitting, she'd be around more often. I could whip out this closet in a couple of days. Anybody could. Which made me wonder why she wanted me to do it.

"I have a ton of other work to catch up on, so it would take me a lot longer to finish than someone who didn't have to fit it in between other projects."

"I'm the reason you have so much catching up to do, so no problem."

"If I can't finish it by the time Liz gets back, how does she feel about having a strange man in her bedroom closet?"

"Who doesn't love having a strange man in their bedroom?" She laughed. "Is two weeks enough?"

"Should be."

"No pressure, but pleeeease?"

Fuck the overhead lighting, her damn smile lit up the room. Good thing we'd never date because I didn't think I'd ever be able to say no to her.

"Yeah, I'll do it."

With a tiny squeal, she threw her arms around my neck. I grunted when we collided, but I didn't move. Besides the cheek kiss and accidental brushing of body parts, this was the first time we'd really touched, and my body reacted accordingly. Without deciding to, I wrapped an arm around her and took in her scent—heaven with a touch of lavender.

With our faces inches apart, I watched her expression go from superficial excitement to the shocked realization of the position she'd just put herself in. But she didn't pull away. I slipped my hand around the back of her neck, the muscles in my arm taut.

She stared at me, eyes wide and unblinking. Slowly, so fucking slowly, I pulled her even closer, giving her time to decide if she wanted this as badly as I did.

No one on earth could possibly want this as badly as I did.

Her breath stopped when her breasts pressed against my chest, or maybe that was the moment she felt my erection.

I was already staring at her lips when she whispered my name, her voice low and seductive. "Cooper?" Her hands slid down my shoulders onto my chest.

"Yeah," I whispered back.

"We should finish talking about the project."

I shut my eyes and laughed—silently and bitterly. Fuck yeah, I was disappointed she could still think clearly, ignore the moment, the heat, the perfect way our bodies fit together. I sure as hell couldn't, not with the way she looked at my mouth, the speed of her heart, the heaviness of her breath. But I wasn't going to take anything she wasn't willing to give.

"You'll let me know if you're ever in the market for something casual, right?"

"I'm not," she said.

"But if you were . . ."

"Why?" She stood up a little taller and slid her hands onto my shoulders, bringing her lips that much closer to mine. "Would you give me your brother's phone number?"

Groaning, I let go of her and stepped back. "Oh, the pain."

"Now, if we can get back to work." She said it seriously, but I could tell she wanted to crow a little for that one.

"Right after I find my ego." I searched the floor. "It's gotta be in here somewhere." After another second, I followed her back into the bedroom.

As I adjusted my cock, the only reason I didn't start weeping was because I could tell she was suffering just as much. The light had changed, but her pupils were still large, her face flushed, her breasts rising with every breath.

"I'm going to need a couple minutes," I said, heading for the bathroom in the hall. She'd taken me this far, I'd probably need less than five to jerk myself off, less if she came with me.

As soon as the door shut, I leaned against the counter, taking deep breaths until my body calmed down. I splashed some water on my face and checked out the shower just in case I needed a cold one later.

"Better?" she asked when I came back to the bedroom.

"Marginally. You?"

She shrugged. "Just like normal." Except there was a lot more tension in her voice than normal.

"Then you recover a lot faster than I do."

"Doesn't a man always need more time than a woman to recover?"

I laughed. "Depends on the man."

Her gaze lowered down my body, possibly to check how well I'd recovered, and then spun toward the window. "Anyway, once you're done with the built-in, there's another project, a much bigger one. It—"

"Whoa!" I stopped her with a raised hand. "I agreed because this one shouldn't take too long. Meanwhile, Roy will be at the shop alone, doing all the shit we should've been working on for the last couple weeks. His baby isn't due for a month, but I'm pretty sure they pick the worst possible time to show up, don't they? So, one job at a time."

Her disappointment was brief. "That sounds . . . close to perfect."

19

COOPER

Things didn't look promising for cat and dog relations. Sammy's frustrated yipping drove me nuts after about five minutes. Orion had a great time sitting on the counter a good two feet out of Sammy's reach as he casually groomed himself. Then, as soon as Sammy forgot about him and stopped barking, he would peek over the edge just to get Sammy all riled up again. As I was about to put the little guy outside and let him explore the small backyard, Orion gave his thigh one more lick—disgusting—jumped off the counter, and sped off before Sammy even had a chance to figure out what had happened.

"He doesn't like me either, little man. Maybe tomorrow will be better." Probably not though. "I'll call Uncle Aaron tonight and see if he can keep an eye on you."

Speaking of cats and dogs . . .

At the last job, Sophie would stop by and hang out for twenty minutes or so. But she was sticking around on this project.

She sat at the small table across the room, making calls and working on her laptop while I tried to focus on what I was doing. All I wanted to do was stare at her, talk to her, fantasize about things I would never get to do to her on that bed. Every time I managed to forget she was here, she would ask if I wanted a drink or how things were going.

At least she seemed less anxious. I'd like to think it was because I'd earned her trust on the last job, but more likely, her calm was due to her dad not being involved.

"Are you going to be here the entire time?" I asked after she'd hung up with a potential new client.

"Am I bothering you?"

"A little."

She put down her phone and turned her chair toward me. "Should I go into the other room to make calls?"

"You should go into the other room to *be*." When I saw the hurt in her expression as she stood and gathered her stuff, I knew she'd misunderstood my intent. "Wait a sec."

"You don't have to baby me," she said without looking at me. "I'm a grown woman."

"That's why I want you to leave."

"What?"

I took a deep breath and set down my measuring tape. "It's a good thing this job isn't official because what I'm about to say would—and should—get me fired."

She crossed her arms over her chest and stood straight, preparing herself for a fight we weren't going to have.

I didn't know how to put this delicately, so I didn't bother trying. "When you're around, all I can think about is where I'm standing. In a bedroom. With you. And that beautiful monster of a bed over there."

"Oh." Her arms dropped to her sides as her eyes tracked from me to the bed and back. "Oh!"

"If you think *that* was bad, you really don't want to know what I've been choreographing in my head for the last hour."

She swallowed. "I'll be out on the patio."

"Good idea." I chuckled to myself as she hurried from the room.

Thirty minutes later, I realized I'd made a rookie mistake with a measurement that meant I'd have to start one side over completely. But not today. After over two weeks of nearly constant work on the other house, I was exhausted. My job kept me in shape, but that last week had been brutal. Everything ached. Twenty-six had never felt like sixty before. Since Sophie's friend was out of town until next week, there was no hurry. So, I decided to cut out early and catch up on some sleep.

First, I had to clean up and put away the tools I'd left out back where Sophie was playing a weak game of catch with Sammy. She tossed his ball a few feet away and clapped encouragingly when he went for it.

"He's not going to bring it back to you," I said as I walked past her.

"He already did. Twice. You should give him more credit."

"A man's gotta earn it."

"Sammy! Bring it here!" She repeated that a few times. "Come on, Sammy. You can do it." Her final "Sammy" was more of a whine. The dog was lying in the grass on the other side of the lawn, gnawing on his ball.

"He's probably had enough for today." Sophie leaned back in the lounge chair, slipped her hands behind her head, and watched me put stuff away.

I wound up the extension cord and set it under the patio cover to one side. There was no rain in the forecast, but the last thing you could trust was California weather these days. I grabbed the saw and the rest of my stuff and brought it inside. Could I have moved faster? Absolutely. But with her eyes tracking my every move, I wasn't going to. Especially because she wasn't looking at my face.

"Quit staring at me."

"I wasn't staring," she said quickly. "I was looking at your equipment."

"My equipment?" I didn't need to look at her to know she was blushing.

"Your tools."

"My tools?"

"Ugh. You know what I mean!"

"Yeah, I know. You were looking at my hammer. Or my drill. Wondering what it might be like to watch me screw something . . . in. Nail something?" I could go all day. It was one of the perks of the job—an unending supply of puns and innuendo.

"Very amusing, but I meant it would be good to learn more about construction."

"Right."

I held her gaze until her blush deepened, and she turned away. We both knew she'd been checking out my ass. I'd let it go for as long as I could, but why miss out an opportunity to give her shit?

"I'm sorry," she said. "I didn't mean to make you uncomfortable."

"I'm not uncomfortable. I'm just trying to get my stuff together. That's tough to do when you're looking at me like I'm a piece of meat. You do eat meat, right?"

She brushed off the joke with a wave of her hand. "I'm serious. I don't want you to think I don't respect you and the work you do. It would be the height of hypocrisy to make someone feel that way after what happened with Dennis."

I bristled. "The contractor before me? What'd he do?"

"He didn't hit me or anything, although I'm sure he wanted to."

"What did he do, Sophie?"

"Nothing. He was just disrespectful and called me a bunch of ugly names."

"That's not nothing."

She studied me for a minute, her brow tight. "I can handle being cursed at."

"Didn't say you couldn't handle it. I said it wasn't nothing." I sat on one of the patio chairs. "There are lots of assholes out there. Some of them never learned how to properly act around women, especially successful women."

"In Dennis' case, the surprise came from someone being so proud of their misogyny. Usually it's more subtle. That doesn't make it better or less . . ." She didn't have to finish the sentence. Whether the strike was physical or verbal didn't matter—it had still hurt.

Growing up in a house with women as smart and competent as Sophie, I'd seen how shit like that affected them. Sometimes I wondered if it hit strong women even harder, or if they had a harder time letting go of it after it was over. That threat to who they were. The guilt—however misplaced—they took on for allowing it to hurt them.

"Should I kick his ass?" I offered, knowing she would say no. She had to deal with it herself, and I didn't have the right to take that away from her.

"Thanks, but I've moved on. The less I think of him, the better." She stood and stretched her neck. "Besides, if you got involved, there'd be lawsuits and a trial, and you'd probably look awful in an orange jumpsuit."

"I look great in orange," I teased.

"That creates an even bigger problem." She grimaced. "You're too pretty to risk jail."

"You think I'm pretty."

She laughed. "Only a little. Get back to work."

"Yes, boss."

20

SOPHIE

Between designing, budgeting, and talking to prospective clients, I also had to do my regular job—all the accounting, scheduling, setting up photo shoots of the Riverview project for industry magazines, and interviewing contractors for future jobs. I did it all in the kitchen or on the patio—still staying away from the bedroom per Cooper's request. Unfortunately, simply by mentioning it, he'd permanently etched the idea into my mind. I couldn't even be in the bedroom by myself without thinking about him. Needless to say, I hadn't gotten much sleep last night.

That reminded me—I needed to buy new batteries for my vibrator.

It was chilly today, so I decided to work inside. Ironically, I couldn't get through a single phone call without Cooper coming into the kitchen for one reason or another.

"I've been meaning to ask you about something," he said as he dumped some garbage into the bin. "Something Aaron mentioned to me last weekend."

"Oh? How nice that you're spending time with one of my best friends." I rolled my eyes.

"It's an excuse for him to see Sammy that I benefit from." He came over to the table. "He said I should ask about your list."

The muscles in my back tensed.

"I have lots of lists, you know that. Should I tell you about all of them?" I didn't know why I was playing stupid. I wasn't ashamed of the list—why would I be?

"Thanks, but nobody has that kind of time. Or is that masochistic." He sat across from me, stretching his legs out and kicking my foot under the table accidentally. "I think he called it *the* list." The look on Cooper's face told me he knew a lot more than he was letting on.

"He told you about the list," I said, feigning surprise. "How .. . thoughtful of him."

"Sounded like I'm not on it, so am I not supposed to know?"

I paused to consider how honest to be, how each potential word might affect our fledgling relationship. We'd been seeing a lot of each other lately. Even my best friends weren't as comfortable in my house as Cooper was. I wondered if that would change if he saw through my lie and found out this was my house.

I took a moment to consider all the possible outcomes. Unfortunately, the way he studied me was very distracting.

"I'll tell you," I said finally, "if you stop looking at me like that."

"Like what?" A corner of his mouth twitched. "Like I'm wondering what could possibly be on the list that the mere possibility of discussing it with me is causing damage to your psyche?" He put both hands on the table and shoved his chair back. "You know what? Forget it."

"Wait. If you want to know, I'll tell you." I had nothing to hide, and maybe it would settle any lingering resentment he still had about me not wanting to date him.

He sat back down and assumed the same position he'd been

in, legs stretched out under the table, arms crossed, eyes on me, patiently waiting for me to start.

Remembering how quickly Liz and Aaron's jaws dropped when I told them about the list, I decided to go a different route.

I put down my pen. "The list is how I determine if someone has the potential to take an intimate position in my life, to separate the wheat from the chaff, so to speak."

"It's a rating system for wheat. In list form."

I let out a long breath of air. "Rating system implies judgment, which isn't what it's about. It's not about any one man. It's about all men, as a group."

His eyes were wide, but it seemed like he was trying to understand, not make fun of me.

"You're right, that's much less judgmental." He didn't even attempt to hide his sarcasm. "So it's a list of absolute requirements that men either have or don't have. That you track."

"Not exactly, but . . ." I pressed my lips together. "Well, sort of, yes."

"You don't think that's a little . . . weird?"

"Everyone has some sort of checklist," I said, crossing my arms over my chest. "Maybe most people don't write it down, or go through it every few days, or hold it up to every prospective mate they meet. But writing it all down doesn't make you weird."

"You're absolutely right." His smile grew. "It's all the *other* shit you just mentioned that does."

"Gee, thanks." I knew how unusual—or as my father would say, *undesirable*—certain parts of my personality were. "I'm an acquired taste. Like a fine wine. Or cigars. Or that disgusting pink fish on bagels."

"You realize you described yourself as disgusting and compared yourself to something most people think smells bad, right?"

"I also said wine. What's wrong with wine?"

"Nothing. Wine's great. Unless it's already opened, and nobody's touched it in a long time." He rested his elbows on the table. "How long has it been since you've been touched, Sophie?"

I uncrossed my legs, leaned forward, and wagged my eyebrows. "Why? Are you thirsty?"

"I'm always thirsty. But I try to stay away from anything unsatisfying or that'll leave a bad taste in my mouth."

"I wouldn't—" I snapped my mouth shut.

He laughed. "I would gladly take a swig of whatever you're offering, anytime, anywhere. In fact, if you're up for it"—he slammed his hands down on the wood—"I bet this table right here is sturdy enough to hold us."

"You're a pervert," I said. He wasn't, but he'd seemed flattered last time I'd called him that.

"Right now, I'm a pervert at your service. So, if you really want my help—"

"I never asked for your help."

"I need to know exactly what's on this mysterious list of yours."

"I don't want your help. Nor do I need it." I clipped my pen into my planner and closed it.

"Right, you've already been so wildly successful in your quest to find the right guy that you can turn down assistance when it's offered? I've seen your planner. Unless you consider an appointment with your dentist a date, you need my help. Badly."

I grumbled. "You would have to promise not to make fun of me."

"I never make a promise I can't keep. What if I promise to stick to laughing without any side commentary?"

"You're such a—"

"Pervert. Yeah. We already agreed on that." He sat back in his chair. "Come on, tough girl. Show it to me."

I took a deep breath and let it out slowly, preparing myself for the worst. It wasn't as if Aaron and Liz didn't burst into the laughter when I first told them about it. Along with every time it had come up since. I wasn't embarrassed of the list—I was proud of it. There would be a lot fewer broken hearts if everyone had one.

I slid my planner closer to me. "This isn't the typical grocery list of all the things a woman looks for in a man."

"Good, because the idea of there being a *typical* list like that terrifies me."

"You said no commentary."

"That wasn't specifically about you. It doesn't count."

I raised an eyebrow. "It counts."

He held up his hand in submission. "Your list isn't typical. Good. Got it. Keep going." He wrapped his lips over his teeth and pressed them together.

"My list is everything I want and everything I don't want in a man. When I was fifteen, I started a spreadsheet of all the attributes I loved in Robert Pattinson."

Without opening his mouth, he shrugged and shook his head.

"He's the actor who played Edward in the *Twilight* movies," I said in a dull sort of shock. How could anyone get through this much of their life not knowing who Robert Pattinson was? Why would anyone *want* to?

"When I got a little older and started dating," I continued, "I went through a string of not-nearly-Robert-Pattinsons. At the beginning of each relationship, I added all the things I liked about my not-nearly-Robert-Pattinson onto the list. Later, after realizing each one was a complete disaster, I went through that list and moved the applicable attributes over to the 'Everything I Don't Want' column."

"Makes sense . . . in a way." The words obviously caused him pain to say.

"No commentary!"

He zipped his lips back up and motioned for me to continue.

"Doctors were off the table after two weeks. Psychologists after about three days." Without meaning to, I'd turned to the tab in my planner and played with it as I spoke, as if I could see the list through the divider. "Men who go to the gym more than five times per week disappeared about a year later. Binge drinkers—even once—went over my limit last October. Any man prettier than I am went about three months ago." That one had been tough to knock off because I needed more than one sample, and overly pretty, straight men were hard to come by in this part of California. "A great sense of humor is still on there, but not if he makes any bodily function jokes in the first five dates or so. Then he's—"

"Off the list."

He wasn't actively laughing at me, so I let the comment go. Plus, I needed to reassure myself of something more important. Knowing for sure—no matter how awful—was always preferable to not knowing.

"You think I'm nuts."

"Absolutely," he said with an exaggerated nod.

I looked down at my hands, unsure if it would be wise to continue. Why did I care what he thought about me? I had two friends who knew who I was and who put up with me anyway. Maybe that was enough.

"I was kidding," he said. "I don't think you're nuts. You're . . . highly discerning."

I glanced up at him quickly to see if he was laughing. He wasn't. In fact, he looked more sincere than I would've ever expected. Uncomfortable with that, I focused on a small chip in my nail polish. "I'm not sure highly discerning is any better. At least people *like* nuts."

"My guess is you're probably tired of being disappointed by men who don't value you for the right reasons. You've been hurt more times than you should've been, and that's made you wary and, yeah, highly discerning." He waited until I looked him in the eyes. "In a totally normal way."

I sighed. "I know I'm not the perfect girlfriend."

"Because . . . ?"

"Because nothing is perfect," I answered grudgingly. "But is it wrong to expect a man to be respectful, not addicted to anything legal or illegal, and be able to spend a reasonable amount of time with me? Is it wrong to ask that he not psychoanalyze me? Or ignore my phone calls. Or check the pH of my vagina."

"Wait, what?" He leaned forward onto his elbows. "A guy asked to check the pH of your—"

I held up two fingers. "Twice."

"Fucking hell." He grimaced. "He *asked* twice, or he *checked* twice?"

"He was a naturopathic gynecologist—yes, there is such a thing—and I said 'no' both times he asked. However, I like to keep things down there pristine and healthy, so a board-certified gynecologist checks me out once a year."

"Good to know."

I laughed. "You feel good knowing my lady parts are healthy and fully functioning?"

"Hey, I gotta know what I'll be working with." He let the innuendo sit for a moment. "Now, to help you find Mr. Everything from the good side of your list"—he readjusted himself in the chair—"I'm going to need to see it."

My eyes widened. "My . . . lady parts?"

I'd never seen him smile so big. "I meant your list," he said finally. "But after that, we can move on to whatever you'd like."

All my body heat flowed into my cheeks even as I tried to regroup. "You want to see my list? Like, physically?"

"Yep. I want you to put it into my hands and let me read it."

I'd never shown anyone the actual list, not even Aaron and Liz. They knew what was on it but had never seen everything together in print. But Cooper hadn't laughed when I'd expected him to, and I trusted his opinion. I turned to the first page, unclipped the closure of my planner, and took it out one page at a time. My hand shook when I set it on the table between us.

"That's long," he said, sliding it all the way to himself and turning it right-side up. "I didn't expect it to be typed."

"It's easier to update that way. Frequent updates are key to refining my search. With every relationship, I know more about people and about myself." I watched his eyes dart across each line, down each page, not saying a word until he'd scanned all three pages. At least he didn't laugh outright.

"Well?" I asked when I ran out of patience.

"No one can ever accuse you of not being thorough." He slid it back to me. "I'm going back to my 'this is weird' idea."

"Which part?" I clipped it back into my planner.

"Definitely the first page. The second was pretty terrifying." He looked up at the ceiling. "Oh, and the third. Yeah, can't leave out that third page. I think that's it."

Whether he was deliberately making fun of me or not, sharing something personal shouldn't make you feel worse than you started.

"My mistake." I pushed back from the table, stood, and went to the other end of the kitchen. "I shouldn't have shown it to you."

He followed. "I never said *you* were weird. Or nuts. Or

anything other than discerning, which isn't a bad thing. I just don't think a man exists who could check off all those boxes."

"They're circles, not boxes."

He looked at me in silence for an uncomfortably long time.

For a while now, I'd put my search aside, focusing more on my career and friends. But if being around Cooper and his damn testosterone had taught me nothing else, I needed a man in my life. The sooner, the better. Before I made a mistake and ended up with a man who was everything I didn't want.

"I think I can help," he said finally. "If you want me to."

"I don't—" I shook my head. What had I gotten myself into? Why was Cooper so invested in helping me? On one hand, a straight man would understand other straight men better than my friends and I ever could. That went double for a straight man who made his living understanding and fixing things. He was a magician, right?

Except the truth I only thought about late at night or after a particularly awful day was that I already knew why I hadn't found the right man yet. And contrary to what everyone seemed to believe, it wasn't because he didn't exist.

The real problem was me.

How could I expect a man to magically appear who was perfect for me if *I* wasn't perfect for him? Or anyone else for that matter. I still had a lot of work ahead of me to change into someone worthy of the man I wanted, and maybe Cooper was the man who could finally help me do it.

21

COOPER

I thought I'd be pissed off, angry she didn't think I met all her requirements. But it was impossible to feel anything but sorry for her. First, because she'd made spreadsheets when she was fifteen years old. And the list? I didn't know what I expected it to be, but that blew away anything I could've imagined. How much had she missed out on because of it?

I clapped my hands and rubbed them together. "The first thing we need to do is get you to take yourself less seriously."

"If my very expensive therapist hasn't managed to do that after five years, what makes you think you can?"

"Because I have strong doubts that your therapist has suggested you go out and have some really messy, hard, meaningless sex to take the edge off."

Her mouth dropped open. Then she said, "Obviously, my therapist didn't tell me to have meaningless sex. But it doesn't matter because it won't work. I've had sex. Plenty of sex." That last bit wasn't even slightly convincing.

"Missionary the whole time, right? In total darkness. On a soft mattress. And it never lasts more than ten minutes, from start to when he finishes and you don't."

"It's still sex."

"I'm not actually sure it is."

She sighed dramatically. "You said you would help, and that's not helpful." She walked around the kitchen island and leaned up against the opposite counter as if wood and granite would protect her from some hard truths. "Pretend I'm a car or something. What would you do?"

"If you want me to look under your hood, just say it, Sophie."

"Ugh. A fridge, then?"

I liked seeing her uncomfortable. I wasn't trying to be an asshole—I needed to get her to switch her thinking, to be able to laugh at herself, at me, at the rest of the world. To be herself without shame or wishing she were different.

I rested my elbows on the table. "When a fridge isn't working right, you have to find out if it's not cooling at all or if it's running too cold."

Her eyes thinned to slits. "I am *not* too cold."

"Doesn't matter." I tilted my head. "The solution is the same either way."

"Which is . . . ?"

"That edge needs to come off."

"I can't believe you're so bad at this," she said. "What if I were an oven?"

And there it was, the first twitch of a smile. Maybe even a real one instead of kind she always faked.

"First thing I'd do is turn you on. So, you want to try that right now or . . . ?"

"Oh my God, are there any household appliances that don't remind you of sex?"

I paused as if I actually had to think about it. "Nope."

"What about a plumbing problem?" She rolled her eyes. "Never mind. I can already tell you're going to say something crude."

"Something involving pipes?"

"Please forget I asked."

"No more puns." I scratched my chin as I contemplated my options. "Electrical issues don't tap that, aside from the possibility of sparks. And that I just used the expression 'tap that'."

She covered her face with both hands, her shoulders hitching. I'd either made her laugh or cry. I couldn't tell which. People cried when they were happy too, right?

"No more bad jokes," I said. "Promise." I cursed when she dropped her hands. "It was just a dumb joke. I didn't mean to upset—"

"I know. I'm being as dumb as your joke." A smile cracked through. "Almost as dumb. I've just never talked about this before."

"Appliances?" At least that one didn't make her cry again. But she still looked nervous, as if she were about to cop to a felony. "Spill it, Soph."

"You're supposed to be able to fix anything, right?"

Goddamn it. "You're not broken," I said. "You don't need to be fixed."

"I do though. Certain things about me need to be fixed if I'm ever going to be who I want to be."

All the time I'd spent wondering what was real, pushing her to react, and it had taken five minutes of actually caring about her to get through. It was just a crack, but it made me want to get deeper inside. Unfortunately, I couldn't help her the way she wanted me to.

"The world may have dented you up a little because that's what it does, but don't ever think you're broken."

"Then undent me." She rubbed her hands together and interlocked her fingers. "If I want someone great, I need to *be* someone great."

"You *are* someone great."

She was twenty-six years old and acting as if her life was over and she'd lost. There was a lot of shit I didn't understand, but I knew better than to waste time being anyone other than myself.

"Life is messy and absurd, and yeah, it's hard sometimes," I said. "The sooner you accept that, the longer you have to enjoy it."

I'd never seen anyone with more doubt in their eyes.

I sighed. "You have an electrical problem."

"Huh?"

"Electrical problems are usually caused by the person who installed the original wiring doing it wrong. So, although I've never attempted to do anything that involves real psychology before, tell me about who installed your bad wiring."

"You mean Robert Pattinson?"

I shook my head. "He installed your unrealistic expectations of men. Your parents installed your wiring."

"I don't want to discuss my parents." Any progress we'd made disappeared as she shoved away from the counter. "Can't we work on Robert Pattinson first?"

I couldn't fix people, but I could fix problems. Sophie had a problem—a bunch of problems—a few of which I could fix. Aaron told me not to give up on her. I wasn't sure if this was what he'd meant, but it was all I could do. I needed to get her to realize that her list was bullshit and her expectations were off by about a thousand miles. Once she understood her perfect man didn't exist, we could find a decent guy who'd make her happy. Then, at least, she wouldn't have to fake it all the time.

Time to switch tactics.

I glanced at my watch. "We're starting right now. Come on. Leave the purse. You won't need any of the shit you keep in there."

"Where are we going?"

"Somewhere you won't need to check your calendar."

"If it's for dinner, let me call Aaron and get a recommendation for a good place."

I shook my head. "There are multiple reasons why that's not going to happen."

She reached into the small outside pocket of her bag. "It won't take more than a—"

I snatched the whole thing and held it away from her.

"Hey!"

"No," I said, positioning myself in between her and the bag like I did with Sammy and my socks. Both arms outstretched, one hand blocking the creature who didn't understand simple commands and the other holding the object of their unhealthy obsession.

"You're being ridiculous. Why can't I ask him?"

"All due respect to Aaron, but he's not invited. Besides, he's watching Sammy today."

She lifted an eyebrow. "Where are we going?"

I sighed. "If I tell you, you'll spend the whole ride researching it online." I could already imagine how tonight was going to go. Over-examining every man, woman, and drink coaster in the place, and not letting anything go long enough to actually enjoy herself.

"I need you to trust me. I won't let anything bad happen to you . . . tonight." I added the last word quickly because if I hadn't, the comment would've been both sappy and unrealistic. I couldn't promise to never let anything bad happen. Life was hard enough without promising the impossible.

"Can I at least check my makeup before we go?" she asked, her voice coated with sweetness and innocence. I would not be fooled by a pretty face. Again.

"No. You look fucking beautiful. Like always. You'll have to trust me on that too."

I could tell by the tightness in her mouth that she was struggling. When those lips curved into a smile—fake or not—I knew she was ready to go. If it wasn't real now, hopefully it would be by the end of the night.

Tossing her purse all the way across the room onto the table, I grabbed my truck keys and dragged her out the door.

"What if—"

"Leave it."

"This is not good," she grumbled as soon as we pulled out of the driveway.

"Wrong. This is very good." I glanced into the back of the cab to make sure my garment bag was still there. Sophie already looked great and would fit in with tonight's crowd, but I needed to change into something nicer or risk the wrath of my little sister. I probably should've taken a shower, but until five minutes ago, I'd still been hoping to find a way out of going.

Once we were on the highway and it was too late to turn around, I figured it was the right time to tell her what she was in for tonight. "Jasmine has a thing at the university. Students from all over Northern California entered a contest to show off their artwork. It's important to her, so I need somebody to keep me from going insane while I'm there. That's where you come in."

"You think I can keep you from going insane? I thought I drove you closer to it."

She had a point, but I'd ignore that for now. "She said we're supposed to 'dress for cocktails.' I'm not sure if it's true or if she hoped the word *cocktail* would be enough incentive for me to go. It's not, by the way. But I love my little sister."

"When is it?"

"Now."

"Now?" She looked down at what she was wearing. "I can't go to a cocktail party like this!"

"I told you—you're gorgeous. Jasmine's great at throwing something at you last minute while letting you know how much it means to her and how disappointed she'll be if you aren't there."

"That must run in your family."

"If it's too last minute, and you can't handle it, I'm sure we can go man shopping another time."

She turned to me, her eyes wide and her cheeks flushed. "You're taking me man shopping?"

"Did you think this was a date?"

"Of course not. It's just . . . sudden."

I glanced at her. She looked as unhappy as I imagined she would, but that would change. "All varieties of men will be there. Professors, artists, students, bartenders, rich old men who pretend to be interested in student art when they're just interested in students. Maybe even a couple of felons if you're into that."

"I'm not dressed for a cocktail party."

"You're *always* dressed for a cocktail party." I motioned to her body, shoulders to toes. "Black and expensive all the way down. I assumed you deliberately prepare yourself for moments like this as soon as you get out of the bed every morning."

"It's not funny, Cooper. I don't do well with surprises."

"All we're doing is going shopping. You like shopping, right?"

"Yes," she mumbled.

"Then think of this like any other shopping trip. Except tonight is for window shopping. Go in there, look around, and see what's available. We're not taking anything home. Promise." That was a promise I would keep. There was no way in hell I'd let anyone go home with her tonight.

This would be good for her. More than anything, Sophie needed something to challenge her misguided beliefs about men. I wasn't sure how I'd make that happen but trusted I'd come up with something when we got there.

Ninety-nine percent of men could be counted on to make

asses of themselves around a beautiful woman. Tonight, I'd be there to point them out to her. I'd also be there to point out the positives. Hell, maybe we'd even find a guy who didn't turn into an idiot the first chance he got. She'd see how right I was, thank me profusely, and—ta-da—happy ending. Minus all the fun parts for me.

"On second thought—"

"Window shopping," she repeated. "Aside from the cruel and unusual part of not letting me change, this could be fun." She checked her hair and lips in the visor mirror. "Honestly, I thought you were taking me to a strip club."

"You don't like strippers?" I asked, feigning shock. "Or is it the buffets you have a problem with?"

She stared at me without any expression. Then she said, "I'm all for women using whatever they have however they want to use it. I have issues with the men who like strippers. Why do they enjoy being teased by women they don't stand a chance with but then use the word *tease* as a slur for the women? They're paying for the privilege in one instance and irrationally angered by the other. Same situation. The only differences are the amount of clothing the woman wears and how outright the teasing is, and both are opposite from what you'd think."

"Good point," I said. "That alone proves men don't make sense and will never fit in the right boxes."

"Nice try, but not all men like strippers."

I squinted but kept my eyes on the road. "Not all men go to strip clubs. I am not a big fan, and not all men who go to strip clubs have healthy views about women or sex. But all moderately healthy, straight men appreciate what strippers represent."

"Explain."

"If your close-to-perfect guy doesn't think the female body —*your* body—is beautiful, is he really close to perfect?"

She frowned. "He'll love me for more than my body."

"I should hope so, but that's not what I asked. I asked if you want this perfect guy to think you're beautiful, desirable, sexy. If he wants to bring you pleasure just so he can see the exhausted satisfaction on your face and know he had something to do with putting it there."

She swallowed. "Of course, but—"

"You can't have it both ways," I said. "Either he thinks a woman's body is beautiful or he doesn't."

Her frown deepened, incorporating her brow and the rest of her body as well. "Well, of course he does, but that's not all he values."

I pulled into the university parking lot and found a spot near the entrance.

"Trust me, Soph, a guy's gotta be a fucking moron to only value you for your body."

"Thank you," she said. It didn't take a rocket scientist to sense her nervousness. Her shoulders were up around her ears, and she didn't move to get out or look anywhere but straight ahead. "What I want is . . . I want someone who thinks I'm beautiful, but also smart, capable, and kind."

What the fuck was wrong with all the men she'd dated? How could anyone think she wasn't all those things?

"I thought your standards were higher than that. If all you want is a man who thinks you're beautiful and values who you are, I'm surprised you haven't found a hundred 'perfect' guys." Myself included, unfortunately.

"Why are you being so nice to me, Cooper?" She turned to me, and there was something different in her eyes this time, as if she knew what I was thinking.

"Total accident, I swear," I said, smiling. The last thing I needed was for her to think I had any interest in proving I was the right man for her. I wasn't. We were polar opposites. Like a cruise to a glacial iceberg and a walk across the Sahara. Or a kale salad and a Hot Pocket. If I couldn't have her, I'd make sure the guy who could had more going for him than I did. So, I needed clarity.

"Anyway, let's get back to the job at hand. The man you want will think you're pretty, nice, and intelligent." I reached down until my hand was about a foot off the floorboard. "This is the bar you just set. Not impressive, Dillon. What else?"

"He'll believe in me," she added.

"Too easy. Keep going." I raised my hand by an inch.

"He'll have goals that align with mine."

"What does that mean?"

She sighed. "He won't feel threatened if I make more money than he does, or if I'm doing better professionally."

I lifted my hand another couple of inches. "His head can't be up his ass and he can't be totally insecure. Still not even to the bottom of the seat."

She rubbed her lips together in thought. "He'll never force me to go out without my bag."

I laughed. "I want to get back to this later." I waved my hand a little. "So, don't forget where I was."

"At ass level," she said, the sweetness of her smile making the sarcasm more obvious. "I think I'll be able to remember that."

22
____

SOPHIE

Before we got out of the car, I resigned myself to spending the evening in a constant state of discomfort. Cooper didn't want me to overthink things like I usually did, and part of me appreciated it. I'd never been good at living in the moment, at least not without countless hours of preparation and two contingency plans. But had he never heard of baby steps? Surprising me with something so public was more like entering a toddler into a triathlon. People judged first impressions—all people. It was how we'd survived this long as a species.

This was the longest I'd ever been without my bag. It was like a security blanket, something to keep my hands busy when I got nervous, to hold items I might not ever need, as well as vital ones, like money. I never felt safe without a little cash. It was something my mom drilled into me while trying to fit a lifetime of lessons into her last few months.

"Never put yourself in a position of helplessness," she'd said. "Always be prepared to take care of yourself, and never count on anyone else to do it, especially a man."

I never forgot that lesson, at least not until tonight. I didn't have my car or any money to get a cab. Yet, I felt completely safe with a man I'd only known for a short time. There was something about him—his ever-calm attitude, confidence, competence.

"I need a minute." He reached across the truck, unzipped a garment bag that was hanging behind my seat, and pulled back a crisp button-up shirt.

"You brought other clothes?" I scoffed. "That's not fair!"

"Would you rather I embarrass my family—and you—by showing up in a T-shirt and jeans?"

"Of course not, but if you get to change, why couldn't—"

Oh. He wasn't just going to change. He was going to change *here*. In the truck. Two feet away from me. My throat dried up completely when he yanked his T-shirt over his head and tossed it behind the seat. I'd been so right about his body—chest, shoulders, abs, biceps. Yep, he had all of them. All in exactly the right places and all perfectly formed. Flawless even. I think I whimpered when he slipped the shirt on and started buttoning it up.

"Just putting it out there," he said without lifting his head, "but if you're going to stare at me like that when I take off my pants, we may never make it out of this truck."

"Oh!" I spun in my seat and looked out the window. Unfortunately, nothing outside was distracting enough to help me forget what was happening right beside me. Every creak of his seat, thud of a boot landing behind me, his quiet laughter, it all built up images of how he looked without pants. I'd bet his thighs, ass, and cock were all perfectly formed too.

"Are you dressed?" I asked when I heard his door open and then shut. "Cooper, are you dressed or not?" A second later, he opened the door on my side.

After he helped me out, I noticed his shirt was buttoned wrong.

"Your..." I pointed at his chest.

"What?" He looked down at himself but apparently couldn't see what I was seeing.

"Your buttons. They're off." I rolled my eyes and pushed his useless hands out of the way. "I'll do it."

I couldn't start from scratch, as that would involve completely unbuttoning the whole line and risk the possibility that his shirt would come open while my hands were on his chest. I worked slowly, unbuttoning and rebuttoning them one by one without letting my gaze wander away from what I was doing.

When I finished, I patted him on the chest and stood back. "There. Now you're decent."

"I don't think fixing some buttons will make me decent." His smile was sexy as hell. I could stare at him for hours. Days even.

Shit! Get it together, Sophie! I clapped my hands together to stop them from touching him again. "Let's go shopping!"

He squinted. "Don't forget who's keeping whom sane tonight."

I let out a deep sigh as if he was worried for nothing. "It'll be fine."

It wasn't. It was a lot better than fine.

The exhibit hall was bustling with people of all types and ages. Artwork of all types and quality leaned up against wooden easels set-up around the perimeter of the room. Off to one side was a bar area with a bunch of small metal tables and chairs farther on.

Beckett was standing next to a large oil painting with a pretty brunette who apparently was an old family friend. When Jasmine came rushing over, we all said hello and admired the painting she entered in the contest, which was the best in the entire hall. She'd managed to convey so much raw emotion with the man's body position and how she'd used shadow.

"You have real talent, Jasmine," I said, equally amazed by

how good it felt to be surrounded by family even though they weren't mine. There was an instant level of comfort I hadn't expected, like a permanent safety net, ever ready in case one of them fell.

"Did he have to be naked?" Cooper scowled at the painting. "You didn't use a live model for this, did you?"

"We're going to mingle." I dragged him away, deciding we could both use fewer naked men on our minds tonight.

"I don't mingle," he grumbled. "You don't think she used an actual guy for that, right?"

"I didn't want to be the one to tell you this," I said, grabbing him by the shoulders, "but your twenty-two-year-old sister has seen a penis before."

He pretended to gag and led me to the bar. "That was cruel."

After we got a drink and did some people watching, he excused himself to go to the restroom. I stood near the corner, admiring a painting that was just shapes and colors, nothing I understood to be art. I felt uncharacteristically alone in the sea of strangers. Ten minutes later, Cooper still hadn't returned. I didn't know what had distracted him, but it wasn't as if we were promised to each other. Plus, like he said, there were a lot of varieties of men here. So I took the napkin and my plastic cup of white wine and went shopping.

"What do you think?" a man in his forties asked as we stood next to each other and stared at the same painting. I had nothing against older men, and this one had a hot dirty-professor vibe.

I turned back to the painting. "I like—"

"The light carried through the whole piece is lovely, if a bit too on the nose." He seemed to know what he was talking about, and maybe he hadn't heard me. "I wonder if the artist did that accidentally or on purpose."

"Well," I said, "I—"

"Regardless, it shows real talent. I'd love to see an entire collection with that theme."

"What did you say—"

"I'm Roger Lamb," he said, putting out his hand.

I put my drink into my other hand and shook his, more because I didn't know how to avoid it than wanting him to know my name. "What—"

"I work in the History Department."

"It's nice—"

"Who are you?"

He had to be doing this on purpose, right?

I looked around, expecting to see Cooper laughing his ass off and holding a pile of bills he'd promise to give Roger Lamb for messing with me.

"I'm Sophie Dillon. It's—"

"Music Department, right?"

"No, I don't work at the—"

"Thea—" As soon as he opened his mouth, I shoved my drink napkin into it. Both of us froze in shock.

I took a deep breath and said, "I'm-Sophie-Dillon-and-I-don't-work-at-the-university. I'm-here-supporting-a-friend. I-like-this-painting-but-feel-it's-a-bit-derivative-of-Yayoi-Kusama's-work-who-as-I'm-sure-you-know-is-still-very-much-alive. I-always-find-that-a-bit-cheeky." I finally sucked in another breath. "Don't you?"

He pulled the napkin from his mouth and shoved it into my hand. Then he stormed off. Touching as little of it as possible, I dropped it into my wine with a shaky hand. *Why did I do that?* The only reason I could think of was that Cooper had forced me to be spontaneous and put me into a situation I'd been unprepared for. It felt good to blame him for something.

"I heard there was a man here tonight who always knows just what to say," a low voice said behind me. "That must have been him." The body that belonged to the voice was tall, expensively dressed, and holding out another cup of wine. "I tried to get here earlier, but I stopped to get you this."

Not bad. "I appreciate the thought, but I don't take drinks from men I don't know."

"Then let's get to know each other." He took my cup and tossed both into a garbage can. "Let's get another drink too."

As he led me to the bar, his hand on my lower back, I wondered what Cooper would say if his shopping trip had exactly the opposite effect from what he'd wanted it to.

"I'm Paul Sheffield, and you are?"

"Afraid you won't give me a chance to answer."

His laugh was boisterous as he grabbed a napkin off the bar and stuffed it into his mouth, nodding that he was ready.

"I'm Sophie."

He grimaced as he took the napkin from his mouth and threw it away. "It's nice to meet you, Sophie."

We talked about art, his job as a financial analyst, my job, which he actually seemed interested in. He was here for his nephew who apparently didn't stand a chance of winning the contest but was a great kid.

By the time I started getting the big-fat-spooky-liar vibe from him, we'd already found a quiet table away from the crowd. He was about five obvious lies in and who knew how many less noticeable ones. Typical. This was why I hadn't had much sex. Unfortunately, I'd let it go far past the point I could pretend I hadn't planned on talking to anyone and depart without any awkwardness or complicated excuses.

"Your brother?" I shifted in the plastic chair. "I thought you said you were here for your nephew."

His eyes widened momentarily. "I did. My nephew is the artist—the son of my brother, who's also an artist."

"Artistic family." *Right.* He probably lived out front and only left his windowless van to crash parties. A few minutes ago, I'd felt lucky Cooper had his family here to keep him occupied. Now not so much. I looked around the room for him.

"Where's your nephew's piece?" I asked, standing up. "I'd love to go see it."

"He took it down once he saw the other paintings and knew he couldn't compete."

"That's too bad. Well, it was nice talking to you, Paul, but I should go catch up with my friends."

"Wait!" He grabbed my wrist. "Let's get outta here and go have some fun."

"Not going to happen." I yanked my arm away.

"Has she gotten to the part about reassuring you that you're interesting yet?" Cooper said from behind me.

When I turned, he was looking far too handsome and pleased with himself.

"Because I can come back later," he said.

"No!" I blurted. "Actually, we should go . . . back to my place." I looked at Paul. "Cooper is my date."

"I don't mind sharing though." Cooper grunted when I elbowed him in the stomach.

Without another word to Paul, I grabbed Cooper's arm and left. "Where have you been?"

"I didn't want to cramp your style. Loved the napkin trick, by the way. It took you a long time to figure out how creepy that second guy was though. Is that normal for you?"

"You were watching me," I said slowly.

"I got one word for you . . ." He slipped his arm around my waist as if that were something we did. "Subterfuge."

"You misunderstand." I turned toward him. "You've been watching me all night, and you don't find that creepy too?"

"At least I'm not uninteresting." Had to give him that. "I was just making sure you were alright."

He'd been there, not because he didn't think I could handle it, but because he didn't want me to be hurt. Possessiveness versus protectiveness.

Apart from my two best friends, no one had ever protected me, not my boyfriends, not my father. I was something to be controlled, their care based on jealousy rather than trust, even when it turned out they didn't really want me at all. They just didn't want anyone *else* to have me.

Even though it had hurt like hell the first dozen or so times, their proprietorial behavior inadvertently taught me I needed to take care of myself and deal with my own problems.

"I didn't need your help," I said as we walked toward his family.

"I know."

"I appreciate you having my back though."

"Yeah, well, if you let me," he said, his eyes still straight ahead, "I'd have your front too."

Maybe I would.

23

COOPER

My stomach was actively growling, but Sophie said she'd be fast. She felt bad for not feeding Orion before I dragged her from the house earlier, and guilt rarely got better if you ignored it. The one time I'd forgotten to feed Sammy, he'd been pissed at me for two days. I think. It was hard to tell because his face wasn't that expressive.

"Feed the hunter," I said, "and let's go get some human food."

"Your treat?"

"Don't push your luck." Of course, it would be my treat.

"Fine. Since you picked up the lunch tab a few times."

"I used the company credit card, so, really, my father paid."

I grimaced as I pulled into the driveway. "Your dad bought me lunch? Good thing it wasn't dinner, or he might think I'll put out."

"I don't think that's something you need to worry about."

I wiped nonexistent sweat off my brow.

"I need to change into something more comfortable too."

"A restaurant-appropriate negligee?" I asked hopefully.

"Those two things are mutually exclusive."

"Not if you wear a trench coat over the negligee and let me be the only one who gets to peek."

"Two *more* things that are mutually exclusive."

I could've waited in my truck while she fed Orion, but that would've stopped the conversation. She seemed to be under the impression it was her fault she attracted the wrong kind of men instead of just accepting there were a lot of assholes in the world, so statistically, she was going to meet a bunch of them.

"I don't know what it is," she said as she unlocked the door. "Men either treat me like my sole purpose is their sexual satisfaction or like I'm not a woman at all."

As soon we walked in, Orion lunged at us, meowing as if he were starving to death. She picked him up, handed him to me, and went to the fridge for his food.

"Come on. You seriously think men don't notice you're a woman?" I asked, my eyes never leaving Orion's. I sat on a stool to keep him on my lap, knowing if I let my guard down for even a second, I'd have Wolverine-style gashes down the side of my face.

"They *act* like it. You saw those two men at the party. It's one way or the other."

Orion wiggled out of my arms as soon as he saw the open can, beelining it to his bowl.

I followed Sophie down the hall toward the bedroom.

"I need to figure out what kind of vibe I'm putting out and change it." She stopped in the doorway, turned around, and shoved me in the chest. "But first I need to change."

I stepped back just in time to avoid getting smacked in the face by the door.

"There's a lot to unpack here," I said loudly, leaning against the wall. "So, let's start with: Why do you always think it's *you* who needs to change?"

"Because I'm human!" Her voice was muffled. "All human beings—other than you—have hopes, dreams, ambitions."

"None of those things have anything to do with changing who you are," I said, ignoring her dig at me.

"If I stay the person I was yesterday, how can I get to where I want to be with the person I want to be with?"

How could I convince her that mindset wasn't the same as identity? One she could change if she wanted to. The other she shouldn't want to. I couldn't give up, not yet. Because that was the person *I* was.

"You want to change? Then cha—"

When she opened the door, she was wearing something completely different in everything but color. This outfit looked more uncomfortable than the last one—black slacks, a matching black blazer, and a black turtleneck with a thin strip of white trim across the edge. Did she think I was taking her out for dinner and a funeral?

"Trust me"—I pushed off the wall and followed her back into the kitchen—"what you wear or how well you flirt isn't going to do shit."

She turned around with her brow furrowed. "What's wrong with what I wear?"

"Fuck. Of course, that's all you heard." I should've known she'd focus on the absolute least important thing. I ran my hand through my hair. "Fine, you want to do this? Let's do it."

Most of the clothing she wore showed off her curves, catching the side of a breast, gently tugging across her ass. But her "something more comfortable" outfit was fucking depressing. Stylishly depressing. If it wasn't already a thing, it should be, and she'd nailed it.

I took her by the hands and lifted her arms up, giving myself total permission to study her body while she looked on nervously. That she could wear expensive looking yet shapeless clothes and still make my cock hard was a tribute to how great her body was.

"Hmm . . ." I circled around her so I could get a good look at her ass.

"Hmm, what?"

"You want to know what's wrong with what you wear? Why the right man—whoever he may be—isn't falling all over himself to get to know you? Could it be because you look so bottled up a light breeze could set you off, and he might not survive the ensuing nuclear winter?" A bit of an exaggeration, but if I went far enough into the absurd, she might get my point. Nothing rational had gotten through, so why not?

"Armageddon all because I don't wear plunging necklines and short skirts. Got it."

"It's not about how much skin you show. It's about letting go and seeing what happens. Taking a risk now and then. Being approachable." I came back around to her front. "Seriously, do you even own anything that's not black and looks like something a nun might wear on her day off?"

"Black gets along with everyone. It's flattering and can be edgy or professional."

I nodded. "And wearing it head-to-toe every single day is totally appropriate if you're an angsty teenager. Except you want a man, right? Men don't want to date a woman who thinks flashing a little ankle will bring shame to her entire family. I'm not telling you to walk around naked"—although I wouldn't tell her *not* to either—"but what about trying another color and something that doesn't cover every square inch of skin?"

She looked down at what she was wearing, as if she didn't already know what she'd see. "I want to be taken seriously, be judged for more than my breasts."

"If that's the goal, you're doing a hell of a job. Because that jacket is making me wonder if you even *have* breasts."

"I don't see how taking off a jacket will change anything."

"Me neither. I'm also confused why you think men don't see you as a woman. So, maybe you start by showing them you are one."

"Not men in general, just the *right* man." She grumbled for a minute but then shook the jacket off her shoulders and laid it neatly across the back of the couch. "Better?"

"No," I said, motioning to the shapeless, long-sleeve turtleneck that had been under the jacket. "Lose the shirt too."

Her eyebrow popped up. "You want me to take off my shirt? Right now? In front of you."

That wasn't what I'd meant, but . . .

I almost said no. I should've said no.

"Yep." Yeah, that's right. I said yes, and I'd call bullshit on anyone who claimed they wouldn't have done the same.

What was the harm of pushing her when I knew she'd back down and call me a pervert? Then, when I stopped laughing, hopefully she'd see how dumb this was and be ready to really talk shit out. Even if it was uncomfortable.

"Doing something spontaneous and outside your comfort zone would be good for you."

With her hands on the bottom of her shirt, she hesitated, waiting for me to stop her. She should know by now I wasn't the backing down type.

"What's the hold up, Soph? Just do it."

"I will." But she didn't move. "I'm not a prude."

"I never said you were." The corners of my mouth were getting twitchy, and I wasn't sure how much longer I could hold back my smile.

"I've gone skinny-dipping before."

I gave her a thumbs-up. "I hope you had fun."

Her eyes narrowed. "You don't believe someone like me is capable of doing something fun or crazy."

"You mean like taking off your shirt?" I almost laughed at how serious she was taking this, how badly she wanted to prove I was wrong about her. Except I wasn't wrong. Sophie was always in control, of herself, her environment, her emotions. What she needed was for someone to shove her out of that control long enough for her to realize she wouldn't die without it.

"I'm going to do it," she said, her breath speeding up.

"Then you should do it."

Holy fuck! She was doing it. She tugged her shirt out of her pants and kept lifting. All the immature amusement and teasing drained out of me. My eyes got stuck on the smooth skin of her belly until the shirt moved higher and exposed more skin. Then a little bit of bra—black, obviously. Then two full cups of pure gorgeousness.

Blind me now because nothing I'd ever see in the future would be this good. Actually, hold that thought, at least until she took off the shirt completely.

She whipped her shirt over her head, tugging it off when it got caught. The force knocked her bun loose, letting her dark hair tumble down over her shoulders as she freed herself from the fabric.

I didn't deliberately step closer, but it happened anyway.

"Now what?" She tossed the shirt on top of her jacket and put her hands on her hips, as if I didn't know they'd be shaking without anything to hold on to. Pride radiated off her, and rightfully so. She'd not only called my bluff—she'd shocked me stupid.

"What now, Cooper?" She looked up at me with terrified determination.

"Now . . . " I was a man. She was a half-naked woman. She *had* to know what was coming next. "The pants."

Without a word, she unbuttoned her pants, then slid the

zipper down. Slowly. Painfully so. Her panties were black, simple but still highly damaging to my self-control. I ached to help push her pants over the curves of her hips, for my thumbs to graze her skin.

"Do you still think I look like a man?" she asked.

I almost missed her question—too focused on the image two feet away and all the things I wanted to do to it.

"I never once thought you looked like a man." I swallowed. "But you've provided excellent proof I was right." Yet, I couldn't have been more wrong about the direction the night would take.

She stared at me for a minute, blinking rapidly. "Do you want to have sex with—?"

"Fuck yeah," I said, before she'd finished speaking.

"That's nice."

I shook my head. "That's . . . beautiful." My eyes followed the rise and fall of her breasts as she took a deep breath and let it out, the tremble as a shiver going through her whole body.

Shit. What now? My brain had stopped working with that first flash of skin.

"I value our friendship," she said. "A lot. When I'm friends with someone, I tend to be very direct. With only good intentions though. I think you're great, so you shouldn't take this the wrong way—"

Goddammit. I knew what was coming.

"But you're not someone I would carry on a long-term romantic relationship with. You have none of the key qualities I'm looking for in a man."

"I think you've been very clear about that." It might have hurt more if I hadn't been so distracted by the rest of her. The sentiment was nothing new though. According to her list I didn't cut it. Fine by me. I was pretty damn happy with the spot I was currently in.

"Hang on." She put her hand over my eyes, blocking my view.

"Aww, come on," I said with a smirk. I put my hand on top of hers but didn't pull it away. "That's not nice. You're making me miss the one part of this conversation I'm enjoying."

"I need you to hear me."

I didn't fight her. It was probably safer for both of us anyway. You had to cover a horse's eyes to leave a burning barn otherwise they'd be too freaked out or distracted to move. Same basic idea.

"Can I finish what I was saying?" she asked.

"By all means, please finish telling me what a horrible excuse for a man I am and how much you dislike me."

"I don't dislike you, and you're a perfectly fine excuse for a man."

For whatever reason, her laugh did a beeline to my cock and made my pants even tighter than they'd gotten at the start of this.

"I just don't see us in that way," she continued. "However, standing here in my underwear, seeing that look you had on your face—"

"*Have*," I corrected. "You can't see it, but trust me, my expression hasn't changed at all."

"With the look you *have* on your face has made me realize we might be able to add something to our platonic relationship that we both might benefit from. Getting the milk for free, sort of thing."

"Meaning?" I prayed we were thinking the same thing.

"Meaning that because I don't see you as romantic relationship material, I've never felt the need to change you. Your obvious faults don't matter because they can't affect my long-term plan or happiness."

"My obvious faults," I repeated. Damn. I accepted she didn't see me as "romantic relationship material," but she could've left me a little of my pride.

"You said you wouldn't take it personally," she huffed.

"Actually, you *told* me not to take it personally. Since I didn't agree to it this time either, I can take it as personally as I want to." Which was pretty damn personally. Until the rest of what she said started sinking in.

Getting the milk for free.

I took her hand away from my face. "You want to fuck me." Not in the abstract—she actually meant it.

Her eyes widened, but she didn't disagree. So it was probably my choice of words rather than their meaning that had surprised her.

"You, Sophie Dillon, want to fuck me." I took a step closer until there was no more space between us. "I'm not good enough to date, but I'm good enough to fuck. That's what you meant, right?"

In one moment, my ego bounced right back to its original level, maybe even higher. She didn't think I was relationship material. I didn't think so either. That hadn't changed. But now we were on equal ground.

"You said I have *obvious* faults."

"I didn't mean it that way," she said guiltily. "I have obvious faults too. Lots of them."

"None that I can see."

She tried to hide her smile. "I was trying to say it's nice to be with someone who doesn't expect things I can't give them and whom I won't want to change. You are who you are—"

A man a foot away from an incredibly attractive woman in her underwear who's struggling to apologize for offending me.

"—and you're content with that," she said. "It's not something I'm used to."

Was that a good thing or a bad thing?

"I really like it." She picked at the edge of her nail. "It makes you easy to be with."

"Good." I wondered how long it would take her to get around to apologizing, so we could move on to other—better—things.

"I'm sorry for what I said before. I didn't mean to insult you."

There it was.

"You done?" I asked to make sure.

"If you accept my apology."

"Accepted. For future reference, if you ever really *do* want to insult me, it would probably work a lot better if you weren't almost naked and offering me sex while you do it."

"Understood." she said quietly. "So . . . ?"

"So, you want to skip buying the cow and have free milk." I'd never been called a cow before. Surprisingly, I didn't mind it at all.

"If you're understanding the metaphor right, then yes. I'd like the milk for free."

"I understand the metaphor," I said. "And you can have all the milk you want."

I knew all about her ridiculous expectations of the right guy. Why the fuck would I want to be held up to those? Be a contender for a long-term romantic relationship with her? Be the fucking boyfriend who had to put up with her all the time? Not likely.

Then why did I have a sneaking suspicion that was exactly what I wanted to be?

Even as I wrapped my arm around her and pulled her in, I knew, deep down, this was a bad idea.

I leaned down until our lips brushed, feeling a shiver go through her.

"Great." She already sounded out of breath.

"It's going to be."

She let out a long sigh as I slid my hands down her back, past the silkiness of her panties, until I could cup her ass and bring her closer, tighter, to me.

Goddammit. With my cock pressing into her belly, I knew this would only confuse and complicate things.

Then again, maybe, just maybe, it wouldn't. Maybe it would be free milk and cookies for both of us and never turn into anything more than that. I preferred *that* theory. Yeah, I'd go with that one. Besides, I couldn't have stopped myself if I'd tried.

I'd never wanted someone's body as much as I wanted their mind. The beautiful mind that would always be thinking about a three-page typed list I'd never be on.

24

———

SOPHIE

Now that Cooper's hands were on my ass, his lips an inch from mine, and his erection stabbing me in the belly, it probably wasn't the best time to start wondering if this had been a good decision. True, I wanted him, and he obviously wanted me, but it was no longer a hypothetical or another stupid idea Liz had put into my head. This was real. And happening.

What if I didn't live up to his expectations? What if my practically untested skills in bed were a disappointment? Or just . . . bad? I hadn't thought this through nearly enough. I pushed him away—or *tried* to anyway. With his body fully engaged, he didn't budge. He was big. Like, *everywhere*.

"I thought you wanted to eat something," I said, turning my head to the side.

"I plan on it." His lips danced across my cheek to the corner of my mouth, forcing me to turn back to him, to reach his teasing lips. "But let's not get ahead of ourselves."

Shit. It was as if the words came out of his mouth and went straight into my panties. Unfortunately, I was even less confident in my oral skills—giving or taking.

"I meant food," I said quickly. "Going to get food."

"That was before you got naked and told me you wanted to fuck. Shockingly, going out doesn't seem as important anymore."

"You're not even going to buy me a drink first?" I faked a laugh.

"We're not dating. Remember? I'm only good enough to fuck."

At any other moment, I would've corrected him. Made it clear that he *wasn't* only good enough to fuck. But the idea of using him solely for sex, of him *wanting* to be used that way, turned me on even more, and I didn't think he minded.

I could feel his body vibrating, but beyond that, he didn't move, didn't kiss me, or press his hips harder into mine. He didn't let go either, frozen in the same position, waiting for my permission to do what he wanted. Somehow sensing my uncertainty.

I was almost ready. Just needed to gear up a little more.

"Hold up." As if waking from a trance, he let go and pulled back, looking at me with a furrowed brow. "You didn't plan this all out like you usually do, did you? You're going in blind. That's why you're trembling."

Trembling? I'd thought that was him.

As soon as I looked away, he cupped my jaw in both hands and gently guided me back.

"You can tell me to stop, Soph, but you don't get to shut down and just go along with it as if it's something you *have* to do. As if you're not allowed to change your mind or admit you made a mistake. If you don't want this, tell me."

"I *do* want it. I want you. I just feel . . . unprepared," I said, hoping he'd understand something I wasn't sure I did.

He rubbed his lips together, his eyes breaking from mine as he considered what to do. "What if I lead, and all you have to do is follow? Until you decide to take over for a little while. At which point, we can fight about what happens next." The corner of his mouth lifted. "I'm kidding."

I nodded. "I like that idea."

His grin widened. "You'll tell me if I do anything you don't like though, right?"

"Right." Although I didn't foresee that happening.

"I'm going to kiss you now." Holding my face gently, he leaned down just until our lips met and no farther. Letting them rest together for a minute, barely touching. He caressed my cheek with his thumbs, just above where his palms stayed my jaw.

Why wasn't he kissing me? I let out a grunt of frustration because I couldn't close the distance, couldn't press my lips against his like I wanted to. I was finally geared up and ready to go, and he was holding me back.

He must have felt me push against his hands because he laughed lightly, his lips moving even farther away. "You couldn't last thirty seconds before trying to take over, could you?"

"You're a horrible man."

He ran his finger across my lower lip. "Possibly, but remember the plan." His hand kept moving to that sensitive spot just behind my ear and then through my hair to the nape of my neck. "I lead."

"I follow."

"That's my girl." He yanked me in.

Like a wave of warmth and everything good in the world, our lips finally met. No more waiting, no more asking for permission, no more patience as the kiss deepened. He tasted like heat and need with a dash of the coffee he drank earlier. His flavor was almost as delicious as the spark I felt as our bodies grinded together.

I whimpered as his mouth left mine, then let out a long sigh as he gently held my jaw, tilting my head back to get to my neck. He kept his other hand on my ass, pulling me in tighter.

I should be doing something too, not just letting him have his way with me, as lovely as that sounded. Now, I could finally do all the things I'd been too afraid to do before.

Never, ever wanting him to stop kissing my neck, I reached out blindly for the top button of his shirt. Without being able to look at what I was doing, my fingers fumbled in my haste to see his chest, feel the muscles under my palms, against my lips. I yanked the shirt from his pants and spread it open, groaning in frustration because I couldn't see him without losing the warmth of his mouth on my skin.

It wasn't cold, but as soon as I put my hands on his chest, he shivered. Maybe we both did.

He groaned as I slowly traced his abs. Maybe we both did that too.

Knowing he had a body any woman in her right mind would want to touch was entirely different from *being* the woman touching it. Cooper wasn't just fit. He was strong, powerful, built by the real world instead of dumbbells and bars.

I'd seen him in tight T-shirts and even shirtless, but this was better. Only relying on touch forced me to focus on each swipe of his tongue and each muscle as it clenched under my fingertips.

"How are we doing so far, Soph?" he asked, his lips never leaving my skin as they moved up my neck and back onto my mouth.

I hoped the question was rhetorical. The last thing I wanted to do was take my mouth off his long enough to speak. Unfortunately, it hadn't been. He pulled back and waited for my answer.

"Good." It sounded grumpy, irritated, not at all how I felt. I tried again. "I don't know how you're doing, but I'm great. Greater than great. So, can we get back to it now?"

"I'm not sure," he said, smirking. "You don't seem to remember who's in charge around here."

"For now." I yanked him closer by his belt.

"You know, your impatience and bossiness only increase the length of time you won't be in charge.

I slammed my mouth shut and pressed my lips together tightly.

He laughed. "Now excuse me while I get back to my turn."

I nodded, not unclenching my lips until his tongue coaxed them open. With my arms around his shoulders, I moaned as he picked me up and wrapped my legs around his hips, his cock pressed to my core. After another deep, breath-stopping kiss, he looked around the room, his eyes stopping on the kitchen island behind me.

"How horrified do you think Liz would be if she knew I set you on her kitchen counter and had my way with you?"

"Pretty horrified."

"Thought so," he grumbled. "Unfortunately for her, that's not enough to stop me from doing it."

"It's not?" I asked, trying to catch my breath before I lost it again.

"Fuck no." Without letting me go, he walked to the island and plopped me onto the edge of the counter. I squeaked as my nearly naked ass touched the cold granite.

"We should both promise to feel a little guilty later though," he said.

"Feel guilty. But later, right? Not now."

"Oh no, sweetheart. I promise you, for the next few hours, the only thing you're going to feel is good." He slipped his hands between my knees and spread my legs apart. I'd never scooted faster than when he motioned for me to come closer until our bodies were flush again.

Except in the brief moment it took to get his shirt off, our lips didn't part as I ran my hands over his shoulders, down his chest and abs, every inch of him contracted and hard under my fingers.

When I felt the leather of his belt, I followed it to the buckle.

"Slow down a little, woman." He put his hand on top of mine, stopping me from unbuttoning his pants. "I'm still leading, remember?"

"For how much longer?" I pouted.

"Long enough for me to enjoy your body a little." As he spoke, he pulled down my bra, cupping my fullness in his hands. "Remember how I said nothing was perfect? Your breasts are the exception."

Not knowing how to respond, I hoped my body could express my gratitude.

He alternated between dragging his lips and his teeth down my neck, hovering over my clavicle just long enough for his gentle nibbles to get strong enough to hurt.

"Ouch."

He mumbled a quick, probably insincere apology and moved to my breast, taking my nipple between his teeth and flicking his tongue across it lightly until I couldn't handle any more.

"This is the last time I let you lead," I mumbled as I unhooked my bra and ripped it off. With my arms around his neck, my hands in his hair, it was a simple act to yank him closer, forcing more of my breast into his mouth.

His chuckle reverberated against my skin. He pulled away just long enough to grab a stool and drag it behind him. When he sat and ran a hand under my legs, it became very clear what he was planning to do.

My nervous "oooh" sounded like a whistle.

He leaned down to kiss the top my thigh. Then the inside. Teasing little kisses and bites.

Leaning back onto my hands, I watched him slowly, achingly, work his way to my core. The heat of his breath passed through the fabric of my panties as if they weren't there. But damn it, they were. Until he hooked his finger around one edge and gently pulled them out of his way.

When I felt his mouth, my arms gave out. I fell backward, catching myself on my elbows. "Ow!" The pain disappeared as soon as his tongue dove deeper, running up my slit and stopping where I needed him. "Oooh!"

I'd been wrong about how stubble would feel—his didn't scratch my lady bits at all. If anything, it tickled, making me wonder what it would feel like if he had a full beard and already look forward to doing this again to know for sure.

This wasn't the first time a man had ever gone down on me, but it had never felt this good, even after giving the guy clear and detailed directions. I would never doubt Cooper's magic again. He held my legs firmly, but that didn't stop my toes from pointing until they cramped. I held my breath when he lifted his head, not sure how long I could handle his mouth not being on me.

He slipped my panties off and rubbed his lips together as he looked at me, the blue of his eyes even brighter than I remembered. "I found another exception."

"Why are you so good at everything?" I asked breathlessly, not expecting an answer and not getting one.

When he lowered his head again, I gripped the edge of the counter, wishing I could do the same with my other hand but wanting to watch him more. And as clenched as my abdominal muscles were, they weren't strong enough to keep me propped up well enough.

As he reacted to my every moan and shudder, he proved that he understood my body better than I did. Biting my palm, I stifled my sighs, gibberish, and whimpers until he reached up and took my hand away from my mouth as if he wanted, maybe needed, to hear the pleasure he was bringing me. So I let him— along with all my curses and gasps.

He certainly deserved it. His fingers worked me along his tongue, circling my clit and pressing inside me. Spreading me, a reminder that this was just the beginning.

When he started using more pressure, more speed, I lowered onto my back, only then realizing how close I'd come to smacking my head into the metal faucet and not caring. My head was spinning as it was.

He grabbed my leg—probably to stop it from flailing and possibly kicking him—and set it on his thigh. "It stays here. Don't move it."

"Promise." Especially because he was holding it with the hand I so desperately wanted to go back to where it had been.

I tried to savor what he was doing, to focus on each caress, each curl of his fingers or swipe of his tongue. But it all became too much to keep track of, the intensity building until I couldn't hold it back anymore.

With a shout of his name followed by God knew what, I tumbled over the edge and let his touch carry me through what might possibly have been the world's longest orgasm. It definitely broke all *my* records.

I swear, if I hadn't promised not to move, I would've melted off the counter into a puddle of satisfaction at his feet.

25

COOPER

After I watched Sophie come, felt it happen with my mouth and fingers, I didn't want to stop. But when she twitched and pushed my head away as if she were too sensitive, I took away my hand and let up the pressure of my tongue. I kept my lips on her though, gently kissing the smooth skin of her thighs for another minute or two.

My cock was harder than the granite she was laying on and, since I could still taste her, my erection wasn't going away anytime soon. But I'd give her a chance to breathe.

"You . . ." she said breathlessly. "You are a damn good leader."

"I've spent a lot of time planning what I'd do if I ever got the chance." I scooted the stool back and stood.

"If you'd told me how good you were at it, I would've let you." Groggily, she lifted her head to look at me through her open legs.

"I think I did. You just weren't listening."

"Something I now regret tremendously."

Amused and flattered, after a quick adjustment of my cock, I kept my hands at my sides, not feeling right about groping her when she didn't seem to be thinking too clearly yet.

Which made two of us. I'd always been a big fan of oral sex —giving and getting—but feeling actual fear that she'd stop me before I'd had enough of her was new. As much as I'd wanted to see her come, I'd wanted her *not* to even more. Just so I'd have an excuse to stay between her thighs. That was tough to understand or process.

Fuck it. Now wasn't the time for logic or thinking. If things progressed as I hoped they would, I'd have my cock in her soon and needed to focus all my effort on making that last as long as humanly possible.

"Why am I dying of thirst when you're the one who did all the work?" Reaching above her head, she turned on the faucet, cupping her hand under the running water and cursing. "And why do I insist on putting away the dishes instead of leaving a glass out to use whenever I'm in this position?"

"Are you in this position a lot?" That was an unpleasant thought, although I couldn't blame any guy for putting her there.

"Never." She sighed, giving up on the water and turning it off. "But I'm considering putting it on my calendar as a regular thing."

"Would *I* be involved in this regular thing?"

"You *are* the regular thing." As soon as the words left her mouth, her head popped up, eyes wide as she waited for my reaction.

"Relax, Sophie. I took it the way you meant it." *Regular thing* sounded too much like dating or commitment. "And I'm happy to be of service."

I walked around the island and took two glasses from the cabinet by the fridge.

She propped herself on her elbows and watched me fill them with water from a jug in the fridge. "How did you know which cabinet they were in?"

"It's where I would've put them. Wine glasses near the wine rack. Short glasses near the booze. Drinking glasses near the fridge."

She eyed me as I came back around the island. "Most people keep them all together."

"I guess Liz is a smarter woman than you give her credit for." I pulled her up to a sitting position and handed her a glass that she drained in one shot.

"And the water in the fridge? How'd you know about that?"

"Do you think it takes superpowers to figure out you don't like drinking from the tap? Except when you're lying on a counter, I guess." I didn't mind tap water—it was what I filled my bottle with every time I came here—but I knew she would.

"Extenuating circumstances." She set her glass down beside her and slid down to the ground.

I caught her by the waist, making sure she was solid before I let go. "Take your time." I leaned against the counter and watched her a second. "You sure you're ready to take over?"

"Yep. Just needed to hydrate." She shoved her hand down my pants and wrapped her fingers around my cock, instantly reviving my hard-on.

"Whoa! I guess you *are* ready."

"Too fast?" she asked, relaxing her hand but not moving it.

"Too sudden. I like to have a little warning before someone grabs my dick." I paused for maybe a second. "Okay, I'm good." I unbuckled my belt and yanked my pants open.

"Wow," she said, wide eyed as she pulled down my boxer briefs. Without letting go of my cock, she slid onto her knees.

"Oh! We're doing that now." It was her turn, and I really wanted to see what kind of leader she'd be. So, why did this feel too fast? "Hang on a second."

"If I do half as well as you just did," she said, drawing me toward her mouth, "I'm calling it a success."

"It's not a contest. I just wanted to make you feel good." After how long I'd waited for this to happen, the last thing I wanted was to rush it. Unfortunately, I only got one word out when her tongue flicked out, and it wasn't the right one. "Fuuuuck."

Unable to look away or stop her, I grabbed at the air next to me until I touched the stool and moved it close enough to lean on. She slid her mouth up and down my cock, each pass adding more wetness and more depth.

I moaned. Then cursed. Then moaned again, combing my fingers through her hair and wrapping a handful of it between my fingers.

When she looked up at me with those big, beautiful dark eyes, I almost lost it. She was too far away. I needed her lips on mine, her tongue in my mouth, and my cock inside her.

"Damn it." In the history of mankind, had a guy ever turned down a blowjob? If not, I was about to be the first. I pulled her off as gently as I could. "That's not going to work."

"Why not?" She looked hurt, as if she'd done something wrong.

"Because it feels too fucking good," I said, helping her stand. "And I don't want to embarrass myself by coming too fast and making you think that's as long as I'm good for."

"I wouldn't have thought that."

"Doesn't matter—I was kidding." There was no way I'd let myself ruin my chance to feel her come on my cock.

I clenched my jaw, shocked by what I was about to say. "Don't take this the wrong way, but I'm not sure how much longer I can stand not being inside you." Then, to make sure she understood I hadn't meant that in a sad, sappy way, I backed her across the room, shaking off the rest of my clothes and sitting down on a dining room chair.

When I reached out and tugged her hips, she got my hint and slowly straddled me.

I could get used to this. Repeatedly.

"I've never . . . um . . ." Her brow furrowed as she tucked her hair behind her ears. "I've never done it like this before."

"Good." Saved me the unpleasantness of imagining her doing it with anyone else.

"I don't know how well I'll do."

I ran my fingers up her neck and into her hair, pulling her in. As we kissed, something she said earlier popped into my mind —that she wasn't good enough for the man she wanted yet. I wanted to kick the shit out of whoever made her think she wasn't already. Whoever made her doubt herself whenever she did something new or different or unscheduled.

"Do you want to feel good?" I asked, pausing for her superfluous nod. "Do you want me to feel good?" Another nod. "Then you have nothing to worry about."

Holding her hips, I guided her movement, sliding her along my length, showing her how I hoped she'd move when I was inside her.

"Fuck." Poor planning on my part. "Grab my pants."

Instead of letting her stand up and get them, I wrapped my arms around her back and lowered her enough to reach where I'd flung them, pulling her back up as soon as her fist closed. I yanked my wallet from the pocket, found what I was looking for, and dropped everything but the condom and her onto the floor.

"You're in charge," I said, handing it to her. "If you want to stop, now would be the time to do it."

A quick tear of the wrapper, a little anxious fumbling to get it on, and we were ready.

She lifted up just enough to guide me in.

We both froze mid-moan when our bodies met again, my cock deep inside her. Words did not exist that could describe everything going through my mind and body. She looked just as confused. What were the chances she was thinking the same thing I was: How could a single motion make everything feel so damn right?

Pushing the thought from my head, I kissed her, forcing her down onto me to get even deeper, telling her what I wanted without using any words that might fuck things up. I rocked her against me, sliding her warmth and wetness along my cock. My fingers dented the flesh at her hips as she lifted, as if I were afraid each time that she would break free and not come back.

When she started to move faster, it became too hard to breathe and kiss at the same time, so we stopped trying. Instead, we looked at each other. I wasn't sure what she saw, but I watched her intently, studying her. Every shallow gasp as she sank down onto me, every sigh as she pulled away. How she fought to keep her eyes open and on me. The moment she lost the fight and shut them, moaning my name.

She kept the same torturous rhythm as I wrapped my arm around her and took her breast into my mouth. She gripped the back of the chair, pushing against it to press down on me, in the next breath pulling herself up and doing it again. The wood rail at my back groaned louder than I did as she used it—and me—to get off.

There was a good chance I'd have to repair the poor chair before her friend got home, but it would sure as fuck be worth it.

I closed my eyes to concentrate on every thrust and withdrawal, every rock of her hips until it got to be too much for both of us. Arching her back, she cried out, her body clenching mine as she came. I wasn't going to last much longer, not with the way she felt around me.

I stood, catching one of her legs and setting her down on the table.

"We can feel guilty about the table later too," I mumbled, pressing into her to regain the depth I'd lost when we moved. "And all the other spots of this house I'm going to take you."

This time she didn't get a break. This time she got to feel each thrust as I buried myself in her over and over, harder and harder.

I was right—it didn't take long. Especially after I heard her ask, "Can you make me feel like this forever?"

I kissed her—maybe to stop myself from saying yes, maybe because I didn't want to hear whatever she'd say next.

I groaned as I let go inside her, wanting it to last, knowing it was over. At least we stayed connected for a while, our mouths and bodies entwined.

Once my heart and breaths slowed down, we separated a little. Just enough space to look into her eyes and realize I'd been right to think this would complicate things. A lot.

Fuck.

Her brows came together. "You didn't like it?" Just like that, all her insecurity and doubt slammed back in at once, as if the incredible connection we just experienced was a connection only I experienced.

"Are you fucking kidding? I loved it." I brushed my lips over hers. "And in about a half hour, I'm going to love it again."

"A half hour? Really, Cooper?" Her grin proved I'd said the right thing for once. "*I'll* be ready to go in fifteen minutes."

"Remind me," I said, wincing as I pulled out of her, "which one of us passed out spread eagle on the counter and tried to drink water from their hand."

"Screw you." She smacked me in the chest.

"You just did, and you're going to do it again in half an hour."

"I'm taking a shower," she said walking down the hall buck naked without a shred of humility. "You can join me. You know, if you're up to it."

I was. In fact, I was up to it all night long.

26

SOPHIE

Aaron had a date who, according to the text he sent me from under the table at the restaurant, wasn't "worth ordering dessert for," so he might come over soon. Until then, it was just Liz and me on my back patio tonight.

Cooper had left after we'd taken a shower and before the other shower I took to rinse off the smell of the sex we'd had as soon as we'd finished our first one. Although, I was really starting to like that scent and, if Liz hadn't come over, I wouldn't have showered until I saw him again. Hopefully tomorrow. Early.

"The sex, Liz. Oh my God, the sex." I squeezed my thighs together remembering how he felt between them. All this time, I'd been so sure stubble on a man's face would be scratchy and painful. I was so wrong. So very, very wrong. "I thought all the women in porn were faking it."

"They are." She tossed another log into the fire pit and sat back down.

I cocked my head to the side. "Well, they wouldn't need to if the male actor was Cooper." Not that I liked the idea of him pleasuring someone else. "The sounds coming from my mouth were embarrassing. Like truly humiliating. We probably scarred Orion psychologically. I couldn't stop. Thankfully, Cooper didn't seem to mind."

"I bet he didn't."

"Have you ever had sex on a dining room chair?" I asked. "I didn't even know real people did that. It's amazing! A little hard on the quads after a while, but amazing."

"You guys have had sex all over the house, then?"

"Not *all* over." It had only been two days. "The one place we completely avoid is my bed." I didn't know why that was where Cooper drew the line, but I wasn't about to argue. I'd never used other spaces so creatively before.

"Because he still thinks it's my place?"

"Yeah." I nodded, my brow furrowed. "Do you think I should tell him? I mean, it seems a little too late now." Pretend-Liz was supposed to be gone until next Wednesday. To use her metaphor, I wasn't planning to keep the cow, so did it matter?

"Maybe you can find a way to slip it into conversation. Speaking of slipping it in . . ." She looked down on the chair she was sitting on. "Did you guys—"

"No. Not *that* one."

She laughed, covering her face with her hands. "You're all kinds of happy now, aren't you?"

"Is that bad?" This was the first real conversation we'd ever had about my sex life. There'd never been much to talk about before.

"No! It's awesome, and you deserve it."

"I can't stop smiling. For the last two days, I've literally wanted to stop people on the street and tell them how incredibly good at sex he is. I almost blurted out something about it when I was at my dad's last night for dinner. Fortunately for both of us, I held it in."

She leaned forward excitedly. "If you ever decide to let it all out, promise to invite me so I can be there to see your dad's face."

I rolled my eyes. "I'd resent that comment if I weren't still riding that post-amazing-coital bliss."

"Damn you. Now you're just making me jealous, except the part about having dinner with your dad. But two days? I don't think I've ever dated a guy who made me smile that long."

I sat back in my chair. "Cooper and I aren't dating."

"Right." She tripled the normal length of the word. "Why would you want to date the guy you've spent the last thirty minutes telling me such terrible things about?"

"He's not terrible. He's just not—" I forgot how I'd explained it before. "We're definitely not dating."

"Then can I have him?"

"I . . . um . . . that would be . . ."

Liz laughed. "I'm kidding, girl. Besides, he's all wrong for me. What did you call him: 'supportive,' 'smart,' 'self-sufficient'?"

"More sensitive than he'd ever admit," I added without thinking.

"Gross. When it comes to men, those are my four least favorite *s* words. I prefer assholes. Or 'shitheads,' to stick to the *s* theme."

"He can be one of those too. Just not as often as he's really great."

Sighing loudly, she sat back in her chair. "Seriously, if you're really not interested, can you introduce us? Because he sounds fucking perfect."

"Nothing is perfect, my friend. Only close to." Cooper had told me that countless times. Sometimes, in certain instances, he seemed awfully close.

. . .

If Liz hated my smile after two days, I couldn't imagine how she'd feel about the one I sported all weekend.

Cooper never stayed the night, but luckily, we had plenty of time during the day, with him still installing lighting in my closet and me working mostly from home. I felt a little guilty the closet was taking so much longer than he'd originally planned. I probably would've felt a *lot* guilty if the reason we kept getting distracted wasn't so fun.

"Are you going to leave a good Yelp review for my work?" he asked as he started his second break of the day by tugging my slacks over my feet. I was already topless, and Cooper hadn't bothered putting his shirt back on after our first break.

"Five stars." Laying across the couch, I spread my legs to give him space. "Fantastic customer service."

"The work is taking a lot longer than estimated though." He took off his pants and his boxer briefs at the same time.

"Yep, longer." I slowly lowered my gaze to his erection. "Harder too." I stopped laughing as soon as he was on top of me. I stopped breathing when he kissed me.

We hadn't had enough time for the sex to get old or boring, but I couldn't imagine ever getting tired of the way he made me feel.

It made me wonder what was wrong with all my previous relationships. The sex had never been bad enough to make me wonder if there was more to it, or *better* to it, but Cooper was living proof that I'd wasted all eight of my sexually active years on subpar sex and hadn't known it. All my nervousness and insecurity seemed to have been misplaced, or at least that's what he told me. He didn't seem like the type of man who'd be happy with just anything, certainly not with the time and energy he'd been putting in. With Cooper, every time was an exploration of different areas, different pleasures. There was always another area of my body or position he wanted to focus on.

When he flipped me over and yanked my ass up in the air, my face smooshed into the couch cushion, today's focus wasn't hard to figure out.

Doggie style.

"Ouch!"

And spanking.

"Was that supposed to be enjoyable?" I rubbed the spot where his hand had landed.

"Give it a chance before you move it onto your Don't Like It list." He smacked me again.

"Ouch! Chance given. Chance taken away."

He laughed quietly. "Nothing ventured . . ."

It was hard to be mad at someone who was literally kissing my ass, even if it was his fault it stung. Even harder when he pressed himself into me.

"More." I reached behind myself to grab whatever part of him I could.

"Naughty girl," he said, misunderstanding what I wanted. "Third time's the charm?"

"Wai—!"

I screamed when he spanked me again. Except, much to both of our surprise, it wasn't a "Knock it off!" type of scream. It was the breathless, moany, "Please, sir, may I have some more" kind.

"Fuuuuuuuck, Soph. I thought you couldn't get any hotter." He leaned over and kissed my back, lightly rubbing where it stung then dragged his hand around to touch my clit and take any memory of pain—and most everything else—away.

Maybe what had been missing from my life was a man's fierce need to make me come before he did. It was almost as if Cooper thought of his orgasm as a reward he only earned by giving me one. If so, as his thrusts sped and my cries became too loud for the couch to muffle, he earned his reward and then some.

27

SOPHIE

I growled at the phone as soon as I hung up with my father. It had to be about Dennis. What else could he be mad about? It was so aggravating that he refused to tell me over the phone or give me any kind of heads-up so I could prepare my response. He expected me to show up with no plan or clue what he was going to say.

After knowing me for twenty-six years, my own father still couldn't understand I didn't do well with these types of situations.

I was on my way back to bed to scream into my pillow for the rest of the day when I heard Cooper's knock on the door. Although he never used it, I'd given him a key a little while ago. Since we started sleeping together—without the actual sleeping —my fear of him catching me naked didn't seem all that important.

"Stay away from me, woman," he said as soon as I opened the door, his hands out in front of him. "No nookie breaks. I have about another forty-five minutes of work left on that damn closet, and if I don't finish it today, Roy's going to kill me."

"Did I ask you for nookie?" I spun around and started walking away.

"No," he said, grabbing my arm and forcing me to face him again, "but you never ask. You just take. I've never minded before, but—"

"Keep your pants on, Cooper. I'm not interested in taking anything from you today."

"Wow. Why are you snipping at me?"

"I'm not."

"Yeah, you are. Look, you can be snippy if you want to. But since I haven't done anything wrong and neither of us are horrible people, I'm going to give you the benefit of the doubt and assume something not good happened that has nothing to do with me. So, let's hear it."

I let out my breath and slowly released the death grip I had on my cell phone. "You really want to know what's going on?"

"Not particularly. But I'm here, you're here, and this seems like a vent-or-explode-on-the-person-closest-to-you type of situation."

He was right. I did feel close to exploding. Normally, I'd call Liz or Aaron, but they were both at work and couldn't spend an hour trying to talk me down.

"My father invited me over for dinner," I said finally.

"Don't you usually go over to his place on Thursdays?"

"Exactly my point." I didn't think he'd noticed or remembered that. "He called to invite me to dinner tonight—a Monday."

He stared at me expressionless.

"I have to be there at six o'clock."

"Why?" He followed me out to the patio.

"Because that's when he eats dinner." I set my phone down on the table and slumped into a chair. He took the one across from me.

"I mean, why do you have to go there at all?" What wasn't he understanding?

"Because he invited me," I said.

"That doesn't mean you have to go." He leaned back and put his hands behind his head, as if that bit of wisdom solved the problem.

"I can't just not go."

"Why not?" he asked without a shred of sarcasm. "It was an invitation, not an order."

"Since when haven't those two things meant the same thing?" I couldn't imagine even a healthy parent-child relationship being as simple as he seemed to think they were. "This is my father I'm talking about, the guy who holds my future in his hands." That he could crush it if he wanted to. "I can't say no. At least I have to come up with a good excuse."

"Adults don't have to explain their reasons."

I didn't argue, because of course that was true. It just didn't change the facts. If I didn't show up at six o'clock tonight, I'd better have a damn good excuse, like being in a coma or bleeding to death from a stab wound. And he'd still be mad I hadn't given him notice.

"If you really need an excuse," Cooper said, "tell him you have a date."

"He wouldn't believe me." Sad but true.

He stretched his arm across the table. "Give me your phone."

I clutched it to my chest. "No way!"

"Call him up and tell him you're seeing somebody and forgot you'd already agreed to go out tonight. I'll say something in the background, so he hears"—his pitch dropped by a few octaves—"my incredibly masculine voice."

"It's nine in the morning. If I tell him I'm seeing someone and then he hears you speaking, he's going to assume you spent the night." Ironic, since that was the only thing Cooper and I hadn't done.

"Even better," he said with a smile. "You're a grown woman. His discomfort from knowing you had a naughty playdate last night will knock him off his game a little. Make him agree faster so he can get off the phone and stop thinking about it."

I ran through the most likely scenarios. Since tonight wasn't our usual night and he'd asked me with less than his usual twenty-four-hour notice, he might understand. Well, not understand, but he wouldn't demand I change plans I'd already made. He'd probably still be upset I prioritized something non-work related over him, and I'd probably hear all about it on Thursday, but I could prepare myself by then.

"That might work," I said with a nod. "Just don't say anything embarrassing."

He crossed his heart, but his smile showed how insincere that promise was.

"I'm serious. He's very conservative and literally has no sense of humor."

"Apples don't fall too far from the tree," he teased.

I took a deep breath, dialed my father's number, and held the phone to my ear. "Hey, Dad. I'm so sorry, but I forgot I'd already committed to doing something tonight. He just reminded me."

Cooper did an exaggerated thumbs-up.

"So, I . . . um . . . I can't come over."

"Who is he?" One thing about my father—he was always transparent. Even over the phone, I could hear how irritated he was.

I looked at Cooper. Maybe for encouragement, maybe desperation. "A guy I've been seeing."

"A really hot guy," Cooper whispered, laughing quietly.

I covered the phone with my hand and mouthed, "Shut up."

He put his hands up in amused shock.

"Bring him along," my father said after a moment.

Oh shit. "What?"

"You may bring your beau with you to dinner this evening. I'm sure Lucy can make enough for an additional guest." Was he calling my bluff, or did he really want to meet the imaginary man I was dating?

Cooper silently asked me what was wrong when my body language switched to panic.

"That's . . . kind," I said, "but we have reservations and—"

"It's quite simple to unmake a reservation," my father said, his voice unwavering. "Telephone the restaurant and tell them to cancel it."

"I'm not sure that's possible," I said as I stared at Cooper. "It's very nice of you to extend the invitation to my date though."

His face morphed into something that would have been comical at any other time—exaggerated large eyes, a slow shake of the head to go with the broad sweeps of his hands signaling he'd probably rather get a bikini wax than go to dinner at my father's.

"Unfortunately, he already planned something special, and I—"

"Sophie Elizabeth," he said loudly. "You and I need to discuss something. In person. Tonight. I am allowing you to bring your young man with you if you must, but you will be at my door by six o'clock this evening. Understood?"

"Can you hang on a second?" I knew he'd say no, so I didn't wait for an answer. "Be right back." I put him on mute and still covered the phone with my hand just in case. "This was your brilliant idea to begin with, Cooper."

"That was before I knew how dictator-y your dad is."

"What do you suggest I do now?"

"I don't know. Tell him we broke up."

"I'll go alone," I said sadly. My father would probably prefer it that way anyway. It would be easier to make me feel horrible about myself if no one else was there. Quicker, because he wouldn't have to be polite about it.

Cooper sighed and sat back in his chair, not saying anything.

I couldn't expect anything more from him. As if he could somehow, after a couple of months of knowing me, fix the life I'd been living for twenty-six years. Fix my relationship with my father and all my issues with him. Fix my career, my dating life, my house.

I took the phone off mute and held it to my ear. "It'll just be me tonight, Dad."

Cooper let out a deep breath and then said loud enough for my father to hear, "Did you say at six, Sophie? Great. I can't wait to meet your dad." He even managed to sound sincere.

28

COOPER

"You can park in the driveway," Sophie said as we pulled up to the house I'd seen on their website, the one she'd grown up in. Beautiful but also simple and understated, just like Sophie herself. The two-story colonial stood back from the street, its brick driveway framed by the drought-resistant landscaping everyone in California was putting in these days.

Why did I do this kind of shit? At the very least, I should spread the discomfort out a bit and give myself a chance to heal between traumas. I'd allowed two women to put me into positions I didn't want to be in, and I didn't mean sexually. There wasn't a position I didn't want to be in sexually with Sophie, but that was beside the point. I wasn't in a relationship with either woman. In exchange for them not wanting to be with me, I was still dog-sitting, and now I'd be spending the evening being interrogated by a crotchety old man.

I turned off the truck. "Whatever happens tonight, whatever you see or hear, you tell no one. Especially if there's weeping."

She smiled and smacked my arm. "I don't understand why you're so nervous. You're my fake boyfriend, so it doesn't matter if he approves of you or not."

"I don't do well with other people's parents. Never have. And yours is . . ." I almost said, "a case study in dysfunction," but she must've already known that. "Probably going to see right through this."

"Probably," she said with a quick grimace. "At least you got a great suit out of it."

I ran a hand down the lapel of my new suit. As soon as she'd hung up with her dad, she took one look at me and said, "We're going shopping." Not like at Jasmine's party. She meant *real* shopping. Apparently, the suit I already owned wasn't good enough for her dad's dining room set or something.

We'd spent the rest of the afternoon at a tailor who took an off-the-rack suit and transformed it into something that made me feel like I was about to accept a very cool, very important award. "Congratulations, Cooper Wahl, you've just won the award for Best Series of Lies to the Parent of Someone You're Fucking."

I checked my hair in the rearview mirror. I'd let her put shit into it. At least every time I touched it, I thought about the hair gel scene from *There's Something About Mary* and laughed internally.

"Remember when I said I was always honest?" I asked. "It's not because I'm a stand-up guy. It's because I'm a really shitty liar. After many, many tries and fails, I decided I shouldn't bother."

"I'm not asking you to lie. I'm asking you to bend the truth a little. It's not unbelievable that someone like you and someone like me would be dating."

I glanced at her. "It's not?"

"Not from the outside."

"Right." I nodded. "Superficially and sexually, we work. It's everything else that doesn't."

"Exactly," she said happily.

Then why did I hate how quick she was to agree? Probably not a good idea to think about it, especially right now. I needed all the confidence I could manage.

"Sure, it all might come crumbling down around us, but at least we'll look good when it does." I'd even shaved.

"*Very* good."

I wondered if she knew she'd been staring at me ever since she saw the final product. Not that my eyes hadn't been on her whenever the truck wasn't moving. Sometimes even then. There should be a law against driving with her—too distracting.

"We should go in before he starts wondering what we're doing out here," she said.

"You mean making out like teenagers?" I liked that idea.

"Maybe later. In front of another house." She opened her door. "Come on."

Once she got out, I was forced to do the same, my heart setting an impossible-to-follow rhythm as we walked up to the door and then through it.

"Hello? Anybody here?" She set her bag down on the front table and looked at me. "You're doing great."

"I *feel* great," I said, my voice sticky with sarcasm.

"Honestly, you being so weirdly nervous has totally made me forget I was even worried."

"You're welcome. Glad I could help. Can I leave now?"

A forty-ish, dark-haired woman wearing an apron and wiping her hands with a dishcloth came through the doorway on our right.

"I didn't expect your dad to be so short," I mumbled.

She groaned. "This is Lucy."

The woman had already crossed the room and was coming in for a hug. As she wrapped her arms around my waist, Sophie mouthed, "She's a hugger."

"Really?" I mouthed back, patting Lucy's back for a second before she released me. Then she moved in on Sophie.

"Lucy is my father's . . ." she said over the woman's head mid-hug. "What does he call you now, Lucy? His 'everything'?"

"I'm sure he calls me all sorts of things when I'm not around, but I like that—his everything." Smiling, she took a few steps back, apparently to appraise me. "Who are you?"

"This is Cooper, and nobody's really sure what to call him."

"Thanks for that," I grumbled.

Lucy winked at Sophie. "I approve."

I pretended to wipe sweat from my brow.

"Cooper." A man stood in the opposite doorway, leaning on a thick wooden cane.

Even if I hadn't seen a picture of Sophie standing next to her dad on their website, I would've known they were related. Apparently, the Dillon's fashion choices were hereditary. Her dad was dressed in a black suit with a dark shirt and tie. Despite his recent health issues, he had an air about him, a controlled strength.

"You can't possibly be acquainted with more than one person with that name" he said. "Yet you told me you were bringing your new beau with you tonight."

After he turned and walked back through the doorway, Sophie motioned for me to follow.

"Good luck," Lucy whispered to me before returning to the kitchen.

We went into an old-school study—a full wall of books on one side and a grand piano on the other. Two matching uphol-stered chairs faced a coffee table in the center of the room. The lighting was dim and made the room look a little sinister except for an area near the window where a lamp shone directly onto a modern recliner that looked out of place surrounded by all the antiques.

"You must have misheard me, Dad. Cooper and I were supposed to be meeting to talk about work stuff."

I eyed the bottle of amber liquid and the single glass on the bar cart off in one corner as Sophie's dad headed for it.

"You're dating an employee?" he asked, not buying her explanation.

"We're not dating," Sophie said at the same time I said, "I'm not your employee."

"A glorified handyman."

"Is there something wrong with being a handyman?" I asked carefully.

"Jack of all trades"—he poured himself a drink—"master of none."

I'd never met anyone who could ignore the multiple people speaking to them in an otherwise silent room while simultaneously insulting them.

"Cooper's more than that, Dad. He's talented. You should look at his website or ask Sandra and Troy from the Riverview house. They can't stop gushing about what he did for them."

"Or you could call some of my other clients if you'd like, sir. Really interrogate them and see all the dirt they have on me," I added.

"Cooper," Sophie hissed out of the side of her mouth.

"Would you like their phone numbers?" I asked innocently, as if I couldn't see the burning anger in his eyes.

"Enough." He held up his hand as if he were king of the world's smuggest and most pretentious country. "Let's start over, shall we? Let go of any misunderstandings and get to know each other a little."

I gritted my teeth. There were no misunderstandings. The only people who ever said, "Let's start over" and who wanted to put shit behind them were the pricks who started it to begin with.

He didn't know me well enough to hate me. From where he sat, I'd done nothing but help his business. He might not have been thrilled I was fucking his little girl a few times a day and could still taste her from the last time, but since he didn't know about that, he didn't have a single reason to dislike me. The guy was just a dick who treated everyone as if they were beneath him, including his own daughter.

But I was here to help Sophie, not cause more problems for her.

"That sounds great," I said, putting on one of those fake smiles Sophie and Aaron were always wearing.

He turned to Sophie. "My dear, would you go to the kitchen and get another glass for our guest?"

Her gaze flew back and forth between us until I said, "Hurry back though. I'm thirsty." Hopefully, she knew me well enough by now to figure out that was both permission to leave her dad and me alone together and a prayer it wouldn't be for long.

"Ask Lucy when dinner will be ready as well," he said.

She rushed out of the room at the same speed I hoped she'd come back with.

"I don't like you," he said as soon as she was out of earshot. "I don't think you're good for my company. I don't think you're good for my daughter. She doesn't seem to understand the kind of man you are."

"Then aren't we all fortunate that you *do*," I said calmly. Can you eat without a tongue? Because I might have bitten through mine by the time dinner was ready.

"I'm not working with your company, Mr. Dillon. It was one job, I got paid, and your clients are happy. It's over. And I'm not dating your daughter. I do like her though. We're friends who drag each other out for the occasional"—I held up my arms and looked around his study—"evening of wine and laughter. I also think she's smart, savvy. Good with people too, even the difficult ones, like the two men in this room. If she can deal with us, I think she understands a lot more than you give her credit for."

"Yet, she brought a handyman to my house for dinner tonight."

When I laughed, even I—a lowly handyman—heard the anger in it.

I wasn't going to hit a guy still recovering from heart surgery. I walked to the wall of books, putting as much space between us as possible.

He looked at me with what some might call a smile, and I'd call the ugliest, most condescending fucking thing I'd ever seen. How could these two people be related?

"I know my daughter quite a bit better than you ever will, Mr. Wahl. She has many wonderful qualities and, unfortunately, some major faults. Judging someone's character, for instance."

If he'd been anyone else at any other time, I wouldn't have let him finish the thought. But Sophie would be walking into the room any second now and might be upset if she saw my fist in his face.

"Keep it coming, Mike." I was fairly sure I'd seen the name Michael on their website. Honestly, I didn't really care. "You think you're the first patronizing asshole I've met? I'd be happy to stand here in your beautiful home all night long and stare at your smug little face as you let out all your misplaced rage on me." I wiped my hand over my mouth. "But the thing that irks me, that makes me wish I were okay with hitting a sick old man, is the way you talk about your daughter. The little jabs at her intellect or competency. Because I know you do it in front of her too. And she hears it." Worse, she believed it.

"I find it deeply disappointing that of all the men she could've chosen, she picked you."

"Stop, Dad!" Sophie stood right outside the room, a glass I

could've used a lot earlier in her hand. "Stop talking to him like that."

"I'm fine," I told her. I'd never doubted her strength, but something in the way her body trembled told me this was one of a few times she'd stood up to her dad.

"I thought you were smarter than this, Sophie. Better than this." He poured himself another bourbon as if this were just a regular weeknight for him. "Evidently, you're not."

I clenched my fists. This had to be enough, right? I couldn't be expected to put up with more of his shit. Two things had kept me here this long—not wanting the asshole to think he'd won and the thought of leaving her alone with him.

"Thank you for the dinner and delightful conversation I didn't have, Mike. It was great to finally meet you." I walked toward him with my hand stuck out in front of me, wondering if he'd allow himself to be debased by my touch.

"Dad! Shake his hand."

He did, and even though I could tell he wanted to do something stupid—just like I did—we both controlled ourselves.

"I hope this will be the last time we meet," he said, his ugly smile never wavering.

"Not nearly as much as I do." I let go and went to Sophie, who was blocking my way out.

She didn't move, so I had to stop, close enough to prove we'd left a lot out of the "we're not dating" conversation. She didn't seem to care, and I sure as hell didn't.

I wrapped my hand around the nape of her neck and pulled her in until my lips brushed her ear. "I can't be here anymore." I hoped she would go with me, but I couldn't ask her for that.

"What did he say to you?" she whispered.

"Doesn't matter."

She pulled away from my grip and looked around my shoulder. "What did you say to him?"

"The conversation was between him and me, Sophie."

She let out a frustrated sigh. "Then I'm leaving too."

"No, you're not," Mike said. "You and I still have something to discuss."

"Why?" She slipped her hand into mine. "Apparently, all conversations are between you and him."

"I spoke with Dennis. I'd like to hear your side of things before speaking to him again."

"My side of things." That stopped her, but only for a second. "Ask him how much he likes my ass."

29

SOPHIE

"What did he say to you?" I asked as soon as we got in Cooper's truck.

"You heard him."

"No, I didn't. But with you growling on one side of the room and him looking like a cat who'd just swallowed a goldfish on the other, it wasn't hard to figure out *something* had happened." Since I'd seen the way he spoke to people, I knew it was his fault.

I'd meant to grab the glass and be back before any damage had been done. But Lucy needed my help to take the roast out of the oven because she'd thrown out her back earlier while taking care of my father. As soon as we heard someone raise their voice enough to hear in the kitchen, Lucy cringed, and I had taken off running. For all I knew, the poor woman might still be hiding behind the breakfast bar.

I wondered what would happen on Thursday—if he'd bring Cooper up at all or if I would. It had always been so difficult to talk to him and so easy not to.

"Are you going to tell me what he said or not?"

"Not." Before I could vocalize my annoyance, he added,

"Let's just say he still thinks we're dating, and he doesn't like me much."

"I'm so sorry."

He glanced over at me. "That your dad's an asshole?"

"Yeah." If I'd heard my dad call Cooper an asshole—which he never would because curse words were the vocabulary of the unintelligent—I might've had a stronger reaction. "I'm sorry for everything else too."

"You don't get to apologize for something that's not your fault." He reached across and squeezed my hand. I wish he'd have kept it there, his hand on mine. I needed that connection right now.

"It was my fault you were there and had to listen to his bullshit. If I hadn't dragged you along—"

"Good point. Let's do the apology over."

I only saw half of his smile because he kept his eyes on the road.

"I'm sorry for dragging you along and for putting you through that."

"Apology accepted if—"

My jaw dropped open. "You don't get to add conditions onto an apology!"

"Says who? It's my apology now. You offered it to me. But I'm not going to take it until certain conditions are met."

"You can't just let it hang out in the air between us. I gave it, now you have to take it. All the way. That's how it works." Something about him brought out every bit of my argumentative nature and then completely derailed it.

When he turned his head towards me, I saw the rest of his smile and knew I should be afraid of what "if" was. But what harm could he do while driving?

"Alright," I said, "what's your condition?"

"You have to get something to eat with me. I'm starving, and whatever dinner was going to be smelled incredible."

"Lucy is a great cook. My father's lucky she can put up with him."

"Dinner. Yes or no?"

As if either of us didn't already know the answer. "Do I get to pick the place?"

"Of course not. You're still working off your apology."

"You're going the wrong way." We'd already passed the turnoff for my house.

"Oops," he said without any sincerity or intention of turning around. Not that I wanted him to.

"Am I allowed to know where we're going this time?"

"Lots of Luck."

It took me a minute to realize that was the name of the restaurant and not him teasing me.

"My family has been going there since I was a kid. You'll love it."

"Who'll pay?" I honestly didn't care what his answer was.

"It's your apology," he grumbled.

"It's your condition."

He pretended to think about it. "Only because it was my condition. Plus, you left your purse back at your dad's house."

"I *what*?" I frantically searched the floor of the car and reached behind both seats before sitting back in a bit of a daze. "I left my bag at his house."

"Yeah, that's why I said it."

"You don't understand. I *never* forget my bag." It had my wallet in it. All my stuff. It had my fucking planner in it. I'd left it behind because I hadn't been thinking of anything other than getting Cooper out of there.

"Don't worry about it," he said. "I'm buying dinner and, before today went the exact opposite of how I thought it would,

I'd planned to return Liz's house key." The keys rang like bells when he swatted his keyring. "May take me a sec to figure out which one it is though."

He thought I was worried about being locked out.

When I didn't respond, *couldn't* respond, he glanced at me. "Listen, if you're not ready to deal with him quite yet, I'll go with you to get your bag. Let him yell at me while you grab it."

He was willing to go back there. For me. He hadn't even hesitated.

"I'll be fine." I pressed my lips together and looked out the window.

"I know, but that's not why I offered."

It hit me all at once, like a freight train. I almost asked him to turn around and take me home, because I wasn't sure I could make it through a whole meal without crying. This wasn't what was supposed to happen. None of it made sense. Every second of every day for as long as I could remember I'd known what I wanted, and he wasn't it.

Cooper was a fling, the cow I wasn't buying. An interesting, attractive, temporary placeholder until I found the man I was meant to be with.

Maybe this feeling was a reaction to earlier, to what my father put him through. Like the sympathy pains a man felt when his significant other was pregnant. An unforeseen reaction to something I didn't understand and hadn't experienced before. Absolutely nothing to worry about.

I smoothed my hair back and pushed an errant strand behind my ear.

"If you were going to say no to dinner, it's too late." He pulled into the parking lot, the Lots of Luck sign flickering in that oh-so-ungentle way neon signs did.

My closet was already finished, and Cooper had loads of work he'd neglected while helping me, so I had no right to ask him for anything else. I was confused and unfocused, the worst possible time to make a decision.

While all those things were true, none of them stopped me from asking, "Is it too early to ask if you're coming over tomorrow or if you need a day or two to recover from what happened tonight?"

"No to it being too early. Yes to the other two." He looked at me and winked. "I'll need a day or two to recover, and *you* get to help."

30

COOPER

After a grueling morning at my shop, I left early and dropped Sammy off with Uncle Aaron. As I drove over to Liz's house, my mind jumped back to last night. Good, good memories.

I'd gotten a blowjob in a car before, but I'd never gotten that *good* of a blowjob in a car, or anywhere else I could think of. After we'd eaten dinner and I'd driven her to Liz's place, Sophie hadn't wanted me to go. When I told her it didn't feel right to use her friend's house for all the things I wanted to do to her and that maybe it was time to consider going to one of our own places, we compromised and stayed in the car. For a couple of hours.

I didn't blame her for what had happened with her dad, but if guilt made her horny, I'd volunteer to go back to his place any time. That was a lie. The man made me want to punch something, preferably him.

Then I realized I had no idea where Sophie lived, and she'd never been inside my place. I wasn't sure why it bothered me that we only saw each other in other people's homes, but it did.

Although, not for long. Because apparently, her guilt was the lingering kind, so she helped me recover from the minute I stepped through the door until about three o'clock. Then I helped her until four.

That was also the time we realized I had no reason to be here anymore. Liz would be back soon, the closet was basically done, I had a fuckload of work to do at the shop, and Roy's baby was going to come out sooner or later.

I didn't know what would happen now that we didn't have the proximity to grab one another whenever we felt like it. I just knew I wasn't ready for it to be over. Although, I had to admit, I'd expected her to take my professional departure a little better.

"Absolutely not." She sat up on the couch and crossed her arms over her chest, covering her breasts. "You can't leave now."

"Don't worry—I'll put my pants on first."

She grabbed her turtleneck and yanked it over her head. "You told me after you finished the closet, we could talk about the other project I wanted to do here."

"Were you naked at the time? Because I don't remember that conversation."

She was already dressed by the time I'd found my boxers. "It was the first day. You didn't want to hear about it but said we could discuss it after you finished the closet." She put her hands on her hips and cocked one hip. "You've finished the closet."

It wouldn't kill me to spend a half hour listening to what she had planned. "Let's hear it."

She squealed, clapped her hands together, and ran away.

Huh. I wasn't used to women literally running away from me. Especially after sex and squealing.

"Meet me in the bedroom," she called.

"Aw, come on!" I said, groaning. "I just got dressed, and now you want me to meet you in the bedroom!"

"Was that you trying to be funny? Add it to the 'huge fail' list. Hurry up!"

"It was decently funny," I grumbled, buttoning up my pants and heading toward the bedroom. We'd had sex all over the living room, the patio, the kitchen, guest bathroom, master bathroom shower and vanity, and in the closet, but I considered the bedroom off-limits. As much as I loved that goddamn beautiful bedframe, it wouldn't be right to fuck on someone else's mattress. Some things should be sacrosanct.

I'd left out the other part that had nothing to do with Liz or her bed and everything to do with Sophie. I didn't want to get too comfortable. If we fucked in a bed, chances were good we'd want to stay there a while, maybe even nap or—God forbid—sleep together all night. That would move our sexual relationship closer to lines it couldn't cross.

Expectations would start, and I'd fail to meet all of them. What we had was good. Great even. Why risk blowing it?

"Holy shit." I stopped in the doorway and stared at all the sketches and plans she'd laid out, every speck of the bed covered. "How long have you been working on this?"

"A while," she said nervously. "It's special."

Special wasn't the word that came to mind. *Huge fucking, not-the-kind-of-project-I-ever-signed-on-for* was more accurate. I didn't have to look at the drawings themselves to know this job would take longer than the closet and the Riverview renovation combined. That wasn't even counting all breaks we'd take.

It obviously meant a lot to her, so I kept my mouth shut as she explained each drawing, rough measurement, and line of her budget.

When she was finally done, she stood back, hands on her hips, preparing herself for the same kind of argument we always had. Except this time, I had nothing to argue about.

All I had for her was one word:

"No."

Unfortunately, that wasn't clear enough, and she still

believed there was room for negotiation. *Then* we started arguing.

I told her why it could never work the way she wanted it to, but she wouldn't listen. She just went through the whole thing again from start to finish, as if she'd rehearsed it a thousand times, which was probably a gross underestimation. As much as I respected the amount of time and effort she'd put into the project, I couldn't tell her something was possible if it wasn't.

"You way undershot the labor costs," I said. Again. "But even if I did it all for free and we ignored the fact that the final project would *still* cost close to what the house is worth, I'm telling you, it's physically impossible in this space."

"Then ask Roy or Beckett to help you hold the glass panels and use a winch or whatever it's called." She pointed to her drawing and then at the ceiling. As if doing it again would make any difference.

"You're not listening, Soph. It has nothing to do with a lack of strength—which I take offense to, by the way. I'm talking about basic principles of engineering. If you can figure out a way around those, I'd be plenty strong enough to do it. Unfortunately, my perfectly adequate muscle mass can't undo the laws of physics."

When she said, "Okay," I thought I'd gotten through to her. As soon as she started talking again, I realized I'd been wrong.

"I don't want anything to block the view directly above the bed, but what if we added a bigger support beam down the middle and made the side supports larger than they are in the original plan. Not too large but larger." She drew a line in the air across the room.

"It's still not going to work the way you want it to."

I wasn't sure which part of the last five minutes of explanation finally sunk in, but suddenly her expression morphed from passionate frustration to confused hopelessness in three seconds flat.

"Look," I said, "if Liz gives you any shit about it, send her to me. I'll explain why what she wants isn't possible, and how much more she'll love whatever you come up with next."

"She won't. She had her heart set on this idea. It would be a dream come true for her."

I took my frustration out on my knuckles. Once they were all cracked, I tried again. "For the moment, let's put aside that the metaphor revolves around breaking through the glass ceiling, not simply having one—"

"That's not what it's about." I guaranteed not a single person on earth was more stubborn than Sophie.

"Does Liz know that if I could figure out a way to make it happen, it would look ridiculous, make the house impossible to resell, and probably kill her sex life?"

Seriously, who the hell wanted plates of glass that big over their heads? I'd personally installed several mirrors over beds, but an entire bedroom ceiling of glass? No, and for good reason.

"Liz doesn't care about those things. She just wants to be able to see the stars every night."

"She doesn't care about her sex life?" I shook my head. "Does she know she lives in a state famous for its earthquakes?"

No matter how many sighs she made, nothing would change. "Obviously, it needs to be safe. That's why I asked for your advice."

"Then I advise you come up with something completely different. Because I haven't even mentioned the worst part yet. The *worst* part is that this house sits between two giant palm trees. Do you know what lives in palm trees?"

I didn't wait for her to answer. "Birds. Lots and lots of birds. So, not only would thousands of palm berries rain down from the trees onto her insanely expensive and dangerous glass ceiling every year, covering up her view with juice, seeds, and pulp, so would bird shit. Lots and lots of bird shit. Raining down. Since there'd be no easy way to clean the glass and it predictably rains in California for maybe six months of the year, for the other six months, Liz wouldn't be seeing any stars. She'd be seeing—"

"Bird shit. Okay, I get it." She turned away and crossed her arms over her chest. "Does anything matter to you? Don't you have any empathy at all?"

Wow. That was a more personal rebuttal than I expected. "It's a ceiling, Soph." I threw up my hands. "The only time anyone should ever care about their ceiling is when it's leaking. Other than that, I'm not sure what there is to be empathetic about."

"Since you obviously can't do it, I'll find someone who can." She briskly and angrily snatched up every drawing and design board one by one and stacked them on top of each other. I didn't notice her eyes had welled up until she was done.

"Just . . ." I rubbed my hands over my face, not knowing how to make facts any more believable. They were *facts*. "Let me try drawing up something she'll like even more than sleeping under an entire ceiling made of glass."

I continued when it seemed like she was too busy being skeptical to respond, "My work has impressed you before, right? Let me take a swing at it. Then you show her what I came up with, and we see what she thinks. Deal?" I stuck out my hand.

She grudgingly took it. "It better be *very* impressive."

"I think we both know how impressive I can be when I put my all into something." I winked suggestively.

"How do we know that?"

"Ouch." I pantomimed stabbing myself in the heart. "My

feelings." They hurt all the way up to the moment a grin pushed through her frustration and she kissed me.

"*Very* impressive," she whispered.

31

COOPER

After a quick dinner of pasta, bread, and awkward silence, followed by over an hour of the hardest thinking I'd done in a long time, I stood back and gave Sophie a chance to soak it all in. Her original plan had about a ninety-five percent chance of ending with a couple hundred pounds of shattered glass on the floor. My idea would work. I'd had to make major alterations to her design, but the *feeling* she'd been going for was still there.

I was surprised she hadn't hugged me yet. Thrown her arms around my neck and given me a full-body squeeze. After getting naked. No, that wasn't why I agreed to do it. I'd agreed because she'd been so earnest, so sure I *could* do it, and she didn't offer that kind of trust to many people.

"So . . . ?" I said when I got sick of waiting for my kudos.

"Start over." She walked out of the room.

My smile dropped like a hammer, my pride right after. "Are you kidding? It's fucking brilliant." Some of my best creative thinking if I did say so myself. *To* myself since she was already walking away. "I did the impossible."

When I caught up with her, she was leaning against the kitchen counter with her arms crossed over her chest. "It's nice, but it's not what I asked for. The size of the panels is too insignificant."

"Nice?" And let's not forget, "Insignificant?"

She squished up her nose as if catching the scent of something vile. "Those posts are—"

"The glass has to be supported, Sophie. I don't draw as well as you, so maybe they don't look great, but trust me, no one will ever notice them once it's all done."

"*I'll* notice them."

Pride in your work was one thing. Demanding everything to be exactly the way you wanted and not being willing to compromise was another.

"It's not going to be a problem." I took her by the hips and ducked down to look her in the eyes. "Trust me. No offense to Liz, but I know homeowners like her. It's all for show. Anything they don't see doesn't exist. If you're still worried about what she'll say, let me meet her and explain why it has to be this way."

"You've already met the owner," she mumbled.

"No, I haven't." I could be pretty stupid, but I'd remember meeting the owner of the house Sophie and I had fucked all over. If for no other reason than I'd probably have a hard time looking her in the eye without thinking of Sophie spread out on her kitchen island.

She sighed, waiting for me to put something together. I looked around for anything that would clue me in on what seemed so obvious to her and I'd missed.

"Me, Cooper. You've met *me*."

I blinked. A couple of times. "This is *your* house?"

Her silence was all the answer I needed. Too bad it hadn't happened weeks ago.

"You're not house-sitting. This is *your* house. No wonder that cat likes you so much. Cats don't like anyone."

I took a few steps toward the bedroom, then turned around

and took a few more toward the kitchen. I stopped when I realized nothing in any direction would've shown me this was her place.

"This entire time, I've been in your house, working on your project, and you never thought to mention it?" I couldn't figure out why she would have kept that from me.

"Do you remember the first thing you said about it?"

"Not exactly, but it probably wasn't good." What was the word I'd used? *Pretentious*? Or was it *cold*? A lot of unfortunate adjectives had been going through my mind in the moment.

"It's not as if you couldn't have figured it out on your own," Sophie said. "The calendar near the fridge literally says, 'Meet with Cooper'."

I walked into the kitchen to look for the calendar. Sure enough, "Meet with Cooper" was written in blue on the first day I'd come here. She'd drawn perfect little blue stars on most days after that, including today. Shit. Had I really been coming here that much?

"At least you know I don't pry into other people's stuff, right?" I smiled, hoping a joke would make her forget how stupid I was.

"I should've told you to begin with, but I didn't. Then I was curious how long it would take you to figure it out. Obviously, back then, I didn't think we'd be seeing so much of each other."

"Seeing so much of each other's bodies or seeing each other so often?"

She rolled her eyes. "Both. Although, definitely more of the former."

"This is your place." I took another tour of the house, looking through each room again but in the new context. "Sophie Dillon lives here."

"For the past four months anyway," she said, following me down the hall.

I stopped in the doorway to the bedroom. "Wait a second. If this is your house, why the fuck aren't we using the bed?"

She shrugged and looked at her feet. "I was hoping you wouldn't ask that."

"Why?"

"Remember when you joked that I'd never had sex with the lights on, in any position but missionary, and anywhere other than in a bed?"

I nodded. That conversation would be forever branded into my memory because of what it eventually led to. Lots of sex. Lots of lights. Lots of positions, including—but definitely not limited to—missionary.

"I know you were trying to get a rise out of me, but you weren't that far off. So, I enjoyed how creative we had to get to avoid the bedroom."

It sucked she hadn't felt comfortable telling me a minimally important truth, but as defined, it wasn't a huge deal. As long as she could be honest with me now.

"No more lying or half-truths, or you will be punished."

She smiled, her tongue between her teeth. "You know where I live now."

"Yep. And I know where your bed is."

"That's also true."

"Then can I finally fuck you in it?"

"Yes, you ca—aaagh!" She squealed when I picked her up, carried her down the hall, and tossed her onto that gloriously giant bed.

Weeks of fantasizing about what she'd look like spread out on it didn't do a bit of justice to the image before me now. It didn't even occur to me that I was breaking my own rule until I'd already gotten both of us naked and was inside her. When not a thing on earth could've moved me from that spot. The way her body clenched around my cock, harder and harder the closer she got to her end didn't allow much thinking at all.

By the time she screamed her release, I didn't care anymore. All I knew was how fucking amazing she felt and how gorgeous she looked post-orgasm. The drunken grin of satisfaction, the flush of pink on her cheeks, the hair she always kept pulled back so tightly now a chaotic mess across the pillow.

I groaned as I let go inside her. As soon as I collapsed at her side, I let out a few silent curses about the easy way she curled into my arm and rested her head on my chest. Hating myself for wanting her there.

"I gotta get up. Take care of . . ." I motioned down to my cock, but she either didn't care, wasn't listening, or was already asleep.

I carefully pulled my arm out from under her, set her head on a pillow, and tried not to think too much while I went into the bathroom to get rid of the condom.

One night sleeping next to her wasn't the end of the world. No one would die or have their heart broken from a couple hours of sleeping next to each other under a blanket on a bed that, until an hour ago, I hadn't known was hers. Hell, the fact she hadn't told me this was her place conveyed how attached she was to me.

Just because I'd never been so comfortable, so careful with anyone—pulling the blanket from underneath her, checking to make sure she was totally covered when I laid it back down, slipping in next to her, and then moving her into the curl of my arm and her head on my chest so we'd be in exactly the same position as when I got up, all without waking her—that didn't mean anything either.

Anybody would do that.

Right? Right.

Oh fuck.

·　·　·

A half hour later, the irony hit me—I was so worried about what sleeping next to her for one night might mean that I couldn't sleep. She mumbled something and wrapped her arm around my torso, pulling herself closer.

Once she'd settled again, I kissed the top of her head and stared at the ceiling above us. There was way too much shit going on in my mind to close my eyes. I was too fucking comfortable, and it was going to hurt like hell when it ended.

Eventually, I gave up and gently pulled my arm out from under her, making sure the blanket covered all of her before getting out of bed. When I pulled on my pants, I glanced at my drawings for the ceiling. The ones she'd hated. I couldn't give her what she really wanted. It wasn't possible.

"Why are you up?" Her voice gravelly from sleep, she raised herself onto her forearms to look at me, squinting.

I sat next to her. "Why do you need to see the stars from your bedroom?"

She pulled herself up to a sitting position and drew her knees into her chest, wrapping her arms tightly around them.

Sophie had never been one to appreciate silence, so the delay in her response told me we weren't talking about just another project. This one meant more.

"My mom never wanted to be part of Dillon Design," she said, tracing around my hand on the blanket with her finger, not looking at me. "Back then, the company was just gaining ground in the industry, and she brought in a steady income as a nurse. When I was little, she worked nights so she could spend more time with me during the day. After giving me dinner, she'd go to work and not come home until, like, four in the morning. She said no matter how quiet she was, I always knew and would get out of bed to keep her company while she heated up leftovers. Then we'd go out to the back patio and look at the stars while she ate."

I stretched out beside her on the bed, my chin in my hand.

"Are you sure you want to hear this?" she asked.

"Do I not look sure?" When I smiled, she smiled back, but it wasn't her normal ear-to-ear, everything's-fine-even-when-it-isn't grin.

"I was eleven when she got sick. At least, that's when she couldn't hide it from me anymore. By then, Dillon Design was doing well. My father was always working, and even though she quit her job, she was always tired. One of her medications gave her insomnia, so she rarely slept through the night. Somehow, I always knew when she got up and would go find her. I'd make her food that I'd end up eating, and we'd go outside to look at the stars.

"The sicker she got, the more time we spent out there. Most of the time, I'd fall asleep with my head in her lap. One night, while we were stargazing, she told me that if it turned out she got to choose, that's where she'd go. To the stars. So, whenever I needed her, all I'd have to do is look up."

"What constellation?"

"You mean which one we were looking at when she said that?" She waited until I nodded. "Orion's Belt. Cassiopeia was up the night she died."

"That's why you want to be able to see the stars."

"It's an idea that's been floating around my head ever since." She shrugged and lay down next to me. "Kids are weird."

Knowing I wasn't going anywhere tonight, I brushed the hair from her face and kissed her forehead. "I'm sorry I can't give you what you want. If I could make it happen, I'd—"

"It's okay, Cooper. You're right. I'd never considered the bird shit." She tucked her head as she laughed.

Not her old laugh, not her old smile. These were genuine. Beautiful.

She let out her breath slowly. "Some things just aren't meant to be."

Maybe not. But that didn't make the tears in her eyes any less real. Or any less painful to see.

32

SOPHIE

Early the next day, I gave up trying to live without my phone and planner. It just wasn't possible. I was surprised I'd lasted this long. A digital calendar could only do so much, and I couldn't borrow Cooper's phone all day. Eventually, he had to leave my house.

I waited impatiently until two o'clock, leaving enough time for my father to eat lunch and for his pain pill to kick in. I tiptoed inside the house, grabbed my bag, checked on Lucy, and was gone before he woke from his afternoon nap. I'd worry about our Thursday night dinner on Thursday.

Luckily, Cooper made it easy to forget which day it was. I'd never known anyone like him. So true to who they were. So unapologetic about it.

After he'd finished at his shop, he came over to make sure I was still happy with the closet and didn't want to make any changes. Since I hadn't moved my clothes into it yet, he declared it a "clothing-free zone," and tore off everything I was wearing before doing the same to himself.

Eventually, we ended up on the bed, happy and satisfied, and unable to move for the next six to seven hours. It felt good to sleep next to someone, even if it meant having to share him with Orion the first night, and Orion and Sammy the second. I couldn't remember if I'd always slept so well after sex or if it was sex-with-Cooper level exhaustion I'd never felt before.

Despite my fervent denial, Thursday came anyway. I hadn't given a single thought to what I would say to my father. So, I did what any intelligent, mature woman would do—I pretended I forgot what day it was.

Since Cooper *did* remember and could tell I was trying not to, before he left for work, he invited me over to his place for dinner if I wasn't going to "that other place." Apparently, he could cook. Although, he may have been kidding about that.

It didn't matter, and it wasn't Thursday.

I spent most of the day wondering what would happen *after* dinner at Cooper's—if he would ask me to stay over or if that would be expecting too much. From both of us.

I decided to enjoy whatever we were doing for however long we were doing it. It felt good not to overthink something, not to worry about what it meant or wonder how to make it better. To just be happy for a little while. To just *be*.

I got the call an hour before my usual Thursday night appointment.

"Hi, Dad. How are you doing?" Since I could practically hear his jaw grinding, I knew he hadn't hung up. "Are you alright?"

"You need to get your rear over here now, Sophie. I don't care what you're doing. Don't bring that man."

At least all that audible anger meant he wasn't having another heart attack. Other than that, I had no idea why he'd be so mad. I wasn't the one who'd been a jackass.

"Are you going to tell me what's wrong?"

"Now, young lady." Then he hung up on me.

"Great. See you soon." I had to deal with him eventually and putting something off never made it any easier.

Cursing a lot, I shoved my phone and my planner into my bag and left. I called Cooper from the car and left a voicemail canceling our dinner plans and asking for a raincheck.

After I had stormed out with Cooper, my father didn't call me immediately after or in the days following. I hoped that he'd had time to cool off and reconsider his actions. Then I remembered who my father was and knew he'd merely been biding his time and replenishing his spite.

Except he'd never paid attention to my private life before. As much as he disliked the idea of Cooper and me dating, he didn't care enough to spend three days thinking about it. This had to be something else, something business-related.

As I drove, my mind bounced from one worst-case scenario to another. Was something wrong with Riverview? Or the new project I'd just started? Maybe Dennis was causing more problems.

Then I remembered the date. Yesterday, this month's issue of *Northern California Home* magazine was supposed to come out with a three-page feature on a foyer-great room remodel we'd done a few months ago.

I tried to remember if I'd said anything in the interview that could've been misconstrued or sound terrible if taken out of context. I'd been so careful though, sticking to the same bullet points we always used in features.

By the time I pulled into my father's driveway, I was no closer to figuring it out.

I went straight to the kitchen. It was empty. I checked my watch again. At five o'clock, Lucy cooked. Always. So, where was everyone?

"Lucy? Dad?"

"In here."

I found him sitting at the dining room table, scowling at the magazine in front of him.

"Sit down."

"Is it the interview? I don't remember saying anything I shouldn't have. If there's an error, it's not—"

"Sit. Down."

I did, but at the edge of the seat, my arms wrapped tightly around my bag as if my subconscious wanted me prepped to flee if necessary.

He slid the magazine over to me without a word of explanation. It was opened to our feature. On any other day, a three-page spread would be cause for celebration.

After glancing at the picture on the first page, I started skimming the article quickly, looking for words like *ugly*, *talentless*, or *hard to work with*. Words that could hurt a design firm more than any amount of great photography could help.

"The pictures look great. I'm glad they used one from the second floor."

"Turn the page."

I flipped the page, my eyes still flying over words and photos without seeing what he was so upset about. "I don't under—"

The article after ours began with a full frame picture of Cooper standing in front of a beautiful colonial home with his arms across his chest under the headline:

Getting It Done

Cooper Wahl: The New Generation of Contemporary Design

"Wow." I knew his business was doing well, but I'd completely underestimated *how* well. No wonder he'd never shown any signs of competitiveness. The company he deliberately kept small was getting more attention and kudos than the one my father spent the last twenty-three years building. That didn't even touch on what people were saying about him online.

I skimmed the article for something upsetting, but it all seemed complimentary. More than any of our features had ever been. The magazine spotlighted a few of Cooper's builds and, although my gut clenched when the writer expounded how handsome and talented he was, I couldn't imagine that would bother my father.

"Did you know?" he asked.

"That Cooper is the next big thing? No. I'm not surprised though. I told you he's really good at what he does."

"People like him make the entire industry look bad. Did you read what he said?"

Reading through the inset quotes quickly, I found the one my father probably found most objectionable on the second page:

"These days, design firms focus on the same stuff"—*guaranteed Cooper hadn't used the word stuff during the actual interview*—"they did ten, twenty, thirty years ago. It's all superficial. The feeling you should have when you walk into your home should go deeper than a slab of granite or imported tile. There's always a reason why people do what they do, like what they like, and want what they want. As soon I figure that out, I know what they need."

·   ·   ·

He was right. Knowing *why* someone wanted something made it so much easier to give it to them. He was also right to be cocky about his ability to figure that out. Hell, just this morning, he'd known what I wanted before I did, and then he'd given it to me right there on the bathroom vanity.

When I looked up, my father was staring at me. "I don't recall any of it being funny."

I stopped smiling. "I'm sure he didn't mean *all* design firms. Even if he did, he's not entirely wrong. Just because something worked well for you fifteen years ago doesn't mean there's not a better way now."

It certainly wasn't personal. The interviews had been done before we'd even met. It was dumb coincidence the features happened to be back-to-back in this month's issue.

"Four pages, Sophie. Four. *Your* interview only merited three. Imagine how much business we'll lose when people read this."

It was as if I hadn't even spoken. Once his mind locked in on something, nothing I ever did would sway his opinion or his focus. Since putting in less than two hundred percent was unacceptable, he'd dumped everything he had into hating Cooper and never giving him the tiniest chance to change his mind.

I looked at the pictures again. One by one, I saw what they were showcasing and sat back in my chair when I was done. "We'd never have taken those jobs. Ninety-nine percent of what we do is at least double anything Cooper does."

"*Did*," he snapped. "Who knows what he'll do now that you've shown him he can."

"You mean with Riverview?" I asked, annoyed. He was back to blaming me for something I didn't do.

"You hired him without my input. How do you know he's not going to underbid us for every job moving forward?"

"Because he's not like that. If you gave him a chance, talked to him . . . . He doesn't want to compete with you." I shook my head. "You're being paranoid."

"And you're being defensive." He closed his eyes and sighed. "Oh, my dear. You're not still seeing him, are you?"

"No. I mean, we never were seeing each other. Not really."

"It has to stop, young lady. Now!" He slammed his hand onto the table. "There are moments in your life when you have to choose what's most important to you. Choices that determine which path the rest of your life will take and how far you'll go. Whose future are you more concerned with—Dillon Design or your handyman's? Because it can't be both. Splitting your focus is the best way to fail at everything."

I stiffened. "Are you mad because I left with Cooper instead of staying for the fucking pot roast?"

He flinched. "Sophie!"

I blinked back the tears that burned my eyes. No, this couldn't be the actual conversation we were having. Not after all the times I'd bit my tongue and tried to be good enough. I put up with everything because it was what my mom would've wanted, and I was all he had left.

"What are you more upset about, Dad? That I used a curse word? Or that I chose him over you?"

"Don't be naïve. We've worked too hard to be derailed by a handsome, charismatic handyman."

"You don't know him."

"Like you do? Like half the women in this city do?"

I sucked in a breath. "What does that mean?"

"Men like him don't commit, my dear. They take what they want for a little while and then go in search of something more exciting, a greater challenge, whether it be a client, a job, or a woman. Men like him bore easily. When they stop being entertained, they move on, and they don't look back."

I bit the inside of my cheek to stop myself from remembering Cooper saying the exact same thing to me before any of this started.

He bored easily. He loved a challenge.

Was I just a challenge? The girl with a stupid list who'd turned him down.

What was more challenging than that?

And then, after he'd made me question everything I'd ever wanted, what was more boring?

"I don't want you to hurt," he said.

If that was true, he'd failed.

"That's not . . . I don't care about Cooper in that way." I shrugged, wringing my hands under the table and keeping my expression as blank as possible. "I hired him because I couldn't work with Dennis anymore and had to find a replacement fast. Since you've burned more bridges than I could cross in a lifetime, you didn't leave me too many options."

"After all you've learned about this business," he said, "all the time we've both put in, you already know your choice."

I pushed back from the table and stood. "I need to go."

"Sophie!" he called. "Sophie, come back!"

I walked out the door not sure what felt worse—that my father ruined everything good in my life, or that I let him.

33

———

COOPER

"What are you doing in my bedroom?"

I swung toward her voice. "Damn it! You couldn't have come home a little bit later?"

She was the most predictable person I'd ever known, except for the one day I needed her to be. It was Thursday night. She was supposed to be at her dad's place eating dinner or, if she hadn't called to cancel, at my place eating dinner.

With no more official reason to be here anymore, I wanted to come up with something that would make her smile long after she'd moved on. Since, after staring at the ceiling for half an hour, I still had no clue where to start, I might need more time than I'd ever have.

"How's your dad?"

"I don't want to talk about it," she mumbled. "I'd rather talk about what you're doing in my bedroom."

"I'm thinking about the ceiling."

"I told you to forget about it."

"I heard you. But you know how well I follow directions."

She sighed and let her bag fall onto the floor next to her. "I'm so tired. Can we please not do this right now? We can argue tomorrow."

"Sure," I said, watching her drag herself to the bed. She flopped on top of it facedown and then stopped moving. "Can you breathe in that position?" I picked up her bag and set it on top of her dresser then sat at the foot of the bed. As soon as I unbuckled the ankle straps from her shoes, they fell onto the floor.

She turned her head toward me without lifting it off the duvet. "Kind of."

I lay down on my side and brushed the hair out of her face. "Want to talk about it?"

"No. I want to take a nap. For a year or two."

"Sounds entirely reasonable. You want to change first?" I still hadn't figured out how she was *ever* comfortable in stuff like that, but I knew from the last few nights we'd spent together that she didn't like to feel bound by clothing. I never argued because I liked to sleep in the buff too. Plus, you think I was going to tell the naked woman lying next to me to go put something on?

"Can you help me take off my clothes," she asked, "and then not do anything about it?"

"Never have before." I blew out a breath. "I'll try to control myself."

She lay there like a fucking corpse, her arms unmoving until I picked them up, flopping back onto the bed as soon as I let go. She was almost able to hold in her giggles the entire time it took me to get her blazer off. I unbuttoned her skirt and pulled, rocking her side to side to get it down her legs, then yanked it off completely when it was at her knees. By the time I did the same thing with her tights, I was winded.

Her panties were riding up her ass just a little. I loved her in this position. I could move that fabric to the side and slip inside her with barely any effort at all. Since she was facedown, she couldn't see how hard my cock was. I shouldn't have said I'd control myself. That was stupid.

The fancy tank top wouldn't bother her while she slept, so I grabbed the bottom edges of her duvet and laid them over her, effectively wrapping her up like a burrito.

I sat next to her, took a deep breath, and wondered what the fuck I was doing. She could be controlling. I could be thoughtless. I did what I felt like doing. She didn't do anything without a week of prep, her planner, and a couple to-do lists. We shouldn't fit together, but we did. Better than I'd ever fit with anyone.

Shit. I hadn't expected this—to want nothing more than to tell her every reason why I loved being with her, knowing she didn't want to hear it.

"Will you be here when I get up?" she asked quietly.

"If you want me to be."

"I do."

"Then I'll be here." I kissed the top of her head.

"Why are you here again?" she mumbled.

"I'll tell you later." I pulled the blanket a little higher and then tried to think of a way to give her the impossible.

34

SOPHIE

When I woke up, the first thing I did was reach for my phone. As soon as I got caught up in the duvet, I remembered Cooper helping me get into bed.

Cooper.

I let out my breath and wondered what I should do about him.

I hated that my father had given me an ultimatum, demanded I choose between everything I'd worked for and a man who'd get bored of me eventually, if he weren't already.

I spent years trying to show my father I was ready for more responsibility. I'd hoped that I'd finally done it with the Riverview project. Along with Cooper's help.

Cooper.

How much did he matter? Sure, I was grateful for his help, but I'd known him for a fraction of the time I'd put into my career. If I had to choose one—if my father *made* me choose one—there was no contest. Cooper was great, wonderful even, but he wasn't even close to being the man I needed.

I unwrapped myself from the duvet and got my bag off the

dresser. Had I put it there or had Cooper? What happened to all my clothes? I found my phone and checked the time. Despite the ninety-minute nap, I was still exhausted.

Suddenly, I heard a noise from my backyard that sounded like multiple people. I slipped on a pair of leggings and went to find out what was going on.

Everybody was out there—Aaron, Liz, Cooper, even Sammy —sitting on my patio, sharing a bottle that might have come out of my wine rack. It surprised me how well my newest friend fit in with my two oldest. Three utterly opposite personalities, all laughing at the same joke.

I shivered when I stepped outside. "Why didn't anyone invite me to the party?" I'd meant it to be funny, to stay with the theme, but it had been too groggy or depressed sounding to make anyone laugh. At least I could still fake a smile like nobody else, even as I racked my brain for a polite way to get my amazing friends out of my house. Especially the newest one.

"Hey there, sleepyhead." Cooper reached down and grabbed something before coming over to me. "I've been trying to get rid of these creeps for the last hour, but no matter what I do, they won't leave."

I didn't want him here. Not until I had a chance to decide what was best for me. With him this close, it was too hard to think clearly about anything but him.

"This is the first time we've ever spoken, Cooper," Liz slurred, letting me know it wasn't the first time her glass had been empty tonight. "I'm the only one who doesn't know every-thing about you. No way am I leaving."

"You okay?" he asked me quietly.

I ignored my friends and focused on him. "Why didn't you tell me you were going to be in this month's issue of *Northern California Home*?"

"Is it out? I wasn't sure which issue we'd be in." His surprise passed almost instantly. "Didn't know and didn't really care. Is that important?"

"It's the biggest home design magazine in one of the most expensive housing markets in the country. But you didn't think it was a big deal?"

"Nope."

"It would've been nice to know someone I worked with—"

"And sucked off fantastically last night," he said under his breath.

"—was appearing in the same magazine issue as my company was."

"You guys were in there too? Cool. Also, yeah, I'm sorry."

I exhaled slowly. "I appreciate you saying that. It was a bit of a shock. Especially for my father."

"I didn't mean I was sorry for not telling you. I'm doubly not sorry for not telling your dad."

"Then why did you apologize?"

"Because I didn't know it was a big deal, and apparently it is. I should probably follow that side of the industry, whether I got into it accidentally or not. It's just a tough thing to get excited about, you know?"

"No, I don't know." Maybe because I hadn't *accidentally* gotten into it. Dillon Design was everything to me. I'd worked my ass off to earn it, and even if my father wasn't ready to hand over the reins to me, at least he recognized the work I'd put in.

"It's a big deal because it's something that excites you." He came closer. "I love seeing how passionate you are about it."

I didn't like the look on his face. It was too smirky, too sexy for the moment. When he slipped his hand around my waist and yanked me into him, I shot both hands up to block myself from slamming into his chest.

"Tonight," he said, his voice low and gravely, "all my dirty talk is going to be about industry magazines."

Aaron held up a half-empty bottle of wine. "Give the woman a drink already, Coop."

"Cooper, not Coop," he grumbled, his eyes still on me. "They showed up out of nowhere, but it seems like you had a hard day, so if you want to be alone, let me know."

That was the moment I started hating him.

Hated.

Offended that he could be so observant, so thoughtful. Offended that somehow he understood me better than the people who'd been my best friends for over a decade. Whom I loved.

I didn't love him. I didn't. And I wouldn't give up everything I'd spent my whole life wanting for him.

He was milk. It just got hard to remember that sometimes.

"How many bottles did you guys bring?" I yelled, faking a grin I'd never felt less sincerely. One that was the only thing stopping me from crying. "I'll go grab a glass."

"I grabbed you one earlier." Cooper pulled the hand that wasn't still resting on my hip out from behind his back, the stem of a full wine glass resting between his fingers. "For when you woke up."

Hated.

I looked around him, wanting, maybe even *needing*, to prove he was full of shit. To know he didn't think of me when I wasn't around, didn't consider my needs or feelings before I had. But instead of being relieved to find out he'd tried to pawn his own glass as one he'd gotten for me, I saw a mostly empty one on the table in front of where he'd been sitting.

Hated.

"Just in case you felt up to it." He handed me the glass and smiled. "Don't worry, I covered it so no bugs could get to it before you did."

Hated.

I took the glass and pushed past him without even saying thank you and went to join my real friends.

35

COOPER

As soon as Sophie sat next to Liz, she seemed fine. Happy even. Or at least she was faking it well. But I knew something was wrong, probably having to do with her dad. I stood in front of the lounge chair I thought we'd share so she could cop a feel whenever she felt like it. Had been looking forward to that, actually.

"What is that?" Aaron pointed toward my crotch.

I glanced down to where he was pointing. "That is my dick."

"No, I meant what's in your pocket."

"It's nothing." I shoved the paper deeper. How the fuck had he noticed it? "And stop looking at my dick."

"Not looking at your dick . . . right now," he said. "I'm looking at the piece of paper that was sticking out of your pocket. Because, from here, it looked like a list."

Liz gasped. "Shit, Sophie, you've corrupted him."

"You mean *converted*."

"Nope, I meant *corrupted*."

Aaron stood. "What's the list, Cooper? I swear if it's not about sexual positions or celebrities you want to bang, I'm gonna start crying."

"It's not. Can we change the subject, please?"

"Not until I know what it is."

I turned away as Aaron lunged for my pocket, but he caught me, first by the belt loop, then by the waist with his other arm. Of course, I could've overpowered him, but I didn't want to hurt him. I just wanted him to leave me the fuck alone.

When I twisted to get free, he lost his footing and we both tumbled onto the grass. Sammy hauled ass out of the way while barking that ass as furiously as he could.

"Get the fuck off me, Aaron!"

"Wow, I think that's the first time anyone has ever said that to him," Liz said.

"Got it!" He sat up, holding the folded-up piece of paper up in the air.

"Fuck!" I lunged for it, but the lanky bastard was faster than he looked. He shoved backward and was on his feet before I could grab him. "Give it to me."

"I will." Aaron stepped back from the beast nipping at his ankles. "*Et tu*, Samuel?"

I was more pissed off than I'd been in a long time, and while I appreciated Sammy's help, I didn't need it.

"Aaron," I growled.

"Don't worry. I only want one itty, bitty peek." He unfolded it as he backed away, his face showing me when he made it past the first line.

"What is it?" Liz asked.

"Nothing important," he said, folding it back up. "Sorry, man." He guiltily handed it back to me and offered his hand to help me up. When I refused, he picked up Sammy and tried to settle him down.

"Aaron, you have to tell us now."

"It's personal. I shouldn't have looked."

"Whatever," I muttered, crushing it into my fist as I stood.

It didn't matter how much of it he'd read. He'd seen enough. Aaron couldn't keep a secret from her to save his life. Or mine.

"Aaron?" Liz pouted.

"It has nothing to do with you, Liz. Back off."

She flinched at his tone. I couldn't leave it there. The two of them pissed at each other over it. Sophie blank with confusion, and Sammy still glaring at Uncle Aaron.

"Tell them."

He shook his head. "No way."

"Tell them or I will." I'd only written it all out an hour ago, never imagining anyone would see it.

"Will somebody tell us already?" Liz asked loudly.

I didn't have to catch Sophie's eyes because they were both already wide and on me. As if she already knew.

I blew out a breath. "It's about you."

"Why?" she asked. Was she surprised I'd made a list period or because I'd made it about her?

"Cooper, you don't have to—" Aaron started.

"Read it." I shoved it into her hand and backed away.

As Liz stepped in close to read over Sophie's shoulder, Aaron grabbed her arm and dragged her toward the door. "We're leaving now."

"Can we take some of the wine with us?"

"No," he said. Then more softly. "I think they're going to need it."

As soon as the door closed, it got very, very quiet. So still, I could hear Sophie's breath change as her eyes moved down the page.

Since I hadn't planned on anyone ever reading it, I didn't know what to expect. But knowing what it was—my very own attempt at a Robert Pattinson-style list that was all about her—I hoped she would at least smile.

When you thought about someone constantly, it didn't take

too much effort to write down all the things you liked about them. Of who they were. Most had been obvious the second we met. She was beautiful, confident, smart, stubborn, tenacious. Others I'd needed some time to figure out—she could be silly, fun, sweet, proud, generous, and loyal. That I loved the way I felt around her, the way she made me feel.

I'd left a lot of lines at the bottom, marked them with place-holders for all the things I wanted to learn about her, things that would take time and patience.

"This is only half a list," she said finally.

"What do you mean?" I'd poured my fucking guts out in that thing.

"Where are all the parts of me you *don't* want?"

"There are no parts of you I don't want."

She pressed her lips together and tucked her head down to look at the list again.

I waited. More impatient than I'd ever been, but I waited.

"I don't—" Her voice shook. "I don't know what to say."

"This is just an idea, but you could say, 'Wow, Cooper. That was great, and I feel exactly the same way.'" I shoved my hands into my back pockets. "Or if that's too much, you could go with something like, 'Wow, Cooper. That was really unexpected and something I need to think about a little before I tell you I feel exactly the same way.'"

She took a deep breath, the kind that meant whatever came next wouldn't be what you were hoping for. "Wow, Cooper. Thank you. That was amazing and took a lot of courage."

And that was it.

So much worse than even my worst-case scenario. "Took a lot of courage?" Score one for keeping all that emotional shit bottled up like I'd planned on doing. Like I'd always done . . . until her.

"I know how hard it is for you to open up like that," she said, "and I respect you all the more for doing it."

"Cool, because that's what I was going for—your fucking respect."

"You don't get to be mad at me for not saying what you wanted me to!" Her voice was raw, hurt and hurtful. But at least she was finally looking at me.

"Every woman I've ever been with always complained I didn't share my feelings. They were right—I didn't. Because I didn't *have* feelings for them, not . . ." I ran my hand through my hair, wrapping it in my fist and tugging. "I finally have some to share, and I'm sharing them. With you. And I think . . . I *thought* you felt the same—"

"I'm glad you can express how you're feeling, Cooper. But it's not my fault you're disappointed."

"I'm not disappointed. I'm pissed." I ripped the paper out of her hand and tore it into little pieces. "Forget everything you read." Everything I felt. "Because it's all been replaced by my desperate fucking need for your goddamn respect."

"Don't be mad. We're good as friends."

"I just admitted I have feelings for you. Not friendly feelings. Not sexual ones." I shook my head. "Not *only* sexual ones. Deeper ones. Real ones. And you want to pretend it didn't happen. You're okay knowing that every time we talk on the phone or text, I'll be thinking about how badly I want to hold you."

I'd never told a woman I wanted more from her, something serious. Normally, even saying I liked them had to be dragged out of me after a few drinks and a blowjob.

"That every minute you're not near me, I'm trying to figure out a way to change that." I heard the tinge of desperation in my voice, but I couldn't stop. "What about when I tell you that you're the most incredible woman I've ever known? That I want to be with you for real, for everything. Can you pretend it doesn't matter?"

"I . . . I don't know." She rubbed her hands over her face. "None of this was supposed to happen." With her arms crossed tightly across her chest, she walked out onto the grass.

"But it did."

"You shouldn't have let it, Cooper!" she yelled at the sky. "You knew what would happen, and you did it anyway."

"Did what? What did I do?"

She wiped her face with her sleeve as she turned her back to me. "I want you to leave."

"Now?"

"Please go."

She'd lied before. If she respected me, she would've at least faced me when she ripped my heart out of my chest.

"If that's what you want." What else could I say? What else could I do? Maybe she needed some time to process. "I'll call—"

"Don't." She tightened her arms around herself. "Don't call. But thanks, Cooper. For . . . everything."

"Right." That didn't cut it, but it was better than saying, "Anytime." I couldn't do this anytime. Or ever again. "Come on, Sammy. Get your stuff. We're leaving."

He trotted over to where he'd left his favorite toy and ran back to meet me at the front door.

"Bye, Soph." I'd laid it all out for her, given her everything I knew how to give. Whatever happened after that was up to her. And apparently, what she wanted more than anything was for me to go away.

SOPHIE

Seven days per week, twenty-four hours per day.

For eleven years.

No crying.

No indecision.

No doubts about what I wanted or the person I was meant to be with.

Every day.

Except today.

Today, he ruined everything.

COOPER

I gave Roy the next day off for two reasons. First, having way too much work for one person to get through meant I wouldn't have time to think about anything else. Second, I didn't want him to see me if I started crying. It worked pretty well for the first few hours. Then I remembered the dangers of combining anger and frustration when using power tools.

"Fuck it." The work could wait. I'd rather not accidentally lose a finger on a saw or give myself a lobotomy with the drill press.

I'd lived alone for almost a decade, and I'd never once been lonely. But when I opened my front door and saw Sammy there —so fucking excited to see me—I felt something break inside. I swept him up into my arms, holding him up so we could look into each other's eyes.

"Fine. I like you. Okay? Are you happy now?" I already knew the answer—he was no happier than he'd been before my confession. Because there *was* no happier than he'd already been. Just to see me, to know I was home.

The little fucker loved me.

"Big mistake there, buddy."

Or maybe that was his pee-pee dance. "Shit. You need to go out, don't you?" I grabbed his leash and took him for a long, long walk, carrying him for the last half hour when his legs got too tired.

He spent the rest of the day and evening sitting in my lap watching TV. Since I wasn't paying attention to much of anything anymore, I flipped it to the Animal Planet Channel and closed my eyes. Eventually, we both fell asleep.

As soon as the doorbell rang for the third goddamn time this morning, I shouted, "For fuck's sake! When will you people understand that I'm fine? I'm always fine. I always *will* be fine."

Across the room, Beckett and Jasmine nodded at me before glancing worriedly at each other.

"Who the hell else did you tell?" I asked my little brother as I got up to answer the door. "If that's Owen or Jackson, I'm moving to Australia and never speaking to any of you again."

Honestly, it was bad enough he'd called my sister. One casual mention that Sophie and I had called off whatever we were doing, and Beckett went full shrink on me, thinking I needed support to get through the trauma or some shit. I would kill the little fucker if he made our two other brothers come into town to pat my back and tell me everything would be okay.

I stopped with my hand on the doorknob and threw him a glare that could melt the polar icecaps. "You didn't tell Mom and Dad, did you?"

Jasmine rolled her eyes dramatically. Beckett didn't react. When I heard another knock, I steeled myself for whatever was on the other side and opened the door.

"You were not who I expected," I told Aaron as soon as I saw him. "That's a good thing. You may have just saved two lives."

"Yay?" he said hesitantly. "I thought we had a date this . . ." His voice fizzled out when he saw my brother. "Oh, hello."

Before I could introduce them, he saw Jasmine. Forgetting all about me and our walking date for Sam, he pushed me out of the way and hugged her. After a quick catch-up, she introduced him to our brother.

"It must have been so hard growing up in such an ugly family." Even without the shit-eating grin, there was no way anyone could've missed Aaron's sarcasm.

"Imagine being the sole woman with four men who all look like them," my sister grumbled loudly.

"Oh, I am." He looked at Beckett and studied him for a moment. "Are you, by any chance, the gay brother?"

I sighed. "Sorry, man. I don't have a gay brother."

"That we know of," Jasmine added, making me wonder if she'd heard something I hadn't. Not that I cared or would continue thinking about it thirty seconds from now, but I'd like to think my siblings trusted me enough to tell me anything.

"I volunteer to be the first person you tell if you find out." Holding up his hand like an overly excited child, he claimed the couch, pulling Jasmine down next to him. Beckett stayed where he was, perched on the arm of the chair with Sammy on his lap.

I stayed near the door. "Aaron, we're supposed to go for a walk." I could use a walk. Or a drink. Since it was eleven in the morning, I'd wait until we got back to start the heavy day drinking.

"This seems like more fun." His gaze moved from sibling to sibling. "What are we doing?"

"We're worrying about Cooper," Jasmine said.

"Oh. That doesn't sound fun." His eyes went wide again. "Wait, is this an intervention?"

"Not sure," I grumbled. "Is an intervention when people who

should mind their own business come over and attack someone who doesn't want to hear what they think about his life?"

In unison, they said, "Yeah," "Yep," and "That's one example of an intervention." The latter came from my overeducated brother.

"Nice try, Beckett. For some reason, every time you try to psychoanalyze me, I have a Pavlovian reaction and stop listening to you. And you two?" I swung around to look at them. "I'm wondering why I listen to you two at all."

"This is about Sophie?" Aaron asked.

"Why are you asking them?" I growled. "If you are all so worried about me, why not ask me why I'm upset instead of deciding what you think I should be upset about?"

Beckett nodded. "You're right. Why don't you tell us?"

"Because . . . I don't know."

Somebody groaned.

I didn't know why I was so upset. "I've been dumped before, but it never felt like this."

"Did you love that person?" Aaron asked softly.

"No, but it's not like I'm in love with Sophie either."

They all shared glances.

"Fuck off, all of you. It doesn't matter if I am or I'm not. Because that woman doesn't do anything unless it's on three separate to-do lists. And I'm not on any of them."

Dogs could be shifty little bastards when you set your food down or when they wanted to sit in your lap. But they could also be smart. When Sammy jumped off Beckett's legs, ran over to me, and scratched my pant leg to get me to pick him up, it was as if he knew more than I did. That I needed something to hold on to.

"We'll be okay, little man," I told him as he licked my face. When I felt my back pocket vibrate, I tucked Sammy into one arm and pulled out my phone, hoping it was a text from Sophie saying something like, "I made a huge mistake. How can I live without you?"

Since, apparently, I'd spent a few previous lifetimes accumulating a huge amount of bad karma, it was from Helen.

Hey, Coop. She knew I hated being called that. *Tell Samuel that his mama is home!* Followed by three fucking smiley faces. Three. Her next text was even worse. *Can you bring him to my place before noon?*

I slumped into a chair, ignoring the worried faces of my siblings and my friend, not caring when they all read the message upside down as soon as I tossed my phone onto the coffee table.

As Sammy ran his disgusting little tongue all over my chin, I held him closer.

"That bitch!" Jasmine snapped. "After all this time, she gives you a half an hour notice?"

It was already eleven thirty.

Wow, it had taken less than forty hours to lose everything that mattered.

The goddamn goodbyes used up twenty of the thirty minutes I had to get Sammy over to Helen's. I finally promised to ask if Aaron could take him for playdates occasionally just to get him to let go.

I didn't have the heart to tell him what was obvious to me now, little hints mixed in with the bitchy stuff in her calls and texts plus my own terrible luck. Helen was moving to Europe and was back to get her shit, including the little shit standing on the seat beside me, trying to stretch his tiny body high enough to see out the window.

I didn't care about the time. Helen had been away almost two months longer than she'd originally said. I just didn't want to drag out the trade-off. Supposedly, dogs sensed the emotions of the people around them. Since Sammy was less than half a regular dog, that meant he was picking up enough of mine to fuck him up permanently. I wouldn't wish that much shit on anyone. Except Helen.

As soon as I parked on the street outside her house, Sammy trotted over to me and climbed up on my lap. I let him lick my chin a little and then wiped my face to get his disgusting drool off. *Right.* Little drops of his saliva somehow got from my chin up to my eyes, and now they wouldn't stop trickling down my cheeks.

It had been a long fucking couple of days.

"Alright, you little bastard, let's get this over with." I grabbed all his crap and him and climbed out of the truck. I made it about halfway up the driveway when Helen and another woman came outside.

How could I have ever thought Helen and Sophie were the same? Sure, they were both objectively beautiful women, but Sophie... Sophie's beauty was so much deeper. It came from a place inside her, one she wasn't afraid to show or be judged by. Not by me, anyway. Not until I'd fallen for her.

"You're late." Helen stayed on the porch, probably afraid she'd embarrass herself by tumbling on the grass in those heels.

I bit my tongue. Sammy shouldn't have to listen to the things I had to say about his mom. I'd spent eight-plus months thinking something was missing in me, that not feeling what Helen thought I should feel meant I would never feel that way about anyone. She was wrong. Sophie proved it.

"This is him?" the woman asked, coming toward me. "He's so adorable!"

"Thanks." I tucked Sammy a little deeper into my arm. "Unfortunately, I'm unavailable at the moment."

When the woman tried to pull Sammy out of my arms, I stopped myself from running away, but I couldn't hide my grimace.

"Cooper, let go of him," Helen said, jogging toward us. "Melanie is the friend who's going to take Sammy."

"Take him where?" Sammy was squirming like crazy, not understanding why two people were playing tug-of-war with his tiny body.

"To her house. She's the one who was supposed to take him when you didn't want him anymore."

"I never said I didn't want him." When Sammy snarled, I growled, "If he doesn't bite you, I will, Melanie. So take your fucking hands off my dog."

She backed off immediately. I wasn't as lucky with Helen.

"What the hell are you doing, Cooper?"

"I'm not letting you leave him behind again as if he doesn't matter."

She didn't deny it. "So what? You're going to steal my dog?"

"No. You're going to *give* me the dog because that's what's best for him. Because he's part of my life now, and because when you left him with me, you knew I'd take good care of him."

Helen shook her head. "I knew you'd take care of each other."

Melanie looked at Helen, then at me, then the dog. "I'm not taking him, then?"

"No." When Helen and I both said it at the same time, we laughed.

"That was the first time we've ever agreed on something," she said, as Melanie left.

"You're right." I felt my shoulders drop back down to normal. "And that's the second time."

"I'm going to live in Europe, maybe permanently, but I'm not sure. I don't even know where I'll be living, so it'd be too hard to bring him with me."

She came over and tried to take Sammy out of my arms. "Let go, Cooper. I'll give him right back. I just want to say goodbye."

"You look good," I said, sitting down next to her on the front step.

"You look like shit. Did someone die or something?"

"Good to see Europe hasn't changed you." I wiped a hand over my mouth. "You're as empathetic as ever."

"Whatever." She set Sammy onto his back and rubbed his belly. "You're lucky—taking care of people with broken hearts is his specialty."

I glanced at her. "How did you—?"

"Because I'm not as stupid as you are. Plus, while you were on your way over, your sister called to yell at me. She let it slip." She gave him one last snuggle before handing him to me, tears welling up in her eyes. "The whole time we were together, I was so sure you were incapable of love. The one thing Cooper Wahl couldn't do. Turns out, it was me you were incapable of loving."

I never thought I'd want her not to hurt.

"Trust me, Helen, there are a lot of people I'm incapable of loving."

"But there's one you are. Don't let her go." Her smile was crooked. "Unless she's a bitch or there are restraining orders involved."

Ten minutes later, the little man and I were back on the road, heading home. "Don't think this changes anything. I'm only going to be expecting more out of you from now on." Sammy was struggling to get his nose to the window. "If you promise you won't try to jump out, I'll think about building a tiny ladder to make up for your stubby little legs."

When he sat, cocked his head to the side, and gave me his dumb puppy eyes, I cursed.

"I'm a fucking dog person now." I should've thought this through better, made a list. "Damn it!"

My emotions had ping-ponged all over the place today, and they weren't done with me yet.

Halfway home, a lightbulb went off in my head. I knew what I had to do. I'd hoped to be part of her life, to spend the rest of my days trying to make her happy. Her nights too. Maybe I could make that last part happen even if I couldn't be there to see it.

When I got home, the three most annoyingly concerned people in the world were still in my living room. At least they'd helped themselves to refreshments and made the place their own.

"Why won't you leave me alone?"

As soon as they saw Sammy, they surrounded us and wanted details. I gave them the gist, leaving out the embarrassing sappy parts.

Aaron held out his arms. Since the little guy was now officially mine, I didn't need to hold on to him so tightly anymore.

"I need a favor," I said as I handed the dog over. "How long do you think you can keep Sophie out of her house? I need as much time as I can get."

Aaron shrugged. "A day maybe? A whole night if I get her too drunk to drive home."

I shook my head. "I need more than that."

"If you brought her to the city," Jasmine said, "we could keep her there all weekend. How drunk do you want me to get her?"

"What the hell, Jaz!" I stared at my sister in horror.

"Why does no one get my sense of humor?" she whined.

"It was hysterical." Aaron slipped an arm around her shoulders, shaking his head and making a face over the top of her head. "Don't worry, Cooper. We got this."

She held out her hand. "If you cover all the booze and taxis."

"Thank you both for your sacrifice." I took out everything I had in my wallet, yanking it away a split second before she grabbed it. "Not *too* drunk."

I pointed at my brother. "You get to go home and do something about that woman of yours. Or is it 'women'?"

"Excuse me?" Jasmine turned to him, her eyes fiery.

"One woman. One friend. That's it," Beckett said. "You make it sound like I have a harem or something. It's not a big deal. It's just that—"

"You're an idiot." I nodded. "Yeah, we all already know. Go home and say hi to Amelia for me."

"Are you going to explain why we're getting rid of Sophie?" Aaron asked.

Their eyes never left me as they waited for an answer.

"I'm going to give her the stars."

38

SOPHIE

I'd spent last night and most of the day wandering around my house aimlessly. When I saw Cooper's old sketch of my ceiling, I burst into tears. Then I went into the bathroom and had a stern talking to with myself in the mirror.

"This is a beginning, not an end, Sophie. You're better than this." I blew out a breath. "Hell yeah, I am." I ripped off my pajamas, showered, got dressed down to the shoes, and did my makeup. All to make me feel strong again. Capable. Independent.

Then I spent the rest of the day wandering around my house aimlessly some more. I burst into tears more frequently though. Just to break it up, I guess.

By the time Liz came over with a bottle of my favorite wine, even Orion looked ashamed of me. While I shoved more kindling under the logs in the fire pit to get it going, Liz grabbed wine glasses and started pouring.

"Are you gonna tell me what his list said, or do I have to guess?" she asked. "I gave you a day and a half of space, but my mind hasn't stopped once."

"Mine either." I smoothed my pants down before I sat, making sure Cooper's list hadn't fallen out of my pocket. It was bad enough I'd carefully taped it back together as soon as he'd left and had read it enough times to memorize it.

The tape stopped it from folding flat, so I was shocked Liz hadn't asked me about the weird thing poking out at my hip. Besides, women's clothing so rarely came with pockets, and when they did, most of them were decorative, not functional. Why was I wasting valuable pocket space on something so ridiculous?

Cooper had neglected to even make a "cons" column. Plus, he couldn't possibly believe even half of the things he listed under "pros." It read more like a list of the woman I *wished* I were.

I mean, where'd he ever get the idea I was flexible? Even I knew I wasn't flexible . . . unless the winking face he'd put next to it meant he'd been talking about the *physical* flexibility he'd witnessed several times during sex versus a character trait I didn't possess.

Oh.

"What did it say?" Liz whined, pounding her fists on her thighs like a cartoon baby. "Tell me!"

I couldn't admit I'd kept the damn thing. I recited the first few lines from memory but left the rest vague. Like after most traumatic events, the brain was quick to blur them, so hopefully I'd forget the whole thing soon.

Liz reacted as I would've expected, minus any confirmation she thought I'd done the right thing.

"Cooper's resilient." Was resilient on the list? Crap. I didn't care. "I think he was just angry about not getting what he wanted."

"You mean *you*?"

I shook my head. "He fixes things, so he doesn't have much experience with things not working the way he wants them to. When I said no, he didn't know how to deal with it."

"Except you didn't say no. You said, 'Thank you,' and that's way worse."

I threw my hands up. I was mad at him for feeling whatever he was feeling and for telling me. I was mad at myself for not reacting better or even *knowing* what I was feeling.

"What was I supposed to do? Tell him I'm madly in love with him?"

"Aren't you?"

"No!" I flinched. "He's the exact opposite of everything I've ever wanted."

As soon as she set down her wine, I knew I was about to hear what she *really* thought. "Why would you ever want a man who's smoking hot and owns a successful business? Gross. He treats you well, supports and respects you." She pretended to gag. "For shit's sake, he went to your *dad's* for you and came back alive. That alone proves he's unworthy and a terrible human being. He thinks you're amazing, listens to you, and makes you scream like a porn star who's not faking it." She grimaced. "Eww. He's the worst. You're so much better off without him."

"I hate your reverse psychology. It never works."

She scoffed. "It works every single time."

"It does." Aaron stood in the open door, looking guilty. "Are you mad at me?"

I shook my head. All the other emotions coursing through me didn't leave enough room for anger, at least not at *him*.

He sat next to me and took a sip of my untouched wine. "Have we figured out what we're going to do about him yet?"

"Sophie is still trying to convince me, and herself, that she doesn't want him."

"It's not about wanting him," I whined. "I just don't want to take the risk of falling for someone who's only temporary."

"At least you can admit you're falling for him."

"*Could* fall for him." If I let myself.

I didn't believe what my father said about Cooper and half the women in the city, not after seeing the look on his face when he told me how he felt. Not before that either. I was so good at faking a smile, hiding behind it, I could tell when someone else did it. Unfortunately, knowing it was all true made things worse.

"We're too different. I want order and stability, and he can't stand it. I hate chaos—he thrives in it."

"As someone who knows you well," Aaron said, "I'm at a loss as to how thriving in chaos made it onto the list of things you don't want."

"I can handle my own problems. I don't need a man to do it for me."

"We know, hon." Liz nodded multiple times. "You're a strong, independent woman who takes care of her own business." Then she looked at Aaron. "Unless it involves vulnerability or uncomfortable emotions."

"Obviously," Aaron said to her as if I weren't sitting right next to both of them. "Then she turns into a strong, independent woman who curls up into the fetal position and waits for it to go away on its own."

"I hate you both," I grumbled. "Ugh." I hid my face in my hands. "Why do I love spending time with someone so opposed to everything I value?"

"Because the shit on that goddamn list aren't values!" Aaron shot out of the chair. Liz looked just as shocked as I was. "They're a bunch of bullshit excuses you made up so you don't have to deal with something you don't think you deserve."

"That's not true."

"You're a smart woman, Sophie. You already know the man

who checks off all your 'pro' boxes and none of your 'cons' doesn't exist." Aaron paced from one end of the patio to the other, using a lot of hand gestures. "But that's okay because as long as you are looking for *him*, you don't have to think about the beautiful man in front of you who wants to love you. It's a perfect defense, really—your whole list thing. Make it impossible for a man to qualify for the position so there's no chance you'll get hurt."

I looked to Liz, hoping she'd stand up for me or tell Aaron he was wrong. One glance told me that wouldn't be happening.

"Cooper is exactly the kind of man you should be with," Liz said. "For some weird reason, he's in love with you."

"He's not in love with me. He's not." I looked at my two best friends who I knew almost as well as I knew myself. "None of us have ever really been in love, so what makes you think we know how it works?"

"Just because I can't do it doesn't mean I can't recognize it," Aaron said. "Like my parents."

"Mine too." Liz shrugged. "They might have weird ways of showing it, but I've never doubted they love each other."

I slid down in my chair, overwhelmed and afraid. What if I'd made it all up, told myself a story of what love *should* be and held on to that idea with every cell in my body until no other explanation could get through?

"I'm a dumbass, aren't I?" When they didn't disagree, I added, "You're supposed to tell me I'm not. Or at least that I'm a dumbass only about this, not everything else."

They looked at each other and nodded.

"I'd go with that. You?"

"Yeah, sounds pretty accurate."

"I hate you both." I screamed as they tackled me. I cried as they held me.

When they let me go, I used Aaron's shirt to wipe my eyes. He feigned horror that I ignored.

"What now?" I asked.

"That's easy," Aaron said. "You figure out what stopped you from sweeping that cute boy up immediately and claiming him as your own. Then you wipe it out of your mind forever."

"You think that's easy?"

"I haven't even gotten to the hard part yet."

When he got up and went inside the house, I hoped whatever he was about to do involved drinking. He passed right by the wine rack. I stood and walked closer to the sliding glass door to see better. "Did he bring another bottle?"

I stopped breathing when he reached into my bag and pull out my planner.

"Oh, shit." Liz held me by the waist as if she thought I were about to attack Aaron and gnaw my planner out of his big traitorous hands.

I stood there calmly, even patiently, as he came back outside.

He held the planner open in one hand, flipping pages with the other. "You know this has to be done."

"Give it to me." I held out my hand. "You don't even know which divider it's under." As soon as I had it, I turned to the tab, clicked open the rings, and pulled out the three pages.

Suddenly, just like that, my friends had nothing to say. No jokes. No teasing. They were probably afraid I would blow up if they breathed too loudly.

"I need to get rid of the digital file too. Don't let me forget." As if I'd forget.

"When you're done, we should get out of here," Aaron said. "Go to the city for the weekend to celebrate your newfound freedom and make a plan for whatever happens after that."

As I held each page over to the fire pit, released it, and watched it burn, a lot of truths finally sunk in.

No more plans. No more lists, at least not about him. They'd almost stopped me from letting Cooper be part of my life. Lucky for me, he'd managed to do it anyway.

"Are we going to the city?"

"There's something I need to do first," I said, turning my back on the fire.

39

SOPHIE

Crisp, cool air blew through the open car window. Once I was focused and one hundred percent in the moment, I called my dad. "We need to talk. I'm on my way." I stopped my finger right before I ended the call. "Oh, and you probably should pour us both a drink."

"What's going on?"

"I'll be there soon," I said, deliberately not answering his question. Why give him a chance to prepare himself when I didn't have one? I'd invited myself over with no notice, hadn't planned out what I was going to say, and the only list I had on me was Cooper's.

It was terrifying.

The ninth or tenth thing on Cooper's list was "brave," something I'd never considered myself. But I wanted to prove him right.

I parked in the driveway, took a few deep breaths, and went inside.

"Dad, where are you?" I found him in his study holding a glass of bourbon. He'd set another one in front of the chair across from him. I didn't want to sit. There was no sense in pretending this was going to be comfortable when I knew it wasn't. I did grab the drink though—that would help.

"When do you plan on telling me what's going on?" he asked calmly. I knew he wasn't calm. My late-night call had thrown him. Good. This shouldn't be easy for either of us.

"You were wrong to give me that ultimatum. You were wrong about Cooper." My eyes were already stinging, so I knew there was no way I'd get through this without many, many tears. That wouldn't stop me. "And you have *always* been wrong about me."

"What are you talking about?"

"I've worked my ass off for everything I have and everything I don't have. But you still don't trust me. Because you decided you didn't want to." After a sip of horrible-tasting firewater, I took a moment to recover. "Like how you decided to hate Cooper no matter what he does, or how much I want him in my life."

"After all I've done to get to this point," he said, "you don't just bring in someone new who could ruin a reputation I've spent my whole life building."

"My life."

"What?" he snapped.

"You've spent *my* life building Dillon Design, not yours. It's been your obsession since I was a toddler. So no, Dad, it's not *your* life that you've given up. It's mine. My birthdays and school events that you sacrificed. Weekends and dinners and home-work questions you weren't there for. When Mom got sick, you sacrificed that too. Time with her as she was dying, and time with your daughter when she was grieving and alone and needed someone to be there for her. So, please—"

I willed myself not to cry. "*Please* don't talk to me about your reputation and all the hard work you've done. All the things you've given up. Because if you think for a second I wouldn't shut all of it down tomorrow for a little more time with my mom or to have a father who gave a shit about me, you're wrong."

"That's not . . ." He looked toward the window, at the darkness bleeding through the soft curtains.

Maybe I should've weighed my words more. Maybe I should've had this conversation at another time in another place when I was less upset, more rested, and thinking more clearly. Maybe I should've waited for him to respond.

But I'd been waiting for him to respond for fifteen years. Fifteen years—5,475 days—of waiting for him to acknowledge any of my feelings.

"I was a child trying to handle something most adults have trouble with." I took another swig of the bourbon. It was just as awful the second time. "You barely noticed when Mom died. Business as usual the day after her funeral. I needed you, and you were at work. Working on this goddamn company you value above all else, including me."

"That's not true, young lady." He rubbed his lips together, shaking his head as if he had something to say.

"Say it." It wouldn't be anything I hadn't heard before. Maybe how ungrateful I was, how I should've done things differently, been less impetuous, smarter.

"Your mother knew."

"Knew what?"

"How hard it is for me to express those types of things. How much I loved you." He stared into his glass, the bronze liquid that comforted him. "She knew how I felt about you both."

"*I* didn't," I said. "I hope that's true—that she didn't die believing you loved a business more than her. But how did you expect a little girl who'd just lost the most important person in her life to understand that?"

"I don't know," he said quietly. "It was easier to pretend it wasn't happening, that it wasn't real. The more I stayed away, the easier it got. How could I help you grieve for your mother when I didn't know how to do it myself?"

I sat back in silence. I wasn't sure I could've answered if I'd wanted to. Part of my reaction was shock, another part overwhelm, and another was understanding him a little better as a man.

"Before your mother passed," he continued, "I'd come home after a particularly late night and find you two on the patio, you asleep with your head on her lap. We'd sit there and talk, and the whole time she'd play with your hair."

I ran my hand over my hair unconsciously, even though the hair my mom touched was long gone. "What did you talk about?"

"What you'd be like when you grew up. What you'd do, who you'd be, if you'd have children of your own. How—" His voice caught. "How much she wished she wouldn't miss it all, even though we knew she would." He drained his glass. "She would've loved who you've become, so proud."

"Thank you for telling me that," I said. "I'm glad she'd be proud of who I've become. Because so am I." As hard as it was to admit.

But why had he waited fifteen years to tell me any of this? Yes, I loved him, and I always would. But he was fifteen years too late.

When I stood, Cooper's list poked into my hip, the universe's way of reminding me it was there when I needed it. That *he* was there when I needed him.

"I'm a lot stronger than you think I am, Dad. Smarter. More tenacious." I let out a tiny laugh when I remembered how badly Cooper had misspelled that one. "And I'm sick of being underestimated more than you could ever imagine."

Cooper made me better—not by telling me all the things I was doing wrong but by celebrating what I did right.

"I'm in love with him." I sighed. Saying it out loud was a relief . . . and also terrifying. "Trust me, I'm just as shocked about it as you are, dad." I pressed my lips together to stop them from shaking. "And I blew it. I was so stuck in what I thought my life should be that I couldn't see the man who was offering me something even better.

"Everything I've ever worked for or wanted has always been so tightly bound to you. To this fucking company. I can't wait around for you to believe in me anymore. I'll always be your daughter, but I'm not going to be your employee anymore."

"Honey, wait. Please." He reached out for my hand, but I pulled away. "I was wrong to ask you to choose between Cooper and the company or treating him as I did. The heart attack, having to face my own mortality, changed me. Before I go, I need to know everything is perfect."

"Nothing will ever be perfect." I set my glass on the table. "But lots of things—lots of *people*—are pretty damn incredible. Good luck, Dad." I smiled as I walked away, then turned to face him again. "To be clear—you were an asshole before the heart attack too. And if Lucy realizes how much more she deserves before you make things right, you'll lose her too. Stop taking her for granted, and whatever you're paying her, triple it. Minimum."

Both Aaron and Liz's cars were still parked in front of my house. Instead of going in right away, I took a little time to think.

Finally knowing what you wanted didn't mean you'd get it.

I'd hurt Cooper when he'd been at his most vulnerable, something I'd never wanted to do. Unfortunately, intentions didn't matter as much as we wished they did. If I couldn't make things right, if he wasn't going to be around anymore, it seemed even more important to take care of the part of him I had. Try to see myself the way he did.

I pulled the list out of my pocket, smoothed it on the dashboard as best I could, and carefully tucked it into my planner. In place of another, outdated and wrong, typed three-page list I didn't need anymore.

I read through the new one again before putting the planner back in my bag. After a few more deep breaths, I went inside.

My two best friends were standing side by side, blocking the entryway, my overnight bag at Aaron's feet.

"What's going on?"

"Toothbrush," Aaron said, "hairbrush, a dress and heels for tonight—you can change in the car—clothes for tomorrow and Sunday, you'll be fine with the shoes you have on now, two pairs of undies—the good ones—"

"Why were you in my underwear drawer?"

"Wait till I'm done," he said, holding up his pointer finger. "Bra..." He looked at Liz. "Is that all?"

"Pajamas."

"Right! Pajamas, and you won't need any cash because it's someone else's treat."

"Where are we going?" I'd hoped to just collapse into bed with a bottle of wine tonight.

"I'm not going anywhere," Liz grumbled, "because I couldn't find anyone to cover me at work."

I followed them both back outside in a daze.

Liz gave Aaron a quick hug and me a longer one. "See you in a few days." I squeezed her harder.

"Come on, we gotta go. I told Jasmine we'd be at her place in ninety minutes."

I slid to a stop. "Cooper's Jasmine? I'm not sure she'd want to see me right now." Siblings tended to be a little grumpy when one of them got hurt, or so I'd heard.

"It was her idea." He tossed my bag into his backseat. "Oh, and we're going to discuss your general underwear situation on the way. No one should wear ugly undies, Sophie. Ever. It's a self-worth thing. And you're worth a lot more than faded black cotton briefs that give you wedgies."

40

SOPHIE

What would normally have been an amazingly fun weekend turned out to be amazingly depressive. For all three of us. It was too hard to fake a smile.

On the first night, we'd stopped at a small grocery for high-carb snacks and drinks on the way back to Jasmine's apartment. Apparently, grocery stores were triggers for me now. They said I hadn't embarrassed them, but that was more because the place was almost empty versus a lack of effort on my part.

The next day was better—more distractions, less crying. We went shopping, and I replaced all my underwear. I also bought a not-black outfit that showed off some skin. Aaron was as shocked as I was. But if this weekend was supposed to be about starting over, wearing something different felt right. Good even. I mean, I wasn't ready for actual colors yet, but white was definitely not black.

Last night was hard though. I wondered if that was my new normal for a while.

We got back around noon on Sunday. I thought the reason Aaron hurried home was so he could get rid of me. That is until I saw Cooper's truck outside my house.

"You know something." I turned to him. "Spill it. Don't make me go in there unprepared, Aaron. Why is he here? To pick up his stuff, yell at me, what?"

"I don't know exactly, but it's definitely not to yell at you." He smirked. "In fact, I think he likes you."

"That's all you're going to give me?"

He leaned in for a hug but went right by me, opening the passenger door and shoving me out of the car. "Good luck, darling!"

I tried to go in quietly, give myself a chance to find out what was going on. As soon as Orion saw me, he let out a meow that could've caused an avalanche. Before I could chuck him in the closet, Cooper walked out of my bedroom.

"Hey," I said.

"You look incredible, Soph."

"Thanks." I glanced down at the new clothes I'd bought as much for him as for me. "So do you."

He looked tired, hot, shirtless, and when he smiled, I couldn't breathe.

"You're kidding, right?" He bowed his head as he laughed. "I can't remember the last time I slept, and I need a shower, but that'll have to wait."

"For what?"

"I want to show you something."

I followed him into my bedroom cautiously, my eyes zigzagging across every wall, floor, and ceiling. Aside from a metal ladder and his toolbox, everything was how I'd left it.

I looked at him and shrugged. "What do you want to show me?"

"Right, you can't see them. Hang on." He ran to the window and closed the blinds, then the curtains over them. "Actually, get on the bed."

"Um . . . you don't want to at least talk first?" Stupid question.

Given the choice, what man would want to talk instead of getting straight to the makeup sex, or angry sex, or whatever situational sex would be appropriate at this moment? I should be thankful, right? If it meant he'd forgiven me for screwing things up and telling him to leave.

"Not until you get on the bed." He walked the perimeter of the room, turning off the overhead lights and shutting the bedroom door. He didn't look in my direction until the room was lit by nothing but the lamp on my bedside table. "You're not on the bed."

Were we going to go back to how things were? Before he told me how he felt about me. Before I knew how I felt about him. I couldn't do that.

"Cooper, what I said . . . I should've . . . I wanted to say . . ."

"You're forgiven."

"I haven't finished apologizing."

"You don't need to."

It must have been just bright enough for him to see my jaw tremble, or my eyes tear up.

"Don't cry," he said, rushing over to me. "This is a happy thing."

"Then why do I feel so horrible?"

"I don't know. This is just as new to me as it is to you." He wiped my tears away with his thumb at first. Then he used his lips. He slowly made his way to my mouth, stopping just before he got there. "I missed the way you smell. How good you feel."

"Me too." I barely got that out.

"I need to be with you, Soph," he whispered against my cheek. "I can't give up on something I know is real. We're right together."

"But we're so different. We don't like any of the same things."

"We like each other."

"That doesn't count."

"It's *all* that counts," he said.

"You want me now, but . . ." I bit my lip to keep it from trembling. "How do you know that won't change a year from now?"

"Because I know who you are now, and I can't wait to see who you become." He kissed me softly, pulled away, and sighed. "Your eyes are too big for your face."

"Excuse me?" I snapped, hating that right now my shock was making my eyes even bigger. "What does that have to do with—"

"They're totally out of proportion with your tiny little nose."

I covered it with my hand. "My nose isn't that tiny! Why are you—"

"I love you anyway."

That stopped me.

Before I could ask him to repeat that last part, he continued, "Last week, when you were singing in the shower, it was so bad I had to cover my ears until you stopped. I love you anyway."

"Why are you telling me you love me while being so mean?"

"Because I need to get it through that beautiful stubborn head of yours that if you add up every single one of your imperfections, your con list wouldn't be a fraction of your pro side. All the incredible things I adore about you." He ran his hands up my arms and grabbed me by the shoulders. "Now, I've been awake and thinking about this for almost forty-eight hours straight, so shut up a second and let me finish."

I did, but only because I had no idea what to say.

He frowned. "You can be really judgy. I love you anyway. I *hate* that you don't have a single unlined piece of paper in this entire house. Hate it but still love you. Your taste in music makes me nauseous." He cocked his head to the side. "Love you. You're total shit at construction. You actually believe people care about having wall colors that flatter their skin tones. You—"

"I get it." I covered his mouth with my hand. "I'm really,

really far away from perfect." I'd never been happier to be insulted.

Before he took my hand away, he kissed it, and he didn't let it go. "Yeah, well, I'm even further away, and I actually like that about myself. Your cat still hates me. I'm grumpy in the mornings and most other parts of the day. I own four pairs of shoes, and until one of them wears out, I'm not getting more."

"Any time you think of a crude joke, no matter where you are, you say it."

"I have no control over that," he said, nodding.

"You're a bit too attractive."

He blinked. "That's a problem for you?"

"Of course, it is," I scoffed. "Plus, your body's too good."

"Yeah, well . . ." As his eyes intensified, he slipped his hand around the nape of my neck and pulled me in. "So is yours."

"You can be a little broody. Not often, but when you are, it's annoying."

"Good to know. So, with all that working against me . . ." He looked at me with adoration, hope, and a little fear. "Will all of that stop you from falling in love me?"

"I . . . no." My heart was going a thousand miles an hour. I could barely breathe, and he asked me that *now*? "Because . . . I already do." I tried blinking the tears away, but it was a total failure. "I love you."

He let out a breath. "Why?"

"Because . . . you're you. And your 'pro' column is infinitely longer than your 'con'."

He nodded slowly.

"You love me." As I said it, the words tickled my tongue. The middle one felt so much different to say now that it was real. "You love me."

"Very much."

"I love you too."

"You better." He smiled.

"I just thought of a couple more. You take up all the room in the shower, and just thinking about your shop gives me nightmares."

"Shut up, Sophie."

When he kissed me, his lips felt softer, sweeter than I remembered them being. As if time wanted me to understand that everything before and everything to come would be defined by exactly this moment—his lips on mine and his words still lingering in my ear.

It only took a few steps to get to the bed, barely any effort at all to drag him down on top of me. When he stood a minute later, bent over at the waist because our mouths were still locked together, I reached for his belt.

"Whoa." He peeled my arms off him first, then my tongue and lips. "Hold that thought." He leaned in for a quick kiss, then backed away again. "Stop pouting—I have something to show you, remember?"

"I thought it was something sexual."

"Nope." He paused. "It's a great idea we'll definitely revisit later though. Hopefully, you'll like this one almost as much." He took something out of his back pocket and lay down next to me, both of us on our sides facing each other. "Look up."

I didn't know what he meant until he knocked me onto my back, then did the same. He wasn't looking at me anymore, he was looking at the—

"Oh my God!" I yelled.

When he turned off the lamp, pitching the room into total darkness, it was even clearer.

What looked like a thousand tiny specks of light shone like the stars above us.

"It's so beautiful," I said in wonder.

"It's Orion."

"It can't be." I sat up, spinning on my knees as I decided where to start. "You made Orion." I found the stars of the hunter's belt right above the bed. He expanded from there. "Rigel, Betelgeuse." I pointed at each star as I traced him. "Bellatrix and Saiph." Cooper had added smaller stars between them, ones that wouldn't be there if we were outside but gave form to the constellation, something we'd otherwise miss because of our perspective.

"You gave me a glass ceiling without the glass."

"Or the bird shit," he said, scooting up higher on the mattress until he could lean back against the headboard.

He'd mapped it out just like it was in the sky. Which meant by the door would be the Northern sky, and over my bed the Southern.

"It's incredible." Without lowering my eyes, I crawled to him. He grabbed me by the waist and guided me until I was sitting between his bent legs, my back to his chest. "How did you do it?"

"They're LEDs. Different sizes. I set them in a little, which is why you couldn't see them when the lights were on. I had to add some filler lights to be able to make it out better. I could've used more time, and some sleep, but it came out well. Take this."

He put something in my hands and closed my fingers around a thin rectangle with a few bumps on it. I didn't know what it was because I wasn't ready to look down yet.

"Press this button on the controller"— he pushed my finger down—"and you get..."

I gasped as everything changed. The Hunter was gone, replaced by a new constellation, this one with the Northern sky over by the door.

"Cassiopeia," I said. "The Greek Queen who was bound to a chair and sent into the Northern sky as punishment for her arrogance."

He laughed as he wrapped his arms around me. "You really

did want to be an astronomer when you grew up. Or was it an astrologer?" He remembered everything. He *gave* me everything. And I loved him for it.

"So, what do you think?"

I leaned back into him and sighed. "It's the most beautiful thing I've ever seen."

"It's just the basics for now, but we can add as many stars as you want."

"No. It's perfect just the way it is."

"*Close* to perfect," he whispered into my ear.

41

———

COOPER

7:00 am Monday through Friday

Occasionally, I convince her to press the snooze button.

Thirty-five minutes together in the shower—just enough time to get clean and then get a little dirty.

Twenty minutes to make coffee—*good* coffee, not the shitty kind—and feed our little beasts while Sophie does her hair and makeup.

Ten minutes to drive to our workspace—a beautifully designed minimalist studio for her right next to the shop of my most chaotic dreams that she refuses to enter.

Saturdays and Sundays

Wake up. Not too early.

Have sex. The warm, lazy kind when neither one of us is totally awake, so we start out slow and just do whatever feels best. Then it turns into more, and we let ourselves go, not caring about what else we have to do that day, or morning breath, or if our neighbors can hear her screaming.

Then coffee and a long shower. With sex. Up against the tile or from behind, I'm not picky.

Hang out for the rest of the day not really doing much of anything. Take Sammy for a walk in the afternoon, watch some TV, then more sex if that's what Sophie wants.

I know nothing is perfect. But this is damn close.

EPILOGUE

SOPHIE

Things weren't perfect between Cooper and me. We still argued, but we'd gotten better at it. Truly knowing someone wanted the best for you, and you wanted the same for them, made it a lot easier to ignore the little stuff. Which most of it was things like which cereal or milk to buy. We each picked our own and compromised on one percent milk.

Our longest argument was what to call our new company. Obviously, Dillon Design was out of the question, but there was no chance I'd do business as Get 'er Done, so it took some negotiation to finally settle on Absolute Design.

Today was the day it all became official. Inside the envelope on my lap was our business license, lots of legal forms, a rental contract, and a key to our new space. We'd picked out the perfect location—a bright, simple studio for me to design and meet clients right next to a giant shop for Cooper. After some reconfiguring and soundproofing so I wouldn't have to listen to power tools all day, it would be perfect.

"You picked up the paint I ordered, right?" I asked as he pulled up to our new building.

"Not exactly."

I groaned. "It's for my studio, Cooper. I get to pick the color, and it's not even close to pink."

"It's not that," he grumbled. "I was just a little distracted this morning."

"I noticed." He'd been weird all day. I assumed it had to do with all the contracts we'd just signed for the business and the lease—all things I was thrilled about. But everyone reacted to commitment differently. "It's going to work. You don't have to worry."

It already had. Thus far, the merging of our businesses had been smooth. I'd refused to poach any clients from Dillon Design now that my father was back at work, but I was slowly making a name for myself.

He brushed it off. "Let's go look at our new place."

After a tour to go over our plan again, I stood in the middle of the room and spun around in a circle. "I love it so much! It's perfect." My joy faltered a little when I saw his expression. "Why aren't you as happy as I am?"

He clenched and unclenched his jaw as he thought about what to say, finally deciding on, "I got a weird phone call earlier."

"Weird how?" I asked, sighing internally.

"A grumpy old guy." He paused. "He wanted to leave you a message."

"Grumpy old guy?" I frowned but didn't see why that would be so upsetting to him. In about fifty years, someone might call him the same thing. "He called your cell number and not our main line?"

He nodded. "I was wondering why he called me too, at first, but then I got it. He wanted the message to come from someone you trusted. Someone you loved. In case you missed it, I'm at the top of that list."

"Really?" I shrugged. "I'll have to update it then." He was all that and more. "What was the message?" None of my new clients were over sixty, and all of them were happy with the work I'd done for them. Was he a disgruntled client from my father's business? Dennis?

"I think the guy's name was Mike. Mike Dillon. Michael maybe?"

My breath caught. "His name is Peter. Why did he call you?"

He cursed. "I called your dad by the wrong name three times the night I met him, and you didn't correct me once."

"Back then, I didn't think you'd be sticking around, so it didn't matter. Why did he call?" I'd heard he was back to work and doing well—which I was happy about—but we hadn't spoken in months. Not even once.

"He wanted me to tell you that he's retiring and is wondering what to do with his client list."

"He wants to sell us his client list?" I asked flatly. The nerve. I helped build that list. I certainly helped keep people *on* the list once they'd had to deal with my father personally.

"He wants us to have it."

I stepped back. "He wants to give it to us?" Client lists were the gold of this business. The treasure my father had planned to retire on when he sold it to a competitor. A competitor like us. "Did he actually use those words?"

"I think it's his way of apologizing. He also mentioned something about getting married, which I tried to ignore because honestly, all I thought after he said that was: Shit, Sophie is going to expect me to—"

I covered his mouth with my hand. "My dad's getting married? To whom?"

"Lucy." He smirked. "Apparently, she did more than housework."

My jaw dropped as I thought back to all the time I'd spent with them. Was it a new thing, or was that what Lucy meant when she told me she could handle him? Gross.

"Good for them," I said. "I'll have to send a card or something." Unless Lucy was fully in charge of the guest list, I doubted I'd be invited to the wedding.

"He wants you to be there—wants *us* to be there. Considering how well we got along, inviting me to his big day is a hell of an olive branch. I think it's time you guys talked."

"Yeah," I mumbled. I missed him like crazy. My anger had disappeared as soon as I realized I'd been the one who was putting the limits on myself—not him. What he wanted me to do or say didn't affect me at all. Unless I let it.

"But back to that other thing . . ." He wrung his hands together.

"Lucy and my dad." I was so caught off-guard by the idea, I almost missed what Cooper said next.

"I told him we were too."

"What?" I refocused. Something in his nervousness told me this was important.

"I told him we were going to get married too."

"That's sweet." I smiled and kissed him. "Although it may have caused another heart attack. Good thing he'll have a couple years to process the idea."

"I was thinking more like one year. Or less, if possible." He reached into his pocket. "A year is enough time for you to make all the lists and schedules you'll want, right?"

My breath stopped when he pulled out a small velvet box.

"Sophie . . ."

"Seriously?" I blurted.

"You don't want to marry me?"

"I just . . . I'm . . ." Speechless. Shocked. Unprepared. I hadn't planned on this happening for a few years. "I—"

He held his hand up to stop all my arguments: What if it was too soon? Shouldn't we focus on the business first? I hadn't even met his whole family yet. Was a year long enough to plan something so important?

"It's a single question that needs a single-word answer," he said. "No negotiations, arguments, or compromises until after you answer. "So, yes or no. Will you marry me, Sophie Dillon?"

Yes or no. There had never been an easier choice.

"Yes . . ." I exhaled slowly to give it a chance to settle in. Then words started tumbling out. "But I'm not sure about the timeline. A year might—"

"Shut up, love," he said right before dragging me in for a kiss that put all others to shame.

The End

THANKS AND MORE!

I hope you enjoyed Cooper and Sophie's story! If you want to receive a special epilogue of *Everything He Isn't and* find out more about Beckett and Amelia's book *Two Doors Apart*, sign up for the newsletter on my website:

www.LaurenStewartAuthor.com

Thank you to everyone who had a hand in getting me back on the horse and bringing this book to fruition. Saying I couldn't have done it without you has literally never been truer. I want to send a special shout out to my eagle-eyed Stewartists - Amanda Crawford, Dayna Hanson, Patricia Kellar, Jessica McCue, and Kathy Van de Wiel - for their encouragement and help in the final stages of this book's creation.

And to all my readers:

Your support and patience with me is everything. I know it's been a long time coming, and I won't bore you with all the emo excuses, but I'm very happy to be back. I'm even happier to see you all are still here with me.

With an uncomfortable amount of love,

Lauren

BOOKS BY LAUREN STEWART

Contemporary Romance

Darker Water

Virtually Impossible

Deeper Water

Immaterial Defense

Everything He Isn't

Two Doors Apart (up next)

Paranormal

Hyde

Jekyll

Strange Case

ABOUT THE AUTHOR

Lauren Stewart lives in Northern California with two teenagers and a cat who doesn't give a shit about anything or anyone. Yes, she inspired Sophie's description of Liz.

Lauren loves emoticons and hates when people speak in the third person, so...

I grew up reading mystery, fantasy, horror, historical fiction, thrillers, and romance (even though, at the time, I didn't know it was romance). I think that explains why I can't seem to stick to one genre at a time.

I strive to make readers think, laugh, and cry (not always simultaneously, although it's great when it happens). Inside each of my books, you'll find elements of other genres, always with a drop of angst, a splash of humor, and a bucketload of sarcasm.

Because what doesn't kill us should make us laugh.

Lauren@LaurenStewartAuthor.com
www.LaurenStewartAuthor.com